## *Little Girl Lost*

About halfway through the album, the photos began to change. Brandi wasn't a wide-eyed little tot anymore, or a young girl on the edge of womanhood. Her smile changed to a sullen grimace. The pink dresses had morphed into ripped black T-shirts and low-slung black jeans. An eyebrow ring hung above eyes ringed in black eyeliner. In the last picture it looked like Brandi had used Easter egg dye to color her hair. Strands of pink, robin's-egg blue, and lime green stuck up in stiff spikes from her scalp.

Abby slid her album aside and reached for the one I had been looking at. She opened it to the last page, to the picture of Brandi with the Easter-egg colored hair. Placing both hands on the photo, Abby lowered her head.

"Water, dark, lost, alone . . ." Abby's voice trailed off as her shoulders shook slightly.

I started to reach for her when she lifted her head and looked at me.

"We need to find this girl fast."

"You're sure she's still alive?"

Abby passed a hand over her forehead as if to rub the images away. "Yes, I am. But she's in danger and we must find her soon."

*Books by*
**Shirley Damsgaard**

THE WITCH IS DEAD
WITCH HUNT
THE TROUBLE WITH WITCHES
CHARMED TO DEATH
WITCH WAY TO MURDER

# SHIRLEY DAMSGAARD

# The Trouble With Witches

## AN OPHELIA AND ABBY MYSTERY

AVON BOOKS

*An Imprint of HarperCollinsPublishers*

This is a work of fiction. Names, characters, places, and incidents are products of the author's imagination or are used fictitiously and are not to be construed as real. Any resemblance to actual events, locales, organizations, or persons, living or dead, is entirely coincidental.

AVON BOOKS
*An Imprint of* HarperCollins*Publishers*
10 East 53rd Street
New York, New York 10022-5299

Copyright © 2006 by Shirley Damsgaard
ISBN-13: 978-0-06-079358-6
ISBN-10: 0-06-079358-9
**www.avonmystery.com**

First Avon Books paperback printing: September 2006

Avon Trademark Reg. U.S. Pat. Off. and in Other Countries, Marca Registrada Hecho en U.S.A.
HarperCollins® is a registered trademark of HarperCollins Publishers Inc.

Printed in the U.S.A.

10  9  8  7  6  5  4

9311

*To Aunt Betty and Uncle Arnie. Thank you for all the wonderful times at the "real" Gunhammer Lake—Crooked Lake, Minnesota!*

# Acknowledgments

With the publication of *Witch Way to Murder* and *Charmed to Death*, the past year has been one of the most exciting years of my life. It's given me the opportunity to meet people I never would have had the chance to meet, and their help in creating this latest adventure for Ophelia and Abby has been invaluable:

The late No Two Horns and my old friend, Bud Murphy, for their insight into the Native American culture. I'm sorry, No Two Horns, that you never saw the publication of this book. I only hope you would have liked the character you named, Walks Quietly.

Diana Abbott for the magick tips.

Ursula Bowler for sharing her stories with me. They fired my imagination, Urs!

Dr. Jerri McLemore and Paul Steinbach of the Iowa State Medical Examiner's Office for, once again, answering endless questions on ways to get rid of hapless characters.

The readers I've met either in person or via e-mail. Because of your response to Darci, she won a trip to Minnesota!

Stacey Glick of Dystel and Goderich Literary Management, Sarah Durand, Jeremy Cesarec, Danielle Bartlett, and the staff at Avon Books—without you, there would be no Ophelia and Abby Mystery Series!

And of course, my family and friends. Without your understanding and support, I never would have had the courage to embark on *my* great adventure!

# The
# Trouble With
# Witches

# *Prologue*

Scattered pictures of a man lay on the table in front of me. The images drifted through my mind as I ran my hand over them. The hot Iowa sun beat down on a couple as they enjoyed a picnic by a quiet lake. The man's dark hair absorbed the heat, and tiny beads of sweat popped out on his upper lip. The woman, smiling, reached out and wiped the beads away. He caught her hand and kissed it.

The scene changed and the man stood alone in an empty pasture. The once green grass was now brown, cooked by the summer heat. Only the cawing of crows broke the silence. The man looked up at the sky and watched while they circled above him. Bowing his head, his eyes traveled to the gun he held in his hand. A sense of total hopelessness filled his heart. And slowly . . .

Opening my eyes, I scooped up the pictures and placed them back in a folder. I snapped the folder shut as if doing so would erase the images from my mind.

"Well?" Henry asked impatiently.

Sliding the folder away, I looked up to see his dark brown eyes roaming my face.

They belonged to Henry Comacho, detective with

the state of Iowa's Department of Crime Investigation. The Iceman. The man who'd suspected me of being involved with two murders. And who now wanted me to use my psychic talent to find a missing man.

His dark black hair glinted in the afternoon sun pouring through my kitchen windows as we sat at the table. His brow wrinkled in a frown while his eyes searched my face. In those eyes, I could see what a struggle asking for my help had been for him. He had a desperate need to find the missing man, but at the same time was skeptical about using a psychic to do so. But the desperation had won. So here he was, with his folder of pictures, asking me for answers to his questions.

And what did I have for him? Nothing.

What had I been thinking? Why did I let him talk me into this? When he'd asked me last spring, after I'd helped the authorities catch the man who'd murdered my friend Brian five years ago, I'd been reluctant. Now I felt the frustration over the lack of clarity that comes with my so-called gift grind at me.

Lowering my eyes, I stared at the folder. Why were the images always vague and couched in ambiguity? A road sign, or something recognizable, would've been helpful in locating the missing man.

"Well?" Henry asked again, startling me out of my thoughts.

Raising my eyes, I rubbed my forehead. "I think he's dead—a suicide. In a pasture."

"Gee, a pasture in Iowa. That should be easy to find," he said with a heavy dose of sarcasm. "I don't suppose out of the thousands in the state you could tell me which one?"

"One with crows."

"That's it? One with crows? No cows, no landmarks like a river, a hill, or woods nearby?"

"Nope," I said, and pushed the folder across the table toward him. "I'm sorry, but I told you I couldn't guarantee that I could help you. Visions are unpredictable at the best, symbolic at the worst. All I know is he was overcome by helplessness and committed suicide in an empty pasture somewhere."

"Crows? Could they be symbolic?" Henry asked, placing a hand over the folder.

"I doubt it, but I don't know for sure." I sighed deeply. "I'm sorry. I really wish I saw more."

A frown creased Henry's forehead. "Yeah, I do, too." He ran his other hand through his hair. "If the guy is dead and if we could find his body, it would provide some closure for his family."

As he said it, I felt a little warmth slip through the shield of ice Henry kept around him most of the time. He really was a compassionate man, but it was a side he didn't let show very often. I'd seen that side of him when he was with his niece, Isabella, and around my grandmother, Abby. But with me, the wall was usually firmly in place.

I covered his hand resting on top of the folder with mine. "I really am sorry."

The flow of warmth flickered, and then stopped. Henry squirmed and pulled his hand away. "We keep looking. Who knows, maybe you're wrong. Visions aren't always one hundred percent right, are they? Maybe we'll find the guy on the beach in the Bahamas."

"Maybe," I replied, my tone sounding unconvincing even to my ears.

Henry picked up the folder and stood to leave. I

followed him to the door, where he paused and removed his sunglasses from his pocket. Shoving them on his face, he turned.

"It was a stupid idea to ask you to look at those pictures," he said abruptly. "If he'd committed suicide like your vision indicated, someone would've noticed his abandoned car, but it's never been found, either. That tells me the guy's still alive."

I rolled my eyes in dismay. A lack of hard evidence had driven Henry to ask for my help, but the truth was, he would never see my gift as anything more than mumbo-jumbo.

He frowned and pivoted away from the open door and me. From the doorway, I watched as he marched to his car, slammed the car door, and pulled away without a backward glance.

After shutting the door, I leaned against it. Scrubbing my face with both hands, I thought about my gift. Would this talent ever work the way I wanted it to? Would I ever be able to help someone before it was too late?

I hadn't told Henry everything. I hadn't told him of the last glimpse I'd had of the man. Only what I saw wasn't a man, it was a pile of bleached bones, picked clean by the crows.

# One

A big black spider sat on Mr. Carroll's shoulder, while a vein in his forehead throbbed as he yelled at me. *He wasn't happy about the library's latest book order. He was sick and tired of all the smut.* Each word was underscored by a constant jangling in the background.

Where was the sound coming from? My eyes left Mr. Carroll's face, searching for the sound, until the pounding of his skeletal fist caught my attention again.

My eyes traveled from his face down his body. The tendons in his skinny neck stood out as he screamed at me, and I could see his bony chest wheeze in and out. His ancient ribs, covered by thin, dry, almost translucent skin, expanded like a bellows with each breath. As my eyes traveled past his chest, I shuddered and said a silent thank-you that the counter prevented me from seeing the rest of his naked, eighty-year-old body.

Whoa—wait a second. What was Mr. Carroll doing in the library nude? And what was *making* that jangling noise?

My eyes shot open and I found myself staring at the darkened ceiling of my bedroom. Thank God, I was dreaming. But why was I dreaming about Mr. Carroll naked in the library? And why hadn't the jangling stopped when I woke up?

The phone, the jangling was the phone. My hand shot out to grab it, and in the process I knocked my alarm clock off the nightstand with a loud clatter. Queenie, my cat, who had also been sleeping soundly on the pillow next to me, gave me an indignant look and stalked off the bed. Lady, my dog, startled by the loud noise, gave a short bark.

I shoved a handful of dark brown hair out of my face and stared at the ringing phone as if it were a snake.

"What?" My tone sounded grumpy, but I didn't care. I didn't appreciate phone calls in the middle of the night, even though they did rescue me from an awful dream featuring a naked Mr. Carroll.

"Hey, know where I can find a good witch?" asked the voice coming from the receiver.

I stared dumbly at the phone. I'd recognize that voice anywhere—Rick Delaney, award-winning investigative reporter with the *Minneapolis Sun*, and a guy who'd almost gotten me killed last fall when he pulled me into his undercover investigation of a drug ring operating in our small town of Summerset, Iowa.

Closing my eyes, I pictured Rick in my mind. Dark brown hair, brown eyes to die for, and a crooked grin that turned most women to mush. I wasn't one of those women. At least, most of the time I wasn't.

"What do you want?" I asked suspiciously.

A chuckle rumbled over the phone lines. "Nice to hear your voice, too, Ophelia."

My eyes narrowed in the dark. "Oh yeah? If it's so nice, then—"

"I know. I'm sorry," Rick said, interrupting me. "I should've called, but I've been really busy. I heard you've been busy, too. Heard you helped catch Brian's killer."

I gripped the receiver in my hand. "How did you know about that?"

"I've still got contacts in Iowa. I heard the killer, Charles Thornton, came after you."

My grip on the phone tightened. Rick was right. Charles Thornton, the man who'd killed my best friend, Brian, five years ago in Iowa City, had found me in Summerset, where I'd moved after Brian's death.

Charles, a descendant of a judge who had served at the Salem witch trials, saw himself as a modern day witch hunter. And Abby and I were the ones he hunted. He convinced himself that we needed to die. His plan had been to kill me at the abandoned hog confinement facility and make it look like a suicide. After I was disposed of, he'd then go after Abby. I ruined Plan A when I got away from him, so he switched to Plan B—kill me and dump my body in the sewage pit. Luckily, after a struggle, it was Charles who wound up swimming in the hog manure, not me. The whole incident ended with Henry and company rescuing Charles and hauling him off to jail, where he was now awaiting trial.

"You didn't answer my question. What do you want?" I asked.

"I need your help."

My snort slipped out before he could continue. "Yeah? The last time I helped you, I got shot."

"I told you to stay out of it, but you had to go off on your own and go snooping around Adam Hoffman's machine shed."

"And you're lucky I did," I argued. "If I hadn't been there, you'd have been alone with Adam and his henchmen, Benny and Jake, trussed up like a turkey and tied to a pole. And remember, I was the one who got us out of there."

"Umm, yeah, I guess you're right . . ." Rick paused. "Except I still don't understand how you managed to do it."

"Never mind." I had no intention of trying to explain to Rick how I'd used the energy throbbing deep in the earth below the machine shed to distract Adam, Benny, and Jake long enough for us to escape. "So again—what do you want?"

"A young woman's disappeared and I need your help to find her," Rick said, getting right to the point. "She's eighteen and the only child of some good friends of mine."

I remembered my failure to help Henry find his missing man. "Rick, I don't think I can."

"Why not? You're psychic. And so's Abby."

"Look, I've tried to explain to you before, the gift doesn't always work. The images can be blurred and hard to figure out. I—"

"Before you make up your mind, hear me out," Rick interjected. "About four years ago, Brandi—that's the girl's name—Brandi Peters—seemed to change. It was right after her grandmother died . . ."

Those words struck a sympathetic response in my heart. My grandfather's death of a sudden heart attack when I was fifteen, and then Brian's death five years ago, had shaped my life in ways I was only now beginning to understand. But I kept my thoughts to myself and let Rick continue.

"She dropped a lot of her friends at school, started to dress differently, spend more time alone—"

"Did she get involved with drugs?" I interjected.

"I don't think so, but who knows? Kids can be good at

hiding things like that." Rick sighed. "It wasn't until she took off after her high school graduation that her mother found a bunch of books about spiritualism in her room."

"You think she was trying to contact her grandmother's spirit?"

"Probably. And I think that's how she wound up involved with a group up at Gunhammer Lake in Minnesota—the last place she was seen. The group is supposedly conducting paranormal research and psychic investigations. You and Abby—"

The phone slipped from my hand.

"—would be the perfect choice to check them out and see what you can learn," I heard Rick say as I returned the receiver to my ear.

"Group? Do you mean cult?"

"Well . . ." Rick's voice trailed off.

"You do. You want me and my seventy-four-year-old grandmother to infiltrate a cult?" I asked in a shocked voice.

"Hey, it's not a cult," Rick said defensively. "Not exactly. The group's not like the Manson group or Heaven's Gate. At least, I don't think they are."

"You don't *think*?"

"Pretty sure they're not. It's been hard for me to learn anything about them. The group does a lot of charity stuff for the town up there, so the townspeople are closed-mouth about anything to do with it."

"And you think the group would accept a couple of witches who happen to be psychics better than a snoopy reporter?"

"Yeah."

I could hear the smile in his voice.

"But you might want to forget the witch part. Just let it be known that you're psychics," Rick said.

"And how do we do that? Set up a crystal ball on the street corner and give readings?"

Rick's chuckle rumbled in my ear. "No, Madam Ophelia, I don't expect you to do that. Something a little more subtle would work better. It's a small town, drop a few well-chosen remarks and they'll seek you out."

"And if they don't?"

"You're resourceful. You'll figure something out."

I was silent while I thought about Rick's request. I understood how the loss of her grandmother might have affected Brandi, but that didn't mean I would be able to connect with her in some way. And I hadn't helped Henry—what made me think I could help Rick find the missing girl? But *no* died on my lips with his next words.

"Brandi never quite fit in, if you know what I mean. She always seemed to be struggling to discover who she was, even before her grandmother died." Rick paused, listening for my response. When I said nothing, he continued. "She wasn't a bad kid, just different, kind of lost. And since she was fourteen, I've watched while she tried to figure out where she belonged."

Where she belonged? Wow, could I understand that concept, and it was another link I had to the missing girl. Most of my life I'd been dealing with the same thing. If I hadn't had Abby to guide me, to understand what it's like to have a gift like mine, I would have been lost, too. Maybe . . .

Rick sensed my hesitation and pressed his advantage. "Her parents are beyond worried. She stopped calling about a month ago and they haven't heard from her since. Like I told you, Brandi is their only child, and they've tried everything to find her. The police have done all they can. I've tried to investigate, but I hit a wall of silence."

"Rick—"

"You two are the only people I know who might be able to find Brandi," he said, butting in. "Look, if I thought you or Abby would be in danger, I wouldn't ask you to do this."

I plucked at the blanket covering me. "Rick—"

"You do have vacation time, don't you?" he asked, breaking in again. "And don't worry—I'll cover all your expenses."

"Yes, I've got vacation time, and it's not about money. It's—"

"Please?"

The *please* and the desperation in his voice tipped the scale. Somewhere out there a young woman was lost. A young woman everyone saw as "different." I hadn't been able to help Henry, but maybe this time . . .

"Okay, I'll talk to Abby," I said with a groan.

As I drove up the lane leading to Abby's house, I saw the August heat shimmer in steamy waves above the gravel. It was only 9:00 A.M., and already the day promised to be a hot one. The heat wave we'd been having was affecting the vegetables Abby grew for her greenhouse. I noticed the pumpkin vines looked sad, as Abby would say. The green leaves seemed to droop toward the black soil at the base of the plant as if they were trying to suck what little moisture they could from the rich earth. If we didn't get rain soon, Abby wouldn't have many pumpkins to sell come Halloween. They'd all have withered on the vine.

Abby's farmhouse came into view when I rounded the

last corner of her lane. The house stood proud, with its dark green shutters shining against the brilliant white of the clapboard siding. And even in this heat the wide wraparound porch looked cool and inviting. During my summer stays as a child and as a teenager, I'd spent a lot of evenings on that front porch, swinging slowly back and forth on the swing, and sipping iced tea with either Grandpa or Abby. My lips twisted in a wry smile—even though Grandpa wasn't with us anymore, I still held his spirit in a special place in my heart. Abby, Grandpa, the memories this house held, they were my sanctuary. And even though I loved my parents, and they had provided me with a good life, Abby's house was and would always be "home" to me. A safe place to go when trouble seemed to surround me. A place where I belonged.

The girl Rick wanted us to find—Brandi. Did she ever have a refuge, somewhere to go when the problems overwhelmed her? Had she thought she'd found that special place with the group at Gunhammer Lake?

My car rolled to a slow stop, and I got out and walked up the path to Abby's front door. After two light raps, I swung the door open and strolled into Abby's wide entry.

"Knock knock. Anyone home?" I called, and sniffed the air. A delicious smell of fresh strawberries greeted me. I knew Abby must be putting up preserves. My nose guided me down the hall toward the kitchen located in the back of the house.

I paused in the doorway, watching my grandmother. She stood at her old wood-burning stove, stirring a steaming kettle of strawberries with one hand, while in the other she held the receiver of the phone. Turning, she smiled, and her eyes, the color of moss, crinkled in the corners. With the hand holding the wooden spoon, she waved me toward the table. I sat and waited for her to finish her conversation.

"Yes, I know. It's going to be hot," she said into the phone.

Even now, after living in Iowa for over fifty years, Abby's voice had the soft, easy tone of someone who'd been raised in the mountains of Appalachia. It was in those mountains where she'd learned the art of healing, using crystals, herbs, candles, and spells. An art taught to her by her mother, who in turn had been taught as a girl by Abby's grandmother. An art handed down from generation to generation, mother to daughter, grandmother to granddaughter, in a line of women stretching back over one hundred years. The art of magick.

But I had no child of my own, no daughter to train in the art. And with each passing year, the chances of ever having a child grew less and less. Unless my life changed, I would be the last of that line. The magick practiced so long by the women of my family would die with me.

The thought saddened me.

"Tsk tsk, such sad brown eyes for this early in the morning," Abby said, pulling my attention to her. "Why such a long face?"

I'd been so lost in my thoughts, I hadn't noticed that she had finished her conversation and now stood watching me as she dried her hands on her apron. Her hair was braided and coiled on the top of her head. And the steam from the strawberries made little tendrils of silver hair curl around her face. Sitting down at the table, she brushed them back.

I shook my head. "Never mind, it wasn't anything important. Hey, don't you think it's kind of hot to be canning?" I asked, and glanced at the row of bright red jars lined up on her counter. "Your woodstove puts out a lot of heat."

"Oh, nonsense." She brushed her hand in the air. "My mother canned in weather twice as hot as this. And without the benefit of electric fans."

Abby had all the modern conveniences—electricity, telephone, the things we take for granted. She even had a computer tucked away in one of the upstairs bedrooms and was becoming quite a whiz on the Internet. But in her kitchen, she preferred the old ways, the ways of her mother, and her mother's mother. Her kitchen looked like it had been transported from an old cabin in the mountains. Dried herbs hung in neat rows from the exposed beams in the ceiling, and the windowsills gleamed with rows of crystals.

I shook my head again, knowing it would be pointless to argue with her.

"So who were you talking to this early?" I asked, changing the subject.

"Arthur," she replied in a shy voice.

Oh yeah, Arthur, better known around Summerset as Stumpy, the owner of Stumpy's Bar and Billiards. And Abby's elderly boyfriend. I don't know; there was just something a little disconcerting about the idea of my grandmother having a romance, so my solution was to ignore it as much as possible.

"When he was here last night, he thought maybe he'd—"

I held up my hand, stopping her. "That's okay. I don't need to know what you were talking about." I felt a hot blush creeping up my neck.

Abby chuckled. "Poor Ophelia. You don't like to think about me being involved with someone, do you?"

"No, no," I stuttered. "It's not that. I like Stumpy . . . ahh, Arthur. I really do. He was great when you were in the hospital, after Charles Thornton had conked you on the head. But I just don't need to know . . ." I winced. ". . . the details."

She chuckled again. "You're worried about too much information?"

"Yup," I replied, nodding vigorously.

She reached over and patted my hand. "Don't worry, dear, I'll say no more."

I blew out a sigh of relief and smiled. "Thank you!"

"Since I had *company* last night . . ." Abby paused, noticing the look on my face, and smiled. ". . . I didn't have a chance to call you and ask you how your reading went with Henry. Were you able to help him?"

"No," I said, my voice laced with frustration. "The missing man is dead, a suicide, but I couldn't tell Henry where to find the body. All I saw was a pasture, with crows flying around. My last glimpse was a pile of bones, so I know they won't find him till next spring."

Abby folded her hands and looked down at them for a moment. "I'm sorry. Not knowing with certainty what happened to him will be hard on the man's family."

"Yeah, that's what Henry said, too." My face tightened in a frown. "Something else happened—Rick Delaney called me in the middle of the night."

Abby's eyes widened in surprise. "Rick. You haven't heard from him in some time, have you?"

"You're right. I haven't. After leaving Summerset last fall, he called pretty frequently, but then the calls became farther and farther apart. It's been, I don't know, at least three, maybe four months, since I've heard from him."

"Why now?"

"He wants our help. A young woman, the daughter of close friends, is missing."

"Is he sending you photos of her to try and trigger a vision?"

"No. I said he wants *our* help. He wants us to go to Minnesota to where the young woman, Brandi, was last seen."

"Why?"

"Well . . ." I said, and traced the pattern on Abby's tablecloth with my finger. "It seems she got mixed up with this group supposedly conducting psychic and paranormal research. He thinks sending a couple of psychics to snoop around would be a good idea."

"And we're the couple of psychics?"

I looked at Abby and smiled. "You got it."

"Hmm. I've never allowed myself to get involved with any kind of an investigation—"

My snort stopped her.

"Well, I haven't," she said defensively. "Not until last fall when we met Rick, and then, of course, this spring with Charles Thornton. But that's different, you were in danger, and I was trying to help."

She had a point. Abby had always kept the knowledge of her talent to herself. She had never done readings or given warnings of approaching disaster to anyone. And to do a spell to direct a specific outcome for someone behind their back, even if the spell was for their own good, was unthinkable. She felt very strongly that to try and influence events without a person's consent was a serious invasion of their privacy. She would give advice, if asked, but would do so under the guise of a "hunch." Whoever had sought her advice never knew it was based on anything other than the wisdom Abby had gained over the years. A very clever woman, my grandmother.

"Does that mean you don't think we should go?" I asked.

Abby gave me a thoughtful look. "No, I didn't say we shouldn't go, but I'm not getting any kind of a feeling about this Brandi."

"Do you think that means she's dead?"

"I don't know. Tell me exactly what happened. From the beginning."

"Okay. I was sound asleep, dreaming I was in the library. Mr. Carroll was there. A big black spider sat on his shoulder. He was yelling at me about the library's choice of books—"

Abby smiled. "Nothing odd about that. Mr. Carroll never likes the books you order. And you've been complaining for months that the library needs to be fumigated."

I arched an eyebrow. "Did I mention he was naked?"

"No, you left that part out," she replied, her smile widening.

I shuddered. "We'll talk more about why I would dream of a naked Mr. Carroll later. Anyway, Mr. Carroll's yelling was accompanied by a loud jangling. The phone. That's what woke me up. It was Rick. He told me about Brandi and asked for our help. That's it."

"What did he say about this Brandi?"

I shrugged. "She's an only child and her parents are very worried. She's been upset ever since her grandmother died. They haven't heard from her in a couple of months, which is unusual. Rick went up to Gunhammer Lake—that's where this group lives—but he didn't learn anything. He thinks we'll have better luck."

"What else did he say about Brandi? There's something about her that bothers you."

"Very astute."

"I'm psychic," she said with a chuckle.

"Supposedly, so am I," I said, shaking my head. "But I'm not really picking up much on this one. All I have is a sense of unease, but I don't know if it's because something's happened to the girl or because, from what Rick said, she has always been 'different.' "

"And you understand that?" Abby asked gently.

"Yeah, I do. If it hadn't been for your understanding of how I felt growing up, maybe I'd have been as lost as Brandi evidently is, or was."

"Well," Abby said as she pushed away from the table and stood, "I guess there's only one way to find out."

I looked up at her. "And what way is that? Some remote hocus-pocus to find out what we should do?"

"No, of course not," she said, crossing her arms in front of her. "We go to Minnesota."

# *Two*

For the rest of the day I stewed about calling Rick. My unease seemed to simmer in my mind like a bubbling cauldron, and I sought things to do around my small Victorian cottage.

Much to the resentment of Lady and Queenie, I gave them a bath and wormed them. After those tasks were finished, and under the distrustful eyes of the dog and cat, I cleaned out all my cupboards and organized my spice rack. I would've alphabetized the spices, but I thought that was carrying things a bit too far. Unfortunately, none of these jobs helped allay the thoughts cooking in my head.

What if Brandi had met with foul play? If so, how far would someone go to keep her fate a secret? From past experiences, I knew the threat of discovery could drive people to do horrendous things. A chill shot up my spine. Like what Adam Hoffman had done last fall when he murdered Butch Fisher and left his body in the woods, on the bank of the stream. Left there for the wildlife to dispose of. And by the time some poor unsuspecting soul—in this case, me—had literally stumbled onto the body, the scene wasn't a pretty one. Did

I want to risk exposing not only myself, but this time Abby, to something like that again?

Maybe Brandi had just taken off with some trucker and was too busy having fun to call home? If that were the case, our assistance wasn't needed. Eventually she'd turn up.

Thinking of Brandi, on the road, in a semi, didn't help my uneasiness. The thought cranked the feeling up another notch.

*Oh, just call Rick and go to Minnesota. Quit dithering about it!* said a voice in my head. But still I hesitated.

Pouring a glass of iced tea, I wandered out to the patio with Lady and Queenie at my heels. By now they'd both forgiven me for the worming and the baths. Pulling out a lawn chair, I propped my feet up and watched the stars flicker on, one by one.

Since last fall, after the incident with Adam Hoffman, I'd finally accepted my heritage, my gift, and had worked with Abby on learning the art of magick. And I was getting better. I still didn't have scrying down, where I'd stare into a flame and try and pick up an image, but I was getting pretty good at using my great-grandmother's runes. Abby had given them to me last fall, and by now I was able to think outside of the box, as Abby had advised me to do. The funny markings on the runes made sense to me now, and my accuracy was increasing.

Hmm, the runes. Abby didn't think remote hocus-pocus would help, but she hadn't said anything about not trying a rune reading. Shoving myself to my feet, I went back into the house to prepare.

After a purifying bath in sea salt, I dressed in a loose-fitting robe and went to the den located in the rear of my house, overlooking the trees that ring my backyard. It was my space, the space I'd created for magick.

I was still damp from my bath while I moved around the room lighting candles. A lot of questions tumbled through my mind, so I lit only the candles that would increase the energy I needed to seek my answers. When I finished, seven candles of black to bind me to the earth, and seven candles of indigo to increase my psychic awareness, lit the room with soft yellow light. My shadow danced across the bookcases as I walked to my desk.

Nestled there on the shiny surface was my collection of crystals. Amber for creativity, green fluorite for balance, rose quartz for love and harmony, emerald for healing; they glowed with the colors of the rainbow. I passed my hand over the shimmering crystals several times, and each time felt their combined energy vibrate around them. Finally, I selected the ones that would help me the most. I picked up a piece of hematite for grounding and an amethyst to increase my psychic energy and placed them in the pocket of my robe.

Walking to the center of the room, I set one silver candle in the middle of the polished wood floor. The energy of the silver candle would assist me in interpreting whatever I saw.

Starting at the north, I walked slowly clockwise while pouring a thin line of salt on the floor, creating a wide circle made of salt around the candle. The circle would protect me against any nasty energy lurking about, seeking a place to call home. But before I could start, I needed a few more things—a notepad and pen to record my impressions, a square of linen, and of course the runes.

When I picked up the worn leather bag that held them from the top of the desk, I felt the stones quiver inside the old sack. Almost as if they were excited to be of use again. Stepping carefully over the circle of salt, I sat down cross-legged on the floor in front of the candle and lit it.

Next I spread out the linen square. Laying the notebook and pen to the side and the runes on my lap, I took the hematite and amethyst out of my pocket. Holding the hematite in my right hand and the amethyst in my left, I concentrated on clearing my mind. And while I did, I tried to pull energy from the earth, up through my body. When I felt at peace and connected with the earth's energy, I framed my question.

*"What will we find in Minnesota?"*

After laying the amethyst and hematite in front of the candle, I reached into the bag and let the stones slip through my fingers until one felt just "right." After placing the stone in front of me on the linen, I repeated the process two more times.

The runes seemed to glow with a light of their own as they lay there on the linen square. A nice straight line of three; the Norns, the Three Sisters. Urdhr—the past, Verdhandi—the present, and Skuld—the future.

I turned the first one over.

Othlia. *"Oath-awe-law,"* I said aloud, pronouncing each syllable slowly to myself. Okay, it means a vision, an ideal, one who might be consumed by the past. Could mean Rick, or it could be the reason Brandi got involved with the group. She was consumed by an idea.

I moved on to the next one.

Ansuz. *"Awn-sooze."* I repeated it as I had Othlia. Hmm, to take the advice of someone. Someone older and respected. Well, that definition certainly fit Abby. So the advice of the runes was to listen to Abby. What a big surprise.

I hesitated before turning over the last rune. It was in the "future" position. I knew enough about magick and the runes to know they didn't lie. Did I *really* want to know the answer? What if the answer was one I didn't like? The future always had the potential of holding some nasty surprises. My hand hovered over the last stone. With a sigh, I flipped it over.

Perthro. *"Perth-row."* I said it softly. Mystery, secrets, the occult. Now what in the hell did that mean? The occult? Because most people associated the occult with witches, and Abby and I were witches? Mystery? No kidding, mystery. We had a missing girl on our hands.

Frustrated, I picked up the notebook and pen. I tapped the pen on my chin while I stared thoughtfully into the candle's flame.

The flame seemed to brighten and dim in a rhythmic pattern, while the air currents eddied around it. The sight was mesmerizing, and I don't know how long it held my attention. When I finally shook myself out of staring at the flame, I was surprised to see how far the candle had burned down. I'd only stared at it for a few moments, hadn't I?

I looked down at my lap at the notebook and my hand that still held the pen. Suddenly, the pen slipped from my nerveless fingers and rolled toward the candle.

Across the once clean, white surface of the paper, written about a hundred times, and in my loose scrawl, was one word. *Magic.*

And I didn't remember writing it.

Monday morning I stood at the bottom of the flight of steps leading to the library and looked up at the old limestone building. Until last fall, the library had been my home away from home. When I'd taken the job of

Summerset's librarian five years ago, after Brian's murder, I used the job to hide emotionally from everyone except Abby. I'd come to Summerset broken, swamped by feelings of guilt over my failure to stop Brian's murder in time. The vision I'd had witnessing the murder had come too late to save him.

It had been Rick and the events leading up to Adam, Benny, and Jake's capture that had finally knocked down the wall I hid behind. I'd been forced to accept who and what I was, to embrace my talent, to follow my destiny. And for that, I owed him.

Now I had to face my next problem. How to explain my trip to my assistant? Darci was a leggy, busty blonde who most people wrote off as an airhead. I shook my head. If they only knew what went on behind those big blue eyes. She possessed a sharp mind and the ability to figure things out faster than most. Sometimes it seemed like she was the psychic, not me. And she always wanted to be right in the middle of what she called "my adventures." And when I told her about Rick's phone call, she would insist on going to Minnesota with Abby and me.

But my answer had to be no.

Reluctantly, I trudged up the stairs. Pausing at the top, I hoisted my backpack firmly on my shoulder and swung open the door.

Darci stood behind the counter, filing library cards. Her long red fingernails clicked against the countertop as she picked each card. When she looked up and saw me standing there, she smiled. "Good morning. Hey," she said, pointing a figure at me, "that eye makeup looks really good on you. Makes your brown eyes pop."

I touched my face self-consciously and nodded. Thanks to Darci, my medicine cabinet was full of things she had assured me I needed—blush, eye shadows, mascara, and all the girly stuff I'd never paid much attention to. And if I didn't use the entire gunk she picked out for me, it hurt her feelings. Now my morning routine had been extended by twenty minutes.

"How was your weekend?"

I crossed to the counter. "Okay," I replied, and stowed my backpack on one of the shelves. "Nothing too exciting."

She eyed me suspiciously. "I doubt that. Didn't you tell me Henry was coming by with some pictures?"

"Yeah, but it didn't work. I didn't see anything that could help him find his missing person. The man's dead. A suicide. But I couldn't tell him where to find the body."

"How did Henry take it?"

"In typical Iceman fashion," I said, picking up my own stack of cards and thumbing through them. "He wasn't going to let on how disappointed he was, but I could tell. He really wanted to be able to give the man's family some kind of answer." I stopped, feeling the frustration pick at me once again. "Some answer other than, 'He's dead and we don't know where.' "

"I'm sorry. I know it's hard when you don't see things clearly."

"Yeah. Well, it's going to be harder on his family while they wait until his body's found." I turned away from the counter and grabbed a pile of returned books from the shelf. Setting them on the counter, I flipped the cover open. "Ahh, Darci, there's something else I want to tell you. Rick called—"

She grabbed my arm. "Really? When? Is he coming back to Summerset?"

I held up my hand, stopping her. "Calm down. He called late Saturday night, and no, he's not coming to

Summerset. Umm, he has a little job for us. He wants us to come to Minnesota and help him find a missing girl."

"Great, when do we leave?" she asked, her eyes sparkling with excitement.

I gave her a pointed look. "Darci, when I said 'us,' I meant Abby and me."

Her face settled into a pout. "Why can't I come, too? You might need my help."

"I also need you to stay here and take care of the library while I'm gone. I've got all the arrangements made with the library board, and we're leaving tomorrow," I said, my tone final.

"I don't think that's fair. You're always trying to keep me away from all of the excitement."

"I'm also trying to keep you out of harm's way. Look, the girl was mixed up with some kind of cultlike group, and I don't know what we'll be walking into when we arrive. I'm going to have a hard enough time keeping an eye on Abby, without worrying about you, too."

"Humph," she said, not buying my excuse. "I suppose I can't force you to take me with you." She stopped and eyed me thoughtfully. "What does Henry think?"

The sudden shift in conversation startled me. "What do you mean?"

"Does Henry think you should go?" Darci asked in an even voice.

"I don't need his permission," I said indignantly.

"You're right, you don't." She traced a finger across the counter. "But I imagine he's not going to like it."

I lifted my chin a notch. "I don't care whether he likes it or not."

Darci looked at me skeptically.

"Well, I don't. And don't be manufacturing another one of your imaginary romances starring me and Henry," I said, shaking a finger at her. "There's nothing between Henry and me. He barely likes me."

She arched an eyebrow.

"I mean it," I said, and paced over to the bookshelves with an armload of books. "I've got enough to think about right now. So much has happened to me since last fall that Henry Comacho is the least of my concerns."

Darci walked over and stood beside me. "Like what? What else is bothering you?"

"This town," I said, shoving a book onto the shelf. "Haven't you noticed all the sideways glances I've been getting?"

"Well, you have demonstrated a real talent for finding dead bodies. Last fall, Butch Fisher, and then this spring you found Gus." ·

I winced when she mentioned Gus Pike. Another friend I'd lost thanks to Charles Thornton. Gus had been a harmless old man, a recluse, and my friend. Charles, in his fervor to stamp out witches, had assumed Gus was a witch and had literally scared the old man to death. Then he buried Gus's body in a ditch, hoping I'd find it. I had. Tripped and fell right on top of the spot Charles had buried the remains. Only Henry, Abby, and Darci knew of the vision I'd had that led me to the ditch and Gus's shallow grave.

"Look," she said, lightly touching my arm. "It will all blow over eventually."

"When?"

Darci shrugged. "Soon. When the next big deal happens. Just don't find any more bodies in the meantime."

"No problem." I shuddered. I *hated* finding dead

people. "But what do you think will happen when it comes out at Charles's trial that he suspected Abby and me of being witches?"

"Nothing." She shrugged again. "He's nuts."

I hoped Darci was right, but I doubted it. What would the conservative little town of Summerset think when they learned that, yes, witches were among them?

# Three

By seven o'clock that evening my suitcases were packed and lined in a neat row in the hallway by my front door. Not that I had many—I'm a blue jeans and T-shirt kind of a girl, and packing a week's worth was a snap. Now all I needed to do was fetch the cat carrier in from the garage. But that would wait until morning. Queenie viewed the box as an instrument of torture, and if she saw it before then, she'd take off and I'd be playing hide and seek trying to find her.

I stood in the hallway, hands on my hips, surveying the suitcases and going over my list of last minute details in my mind when the doorbell rang. Startled, I jumped. Who could be stopping by this time of night? Probably Darci with one last bid to be included in the trip.

When I peeked out the window, I was surprised to see Henry Comacho standing on my front porch. Dressed in jeans and T-shirt, he glanced around the neighborhood before pressing the bell again. Now what did he want? I'd failed so miserably in helping him find the missing man; he surely didn't want me to try again? Nope. I didn't see a folder in his hand. I crossed to the door and opened it.

"Hey, Henry. What can I do for you?" I asked.

He shoved his hands in his pockets before answering me. "Ahh, sorry to stop by without calling, but I wanted to apologize if I was a little short with you on Saturday." He stared at a spot over my right shoulder, not meeting my eyes. "I know you did your best."

Hmm, the Iceman apologizing? I knew the words "I'm sorry" tended to gag Henry, so he must really feel bad. That or he wanted something else from me.

"It's okay," I said, swinging the door wider. "I know you were counting on my help. I'm sorry that what I saw couldn't lead you to the body."

"We, ahh, found his car Sunday. There's a bike rack on it, but no bike. And his wife said his backpack is gone, too."

"So he could be anywhere?"

"Yeah. And if what you saw was the truth, now we know he's dead."

I thought about the pile of bones. "Oh, he's dead," I said emphatically.

"Yeah, well." Henry stopped, pulled his hands out of his pocket and ran a hand through his hair.

I felt Henry's doubt, his uncertainty. My talent was hard for him to accept, so I took pity on him. "Listen, would you like some iced tea? It's too hot for coffee, but I've got sun tea in the fridge."

He ran a hand through his hair again. "Yeah. Sure."

I turned and started to walk back to the kitchen, presuming Henry followed. But when I glanced over my shoulder, I saw he had stopped and was looking at the neat row of suitcases.

"Going somewhere?" he asked.

"Yup." Okay, so do I tell him the truth or not? Abby always said honesty was the best policy, so I opted for the truth. At least part of the truth.

"Let me pour the tea," I said, hustling down the hall, "and I'll explain."

In the kitchen, I poured two glasses of tea while Henry settled down at the table. Seating myself, I took a long drink from my glass, stalling.

"Are you going to tell me where you're going?" Henry asked, watching me.

"Yes," I said, setting my glass down. "Abby and I are going to Minnesota. To Gunhammer Lake."

Henry's eyes narrowed. "Why?"

"Umm, an old friend invited us."

His eyes were narrowed into slits now. "What old friend?"

"Rick Delaney," I said, popping out of my chair. "Hey, would you like some sugar for your tea?"

He reached over and lightly grabbed my arm. "No thanks. Will you sit down and tell me why Rick Delaney invited you to Minnesota? He's the reporter involved with you in that drug bust last fall, isn't he?"

"Uh, yeah," I said, sitting back down and tucking a stray strand of hair behind my ear. "He has a little problem and he thinks Abby and I can help him."

"What kind of problem?" Henry took a long drink of tea.

"Oh, you know. Just a problem," I said, wiping the beads of moisture off my glass of tea.

"No, I don't know," he said, watching me closely. "'Just a problem' isn't very specific."

I should've known it wasn't going to be easy telling Henry only part of the truth. He was a cop, and, I knew from experience, very good at pulling information out

of someone. He tried often enough with me in the past.
Might as well lay the whole story out.

"Okay. There's a missing girl he thinks we can help
him find. She was last seen at Gunhammer Lake, where
she was involved with a group up there."

"Group?" His voice had a distinct edge. "You mean
as in cult?"

I slapped my hand on the table and smiled. "You
know, Henry, it's funny you should say that. I asked Rick
the same question."

He slid his glass out of the way and folded his hands.
"And his answer was?"

My smile faded. "Ahh, he didn't think so?"

"Are you asking me if that's what he said?" He looked
at me intently.

"Well, no." My words stumbled out of my mouth. "I
mean, you weren't there, so how could you know what
he said?"

"You're right, I wasn't there," he said in a tone one
would use with a four-year-old. "I don't know what he
said. That's why I'm trying to get the information out
of you."

"There's no need to be sarcastic about it," I said, taking another sip of tea.

Henry pulled a hand through his hair. It seemed to
be a constant habit of his whenever he was around me.

"Look, just tell what you're planning on doing."

"Oh, all right," I said, and gave up on disseminating.
I looked at Henry with steely eyes. "You're not going to
yell, are you? Lady doesn't like it when you yell."

Lady, from where she was laying on the floor by
Henry's chair, perked up her ears at the sound of her
name.

Henry reached down and scratched her ears. "No, I'm not going to yell," he said, smiling down at the dog.

"Well, then. The group in Minnesota that the girl, Brandi, was involved with is supposedly conducting research into psychic phenomena and the paranormal. We're going to ask some questions; snoop around. Rick thinks—" I was so involved in my story, I missed the look on Henry's face, and I jumped when his voice echoed off the kitchen walls.

*"You're what?"*

"Hey, you said you wouldn't yell," I said indignantly.

"I said that before I knew what a scatterbrained scheme you've gotten yourself into." He pushed back from the table.

"It's *not* scatterbrained," I said, my voice rising. "Rick thinks it's a great idea sending two psychics up to the lake to investigate. Rick also thinks—"

"I don't give a good god—" Henry stopped and tried to compose himself before continuing. "I don't care what Rick thinks. Number one," he said, holding up one finger, "neither you nor Abby are trained investigators." He held up a second finger. "Number two, you have no business bumbling into a situation that could be dangerous. Number three—"

"Look, I understand," I said, cutting him short. "And I take exception to the word 'bumbling.' I do not bumble." I crossed my arms in front of me.

"No, you just fall over dead bodies all the time," he said, glaring at me.

"Only two," I shot back.

"That's two more than most people," he said, leaning forward and crossing his arms on the table.

"Hey, that's not my fault. And finding those bodies helped catch two killers. Did you forget about that?" I pointed out, leaning forward.

"Right. And the first time you got shot, and the second time you were going to be strangled and dumped in hog manure."

He had a point.

"I'll be careful."

"You are not going," he said decisively, and sat back in his chair.

I sprang to my feet and stood as tall as my five-foot-four height would allow. "Listen, you have no right to tell me what I will or will not do. If I want to help find this lost girl, that's my business, not yours." Now it was my voice that echoed in the kitchen. "You didn't think twice about asking me to help you."

By now Henry was also standing. "When I asked you to help me, it didn't require you to be put in the line of fire. All I did was ask you to look at pictures. Not cozy up to some cult." He took one step toward me.

"We're not joining a cult," I said, taking a step toward him.

"No, you're going to stick your nose in where it doesn't belong. Again. And one of these days, it's going to get cut off." He took another step forward.

The distance between us had closed, and we were right in each other's face. Henry's eyes were flashing black fire, and I'm sure mine were just as angry.

"It's none of your concern if I get my nose cut off," I said right in his face.

"Maybe it isn't." He took a deep breath. "Maybe you expect your *psychic* talent will save you," he said, his voice derisive. "Or maybe witchcraft." He snorted. "I hope you do a better job for Rick than you did for me."

I knew Henry had a problem accepting my talents, but his remark cut deep. I took a step back. "You just don't get it, do you? I couldn't help you so that means I'm a fake?" I narrowed my eyes and stared at him. "You had a front row seat to what I can do, but you don't want to accept that there might be more to the world than you can explain."

"What's to explain?" Henry reached in his shirt pocket and pulled out his sunglasses. "Sure, I gave it a shot, to see if you could help me, but it didn't work. I get more results dealing in facts, not hocus-pocus."

The next thing I knew, he turned on his heel and stomped out of the kitchen. The last thing I heard was Henry slamming out of the door and out of my life.

I paced the small space between the beds and the dresser. Queenie lay curled up on one of the pillows, while Lady slept in the corner with her head resting on her paws.

I guess I wore her out with my pacing.

The room Rick had reserved for us at the motel was nice, nothing fancy, but nice. Floral bedspreads covered the two queen-size beds, and a little table, with an armchair positioned next to it, sat by the window. Abby sat in the chair now, trying to read and ignore my pacing. After an uneventful trip from Summerset to the Twin Cities, we had decided we'd stay in St. Paul that night, meet Brandi's family, then drive to Gunhammer Lake in the morning. Right now we were waiting for Rick to pick us up and drive us to the Peters home. And as usual Rick was late.

I paused in my pacing and glanced at my reflection in the mirror.

"My hair," I said while I fluffed the dark brown strands with my fingers, "are you sure it looks okay?"

Abby's eyes met mine in the mirror and she smiled. "Yes, Ophelia, it looks fine. The highlights Darci persuaded you to add are very becoming."

"What about these jeans?" I asked. Turning sideways and sucking my stomach in, I critically eyed myself in the mirror. "Do they make me look fat?"

"No, dear, they don't make you look fat."

In the mirror, I saw Abby pick up her book and start reading again.

"You're sure?" I fluffed my hair again.

With a sigh, she laid her book on the table. "Yes, I'm sure. I'm also sure your hair looks fine, the top you're wearing is lovely, and your makeup is just right."

"Rick's late, you know," I said, turning and leaning against the dresser.

"Yes. I know. Maybe he was held up at the newspaper."

"He could've called," I said, twisting back around to the mirror and brushing a stray hair away from my face. In the mirror, I saw Abby shake her head. "Well, he could of," I said, my tone defensive.

"Would you please sit down? All your pacing and preening is wearing, not only Lady, but me out."

Reluctantly, I walked to the bed near Abby and sat, clasping my hands tightly in my lap.

She watched me with a wry look on her face. "I swear, you're like a spring wound too tight." Reaching over to me, she placed a gentle hand on my knee. "What's wrong with you tonight, Ophelia?"

I tugged at my lower lip. "I don't know."

"Is it meeting Rick again after all these months?" she asked.

"Of course not," I replied, lifting my chin.

A look of disbelief crossed Abby's face. "You haven't seen him since last November."

"So?" I said, popping to my feet and striding to the window. "Rick is only a friend, nothing more." I pulled back a corner of the curtain and peered out the window into the parking lot. Truth was, I didn't know how I felt. Letting the curtain fall back into place, I walked back to the bed and plopped down.

Abby eased back in the chair, lowered her head and studied her folded hands.

"You don't believe me, do you?" I asked.

She raised her head and looked at me. "No, I don't. You and Rick shared a very intense experience, a life threatening experience. That can draw people together, create a bond—"

"Maybe, but whatever bond might have existed last November couldn't stretch over the three hundred miles that separated us." I leaned toward Abby. "And remember, at the time, you told me Rick wasn't the one for me."

"Yes, I did. And at the time, he wasn't. But now . . ." Her voice trailed off.

I leaned closer. "What do you mean 'but now'?"

Abby lifted her shoulders. "Life's pattern can change. What is true one moment, might not be true the next."

"And now? What's true now?" I asked.

Before she could answer, we heard a sharp rap at the door.

Exchanging a look with Abby, I rose slowly and walked to the door. After turning the dead bolt, I opened it.

The light in the hallway made his dark brown hair gleam. His brown eyes were as warm as I remembered them. His face, a little thinner than the last time I'd seen him, wore his trademark grin. And the confidence that had always seemed to wrap around him like a cloak, which had been both annoying yet at the same time endearing, still poured off of him in waves.

Before I could take a step back, he reached out and gathered me in a hug that took my breath away.

I guess Rick Delaney was happy to see me.

# Four

After exchanging pleasantries with Abby, Rick whisked us out of the motel room and to his car. I was still confounded by the massive hug, so I let Abby and Rick carry the conversation, half listening while Rick repeated to Abby what he'd already told me about Brandi. Me? I busied myself watching the suburban landscape fly by.

Strip malls, large malls, car dealerships, passed by one after another. And cars were everywhere I looked—cars whizzing by us on the beltway; cars on the entrance ramp waiting to crowd their way into the rushing stream; cars sitting in the packed parking lots of the malls. So many cars and so many people. The air hummed with the vibrancy of the city. It was such a different lifestyle than the one in our small Iowa town, and it was the one Rick had chosen.

After a few miles, Rick pulled off onto the exit ramp, and after traveling a few blocks, turned onto a quiet street. Large trees stood on both sides. And well-kept houses nestled on neat yards beneath the trees' sheltering branches. It looked like a nice, peaceful neighborhood. But I knew behind the facade of one of those nice, attractive homes lived a couple who had no peace in their lives. Their daughter was missing.

He slowed the car to a complete stop in front of one of the houses. Ever the gentleman, he got out and walked to Abby's side and helped her out. Together we walked up the flagstone path, and Rick rang the doorbell.

The woman who answered the door was probably in her late forties, but she looked older. A webbing of fine lines gathered around her eyes, and deep creases bracketed her mouth on both sides. Her hair, blond with gray streaks, was dull and flat. Lifeless.

But it was her eyes that caught my attention. They were the saddest eyes I'd ever seen, and when they traveled from Abby and me to Rick, I saw the light of hope flicker in their depths.

"Hi, Joan," Rick said, giving her a quick hug. Turning, he ushered Abby and me through the door. "I'd like you to meet Abigail McDonald and her granddaughter, Ophelia Jensen."

Abby quickly stepped forward and took the woman's hand in both of hers. "Hello, Joan. It's nice to meet you."

From where I stood, slightly behind Abby, my senses picked up Abby's energy. She was sending a current through their joined hands and into Joan. She was sharing her strength with the poor woman.

Joan's face seemed to brighten as Abby held her hand, the lines around her mouth less pronounced. She didn't speak for a moment, but then smiled at Abby. "I'm pleased to meet you, Mrs. McDonald."

"Please call me Abby," she answered, releasing the woman's hand.

Joan's eyes turned to me. "Hi, Joan," I said, lightly shaking her hand.

She acknowledged me with a slight bob of her head. "Come in," she said, and waved us into the living room on her left.

The room looked like a picture out of a folksy decorating magazine. Country cute was everywhere. Dried flower arrangements sat on the end tables next to bowls of potpourri. Candles in heavy jars flanked the mantel above the fireplace, and I could smell the faint aroma of apples and cinnamon.

Set between the candles, in a prominent place, was a picture of a young woman. Walking over, I studied it.

The young woman held a graduation certificate tightly in one hand. I couldn't see much of her hair beneath the mortarboard she wore, but it looked to be a strange orange color. Underneath the mortarboard and the orange hair, her face wore a totally bored expression, not a glimmer of a smile, not a look of pride at having completed high school. It was almost as if she posed in the traditional graduation garb to humor her parents.

Joan joined me at the mantel. "That's Brandi. The picture was taken at graduation. In May." She traced a finger slowly down the side of the frame. "We were so proud, watching her receive her diploma. We wanted her to go to college, but she wasn't interested. Instead, she took the money her grandmother had given her for her education and left. She said she needed to find herself, before she made any decisions about the rest of her life. Within a week of moving out, she was living with that group at Gunhammer Lake."

A slow tear crept down Joan's face, and she absentmindedly brushed it away. Her eyes left the photograph and traveled to mine. "Can you help us find her?" she asked in a whisper.

I felt my heart squeeze at the pain and desperation in

her voice. I thought of my failure in locating Henry's missing man, and Henry's reaction. Is this what he faced every day on the job? Worried families frantic to find their missing loved ones? If so, no wonder he kept the wall of ice wrapped around him. He had to. No one could survive serving witness to this kind of distress on a daily basis.

"I don't know, Joan. I—"

"Ophelia, Joan," Rick interjected, "why don't you sit down? And Joan, you can tell Ophelia and Abby about Brandi."

Joan nodded and motioned to the couch. I took my place next to Abby, with Joan and Rick sitting across the coffee table from us in a couple of wing-back armchairs.

"I don't know where to start," Joan said, twisting her hands in her lap.

"When was the last time you heard from her?" Abby asked gently.

"About a month ago. She called from a pay phone near the lake. She sounded upset, but she wouldn't tell me what was wrong. Just things weren't turning out like she expected them to."

"In what way?" I leaned forward.

Joan chewed on her bottom lip for a moment before she spoke. "At first she'd seemed happy with PSI—"

"PSI? Isn't that how some refer to paranormal phenomena?" I asked.

Joan lifted one shoulder in a shrug. "I think so. She mentioned something about how it was an acronym. The letters stand for Psychic Study Institute. Until Brandi got involved with this group, I never paid much attention to that kind of thing."

"Rick said you found books in Brandi's room about

spiritualism. Did Brandi believe she was psychic?" Abby asked.

"Oh heavens, no." Joan's tone was emphatic. "Her father wouldn't have stood for such nonsense." A slight blush crept up her face when she realized what she'd said.

Abby's eyes slid over to mine and one eyebrow lifted. Hmm, the father thought psychic talent was nonsense, yet they were asking two psychics for help?

My eyes moved from Abby's to Joan, sitting in the chair. "Does your husband know that you've asked for our help, Joan?" I asked.

Joan's hands balled into tight fists. "He knows you're going to Gunhammer Lake to investigate Brandi's disappearance."

"Ben's in Duluth right now on an overnight business trip," Rick interjected. "We thought it would be best if you and Abby met with Joan alone."

Abby fixed a look on Rick. "How much have you told her about us?"

"The truth—that you're both very talented psychics." Unspoken words passed between Abby and Rick.

Rick had left out that we were witches. Wise choice on his part. Joan was so anxious to find her daughter that she was willing to believe in anything. But if her husband had problems believing that psychic abilities existed, how would he feel about two women who were not only psychics, but witches, trying to find their missing daughter?

"Let's get back to how Brandi sounded the last time you talked to her," Abby said calmly. "She was upset?"

"Yes."

"But prior to that conversation, she'd sounded happy when she called you?"

"Yes. Happy and excited. She didn't go into details, but she said Jason—Jason Finch, the leader of the group," Joan explained, "was amazing. He could do things she'd never imagined."

"Like what?" Abby asked.

"She didn't go into details, but she hinted that he could talk to the spirits, make things disappear, read minds. I guess things that most psychics can do," Joan said, staring down at her lap.

Abby glanced toward the window. I knew what she was thinking. Although psychic talent covers a lot of different abilities, I'd never heard of anyone who could make something disappear. Talk to spirits, read minds, yeah, but make things disappear? Sounded to me like a parlor trick to pull in the gullible.

"You mentioned, Joan, that Brandi had money from her grandmother. Do you know if she was giving any of it to the group?" I asked, leaning forward.

Joan shook her head. "Not that I'm aware of. We don't have access to her bank account, so I really don't know."

I turned to Rick, who had been silent as we questioned Joan. "What did you learn about the group's finances while you were at the lake?"

"Not much. On the surface, they seem to be financially independent and they give quite a bit of money back to the community." Rick leaned forward, his elbows resting on his knees. "It's an economically depressed area up there, and their generosity has endeared them to the people. One of the reasons people won't talk about them. My instincts tell me this whole deal isn't about money."

"What then?" I felt perplexed. I knew Rick believed if you followed the money, you'd find the solution.

His eyes twinkled and he grinned. "I'm counting on you finding that out."

I rolled my eyes and hoped I earned his faith.

"Tell me more about the group," I said, instead of sharing my thoughts. "How many people and where are they living?"

"I don't know for sure; about ten, I think. Most of them spend all their time at the compound. The most visible ones are Juliet, Jason's wife, and a woman they call Winnie. Winnie's the one I saw the most. She appears to be some kind of a gofer for Jason and Juliet. Short, dumpy woman, can't miss her. And then there's a young girl. I heard she's Jason and Juliet's foster daughter, but I never saw her. Her name is Tink."

*Who in their right mind would name a kid Tink?*

"Did Brandi ever mention any of these people?" Abby asked.

"She talked about Jason, of course, and Juliet. She held Jason in awe, but seemed close to Juliet. And when she talked about this woman, Winnie, she made disparaging remarks. She didn't like her."

"What about the foster daughter?" I asked. "This Tink? Did she mention her?"

Joan smoothed her hands over the arms of her chair. "Once or twice. She described the girl as 'spooky.' "

"In what way?"

Joan lifted a hand. "I don't know. She never explained. Our phone conversations were always short. The group disapproved of contact with the members' families, so Brandi had to be careful about calling home."

Abby stood abruptly. "Do you have any other pictures of Brandi?"

Joan also stood. "Of course. The photo albums are in the den. This way."

Abby and I followed her out of the living room and down the hall. She stopped in front of a set of double doors and swung them open.

"The albums are in here," she said.

Abby paused at the doorway and laid a hand on Joan's arm. "Would you mind if we looked at them alone?"

Joan's eyebrows knitted into a small frown. "No. They're all on the bottom row," she said, pointing to the bookcases lining the walls behind the desk.

"Thank you," Abby said, smiling at her.

Passing Joan, I followed Abby in. It was definitely her husband's room. Very tweedy and masculine. No frou-frou or flowers anywhere. And the air still carried the faint aroma of cigar smoke.

Abby and I each grabbed a photo album, sat down, placed them on the desk and opened them. Mine began with the first months of Brandi's life. As I flipped through the pages, I saw her change from a chubby-cheeked toddler to a little girl in pink dresses with matching ribbons in her hair. Her smile went from toothless to bright and innocent.

"Cute kid," I mumbled as I flipped through the pages showing Brandi as a gawky adolescent.

"What, dear?" Abby asked.

"I said 'cute kid.' It's hard to imagine these are pictures of the same girl as the one on the mantel. The one with the orange hair."

"Take a look at these."

Abby pushed the album toward me and we switched albums. The photos on the first few pages were similar to those in the album I'd already seen. But about halfway through they began to change. Brandi wasn't a wide-eyed little tot anymore, or a young girl on the edge of womanhood. Her smile changed to a sullen grimace. The pink dresses had morphed into ripped black T-shirts and low-slung black jeans. An eyebrow ring hung above eyes ringed in black eyeliner. And the hair—in the last picture it looked like Brandi had used Easter egg dye to color it. Strands the colors of candy pink, robin's-egg blue, and lime green stuck up in stiff spikes from her scalp.

I glanced at Abby. She stood, her head tipped back and her eyes closed as she ran her hand over the slick surface of the photos

"Anything?" I said, watching her.

"Umm?"

"Are you getting anything from her pictures?"

"A happy childhood, a close relationship with her mother, but the father is distant. Too busy pursuing a career to pay much attention to a little girl." Abby flipped to another page. "School is easy, but at the same time hard. She doesn't fit in. She sees the world in a different way than the other children—"

"Psychic?" I interrupted.

"No, but highly intuitive. Her intuition makes it hard to relate to her teachers and her classmates. She begins to spend more and more time by herself." Abby slid the album to the side and reached for the one I had been looking at. She opened it to the last page, to the one of Brandi with black-ringed eyes and Easter-egg-colored hair. Placing both hands on the photo, she lowered her head.

"Water, dark, lost, alone . . ." Abby's voice trailed off as her shoulders shook slightly.

I started to reach for her when she lifted her head and looked at me.

"We need to find this girl fast."

"You're sure she's still alive?"

Abby passed a hand over her forehead as if to rub the images away. "Yes, I am. But she's in danger and we must find her soon."

# *Five*

After leaving Joan, Rick offered to take Abby and me out to dinner. Still mulling over Abby's impressions, I almost missed the invitation, but Abby's quick response caught my attention.

I leaned forward from my place in the backseat. "But Abby, what about Queenie and Lady? I don't want to leave them cooped up too long in the room."

"They'll be fine," she said with a wave of her hand.

"Okay." I settled back in my seat.

Rick chose an Olive Garden not too far from our motel. Once seated, we all ordered the fettuccini, and over the breadsticks and salad, Rick kept the conversation going at a steady pace.

I let the talk buzz around me while I picked at my salad. So many thoughts bounced around in my head that I couldn't focus on one, let alone the subject Rick and Abby discussed. One observation did penetrate my busy brain. Rick hadn't lost any of the easy charm that had made him so popular in Summerset last fall.

I glanced over at him. He looked good tonight, looked every inch a successful reporter. He'd worn an ivory knit shirt with blue jeans that accentuated his summer tan. And his eyes—they'd been the first thing I noticed about him that day in the library when we met. They hadn't changed. They still had the same sparkle, the same hint of amusement lurking there. Last fall those eyes, in spite of my better judgment, seemed to reach out and pull me in.

I guess they still did.

Rooting around in my salad with my fork, I found a tomato and stabbed it. Maybe a little harder than I needed to.

"What's bothering you, Ophelia?" Rick asked, switching his attention from Abby to me.

"Nothing's bothering me," I replied, and popped the tomato in my mouth.

"Oh yeah? You nailed that tomato like you were trying to kill it."

"Did not," I muttered, with tomato tucked firmly in my cheek.

"Did, too," Rick shot back, his eyes twinkling.

"Children, children," Abby interjected with a look of amusement on her face. "Let's not bicker over dinner."

Rick winked at Abby. "She started it."

I chewed the tomato and gave Rick a tight smile. "You are *such* a suck-up," I said after swallowing.

"Only to women as lovely as your grandmother," he said with another wink at Abby.

"Did I also mention," I said sweetly, "that you're full of—"

"Ophelia!" Abby's eyes drilled me with a stern look.

Chastised, I turned back toward Rick. "Okay, okay. I'll be nice."

Rick's eyes met mine and his mouth twisted in a crooked grin. "Sure it won't kill you?"

Pushing my plate to the side, I crossed my arms on

the table and leaned forward. "You know, Delaney, no matter how hard . . ." My voice trailed off when Abby laid a hand on my arm. I looked up and saw the waiter standing next to me, holding a plate patiently in one hand. Scooting back in the booth, my eyes downcast, I placed my hands in my lap while he served each of us.

"Enjoy your dinner," he said brightly, and left.

Looking up, I saw Rick watching me with that stupid grin still on his face. The rat! After all this time, he still liked to tease me, still get under my skin. He thought the waiter overhearing our exchange was funny. I narrowed my eyes, a sharp retort forming on my tongue, but before I could deliver it, Abby spoke.

"As interesting as it may be to listen to the two of you argue, I think we have a more important matter at hand," she said, picking up her fork.

Rick's grin faded, and along with it, his teasing manner. "Brandi," he said shortly. "What happened when you were alone in the library?"

Abby twirled the fettuccini around her fork. "I feel she's still alive," she said, not really answering Rick's question.

A look of relief crossed his face. "She's okay?"

Abby tilted her head to the side. "I didn't say that . . ." She hesitated, stalling for time in order to decide how much information to give him. "She *is* in some kind of trouble."

"What kind of trouble?" Rick asked.

"It's not clear," Abby replied.

"Look, Rick," I interjected. "I told you these visions aren't very specific at times. We need more information about this 'cult.' "

"I think I told you, there are about ten people living at the compound—"

"Ha," I scoffed. "Doesn't sound like much of a 'cult' to me. Only ten people? I thought cults were larger than that?"

Rick gave me a patient look. "I told you I don't know if you could call PSI a cult. They could just be a group of harmless New Agers. It depends—"

"On what?" I broke in.

"On how much control Jason Finch has over the rest of the members."

"In what way?"

"Well . . ." Rick paused. "If he limits their access to the outside world, if he controls their behavior through criticism, if he demands their total obedience to his ideology, then I'd call PSI a cult."

"But you don't know?"

He shook his head. "No. Like I told you, the townspeople wouldn't talk about the group. Winnie and Juliet avoided me once they learned who I was. And the other members were like shadows. I know there were at least three other couples living at the compound, but they're rarely seen in town."

"So Jason could be controlling them?"

"Yes. And a smaller group makes it easier for the leader to *stay* in control."

"Any dissension is easily rooted out," I said thoughtfully.

"Exactly—"

"And from what Joan said, Brandi was unhappy, so she might have been causing a rift in the group."

"And if Brandi had been creating problems," Abby said quietly, "then she would've been either ostracized or punished. That's what you think happened, isn't it, Rick?"

His eyes traveled to Abby's face and his voice sounded weary. "I don't know."

"Hey, Delaney, don't worry about it," I said with more confidence that I felt. "We'll find her, won't we, Abby?"

Abby touched Rick's hand and smiled. "We'll do our best."

A flicker of a grin touched his face. "Thanks."

I picked up my fork and looked at Rick. "Okay, so does everyone live in the same house?"

"No. Here, let me show you."

I ate in silence while Rick laid his fork down and, taking a pen and a small notebook from his pocket, began to draw in it. "The main house is here," he said, making a large square in the center of the page. "From there the land slopes sharply down to the lake." He made a squiggly line to show the lakeshore. "A boathouse with sleeping quarters above the boat storage area sits right on the lakeshore." He drew another box. "Two cottages are located along the long lane that leads from the main road to the property." Two more boxes appeared on the page. "The whole place is surrounded on three sides by a very large chain-link fence." He finished by drawing three lines around the boxes.

"Wow," I said, studying his little map. "That sounds like quite a place."

"It is. It was built in the 1920s by a timber baron named Victor Butler. And according to the old-timers on the lake, he and his wife, Violet, threw some pretty elaborate parties there at one time, but they stopped after her brother, Fred Albert, came to live with them."

I raised my eyes to Rick's face. "I wonder why."

Rick picked up his fork and took a bite of his dinner.

"Don't know. Seems Fred Albert was a recluse who lived in one of the cottages on the estate. According to a couple of the people I talked to, he wasn't quite 'right.' "

"What does that mean?" I looked back down at the map.

"I don't know the answer to that question, either. It could mean he was physically or mentally challenged. Or—"

"Insane?" I said, finishing his sentence for him.

He nodded. "I did hear the word 'spooky' used in reference to the brother."

"The same word Brandi used to describe Jason Finch's foster daughter."

"Yeah," he said, and paused to take another bite. "One more thing," he said after swallowing. "It seems some believe the brother's still there."

"What? That's not possible, is it? If the brother was an adult in the twenties and thirties, he'd be a very, very old man by now."

Rick laid his fork down and pushed his plate away. "People have seen lights, from across the lake, bobbing in the woods around the cottages."

Abby, who had been silent until now, suddenly spoke. "His ghost—his spirit—wanders the estate."

I covered my face with my hands. Great. A missing girl, a cult, and now a ghost.

After Abby's little bombshell about a potential ghost, everyone's appetite disappeared. Rick paid the check and we left for the motel. On the way back he dropped his own little bombshell—we'd be on our own. He'd talked to too many people, asked too many questions during his visit to the lake, and would be remembered. If he came to the lake, it would have to be at night, or he would meet us somewhere nearby where he could be sure no one would recognize him.

I understood his concerns, but why did I feel we'd just been thrown to the wolves?

Late the next morning, we headed to Gunhammer Lake, about 150 miles north of the Twin Cities. Lady, excited to be out of the motel room, ran anxiously around the parking lot, while Abby kept a tight grip on her retractable leash. Queenie, on the other hand, didn't appear excited at all. A series of pitiful yowls were emitted from the cat carrier I lugged in my arms.

Once settled in Abby's SUV, we headed north. As we drove, we saw fewer and fewer malls. Now, instead of parking lots and stores, the scenery consisted of pine and white birch. From my place behind the wheel, I could see the leaves of the birch shiver in the breeze. The leaves changed from green to silver, silver to green, as the wind twisted them on their narrow stems.

"Looks like rain," Abby said, watching the leaves.

I peered out the windshield at the cloudless sky. "I don't see any rain clouds."

"No, but do you see the leaves? See how they're twisted so their underside is facing the sky?"

"Yeah."

"Means it's going to rain," she said matter-of-factly. She rolled down her window, and after taking a deep breath of the pine-scented air, she released it slowly. As she did, I could feel the tension leave her body.

"I didn't realize you were so tense, Abby," I said, stealing a glance in her direction. "Is it Brandi?"

"A little, but most of the tension is from being in the city. They always do that to me. Once, a long time ago, your grandpa took me to St. Louis, and I couldn't wait to get home."

"You don't like cities?"

"Not really. They make me feel hemmed in. All the people. It's like I can't take a deep breath. And the earth—covered up with concrete. I can't feel its energy." She shifted in her seat to look at me. "What about you? Did you enjoy staying there?"

"Sort of. Last night, when we were driving, I enjoyed the vibrancy I felt, the hum of all those busy people. But after a while, I experienced sensory overload. I had a hard time blocking out the random energy thrown my way." I drummed my fingers on the steering wheel. "Umm, what do you think about the ghost of Violet Butler's brother?" I asked, changing the subject. "Think the stories could be true?"

"Of course they could be true. I've never seen a ghost, or even sensed one—it's not my gift—but I've told you before about your great-aunt Mary. She had the gift of communication with the spirits of the departed."

"Some gift," I scoffed. "Seeing headless ghosts wandering around, carrying their detached body parts. Great blobs of ectoplasm oozing out of a medium's nose and ears." I shuddered. "No thank you. I'm having a hard enough time dealing with what I can do."

Out of the corner of my eye I saw Abby's smirk. "You watch too many movies. What your great-aunt Mary did was nothing like that. She said it was more a wisp of energy, a light touch on the shoulder, or a soft voice in her ear. And I don't ever recall blobs of ectoplasm running out her nose and ears. Although she did have a problem with allergies," she said in a teasing tone.

"Very funny." My brows knitted together. "Seriously, what are we going to do if we run into a crazy ghost? I mean, if someone's crazy when they're alive, they're crazy when they're dead, too. It's only logical."

I did a mental head-slap. I'd just said "ghost" and "logic" in the same sentence. Not two terms usually hooked together.

Abby patted my arm. "Don't worry about it, dear. I'm not an expert when it comes to ghosts, but I do know they're usually tied to the earthly plain by some unfinished business."

"Like they're looking for something?"

"Yes, justice, a lost love, a treasured memento. They don't usually harm the living—"

"Usually?" I said, cutting her off.

She chuckled. "I told you not to worry about it. If we do run into anything unusual, we'll simply tell whoever, or whatever, to go away."

"And they'll listen?"

"Probably."

First "usually" and now "probably." Too uncertain for me, and I didn't like it. "Abby, we don't need—"

"We'll deal with it, Ophelia," she said firmly. "One thing you do need to be aware of, if we would run into some type of spirit manifestation, don't ask it questions."

She didn't need to be concerned about any questions from me. I'd be too busy running.

"Tell the spirit to be gone in peace and love," she continued. "We don't want to invite anyone else in by talking to the spirit."

"What do you mean 'anyone else'?" My hands gripped the wheel.

"From what Great-Aunt Mary said, the presence can create sort of a crack between this world and the next. We don't want anything popping through that crack."

"Like a psychic nasty?" My hands tightened on the wheel.

"Yes. Most spirits are benign energy, but some aren't. They can be real tricksters."

Peachy—ornery ghosts.

"What if this Jason Finch is conducting séances and opening that crack a little wider?" I squinted at the road ahead.

She thought about it for a moment. "He could be. Séances could be a source of income for the group."

"Do you believe what Brandi told her mother about Jason making things disappear?"

"Humph," Abby said as she wiggled in her seat. "Sounds like stage magic to me."

Wait a second. "Stage magic?" This time I did smack myself on the forehead. I'd forgotten about that night with the runes and what I'd written on the piece of paper. It hadn't made any sense then. Did it now? Quickly, I told Abby about it.

"Automatic writing. Interesting. And the word was magic? M-A-G-I-C, not M-A-G-I-C-K?"

"Yeah. Without the K. What do you suppose it means?"

"The K can be used to show the difference between folk magick and sleight of hand. But there is a debate on which spelling is correct. I don't know . . ." She paused, tapping her cheek thoughtfully. ". . . yet. It may be significant or not." She shrugged. "I'm sure the message will be revealed in the fullness of time."

Another problem I had with this psychic thing. According to Abby, the answers would come when they were supposed to, and not on my own, personal timetable.

And what about Brandi's timetable? Would we find her before her time ran out?

# Six

I learned when someone says a drive will take three hours, they aren't traveling with a cat and a dog. Lady and Queenie had visited every rest area between the Twin Cities and Gunhammer Lake. The three hours stretched into six, and the sun hung low on the horizon before we reached the road leading us to the lake. Following Rick's directions, I drove down the narrow black-topped road until I came to a gravel lane on the left. Turning the corner onto the lane, I glanced down for a second at the typed directions.

"Watch out!" Abby yelled.

In the road, right in the path of the SUV, stood a man dressed in an old fatigue jacket.

Instinctively, I swerved. Tossed off her comfortable position on the backseat, Lady yelped. And an infuriated squall erupted from the back as Queenie's cat carrier slid forward.

I slowed to a stop, shoved the gear shift into park and turned to Abby. "Are you all right?" I asked, my heart surging with the sudden rush of adrenaline.

"Yes," she said, placing her hand on her chest.

Returning my eyes to the road, I looked at the man who'd almost caused an accident.

He still stood in the middle of the road, but now stared at the SUV. His hair hung in tangled knots down to his shoulders, and a full beard and mustache covered the lower part of his face. And both the hair on his head and the hair on his face was the color of carrots. The same, strange color orange as Brandi's in her graduation picture. Like a deer caught in the headlights, he watched us for a moment longer, then turned and loped off into the woods.

"Who the devil was that?" I exclaimed while I watched him disappear into the trees.

"A rather strange man," Abby replied.

"No kidding. Do you suppose he's homeless?"

Abby shook her head. "It's hard to say, but I think we need to find out who he is. He looked—"

"Don't say it," I said, narrowing my eyes at her.

She said the word anyway. "Spooky."

"Seems to be a lot of that going around up here," I said, putting the SUV in drive and pulling forward.

A few moments later we arrived at the cabin Rick had leased for our use. Surrounded by pine trees, it sat several yards away from the lane. It was gray with white shutters, and a porch extended out on three sides. A plaque in the shape of a pineapple, with the word "Welcome" painted on it, hung above the door.

Getting out of the SUV, I grabbed Lady's leash and snapped it on her collar. Free at last, she made a dive out of the back seat and ran the full length of the leash, her nose pressed firmly to the ground.

After handing the leash to Abby, I went to the back and opened the tailgate. Two green eyes glowered at me from the depths of the cat carrier. I grabbed the carrier and hauled it to the porch. Unlocking the door, I walked inside and set the carrier down. With a flip of a switch, I released the door and swung it open. In a flash, Queenie sprinted out, her tail high in the air, and didn't slow down until she reached the center of the room and well away from me—just in case I changed my mind about her liberation. She stopped there, and with a twist of her head gave me an indignant look. Then, sure that I'd been properly put in my place, she turned away, twitched her tail twice, and stalked off to investigate her new surroundings. I wouldn't see her again until she heard the familiar rattle of cat chow.

Glancing out the window, I saw Lady happily dragging Abby around the yard, sniffing the bottom of all the pine trees. With Queenie off somewhere, enjoying her sulk, I took the time to check out the interior of the cabin.

I stood in one large room. Ceramic tile covered the floor and colorful rag rugs lay scattered about. The knotty pine paneling on the walls gave the room a soft, warm glow. The kitchen area, with cabinets, stove, and refrigerator, sat to my left, and to my right was a large scrubbed-pine table. The living area extended directly in front of me. An L-shaped couch covered one wall and curved out into the room. A wood-burning stove rested across the room from the couch, and behind the stove, large pieces of river rock, mortared together, covered the wall. On the other wall, a bank of heavy drapes stretched across the room at a right angle to the couch. Crossing the room, I pulled back the drapes. And my breath caught in my throat.

The late afternoon sun dipped closer and closer to the thousands of pine trees ringing the lake, and already shadows shrouded the shoreline. And in those shadows, the still water caught the reflection of the pines and the sky above like a mirror.

From a distance, I heard a strange call—a high, repetitive treble. I turned my head, seeking what made that unusual sound. To my surprise, I found myself standing on the deck outside the cabin, overlooking the lake. I didn't remember opening the sliding glass doors and walking through them. Nor did I realize that Abby had joined me until I felt a gentle hand on my shoulder.

"It's a loon," she said softly as the call echoed again over the quiet lake.

A sudden breeze stirred the pines that grew on the slope leading down to the lake. Their whisper seemed to answer the poignant call of the loon.

While I stood there and listened, a sense of complete and perfect peace wrapped around me like a cocoon. With my eyes wide at the wonder of it all, I looked at Abby. "This is a place of magick, isn't it?" I asked, my voice hushed.

"Yes," she said, a slow smile spreading across her face. "I believe it is."

The next morning dawned as bright and as clear as the day before. The rain Abby had predicted had missed us. Not wanting to leave the cat and dog in the SUV any longer than necessary the day before, we hadn't stopped to get groceries. Now, we drove back to Melcher, a small town about eight miles from the lake, to go shopping.

The store we found reminded me of the small corner grocery from my childhood in Summerset. Just like in Summerset, signs in the window of the small brick building advertised this week's specials. A pop machine sat next to the wire rack dispensing the town's local shopper. Bicycles in various sizes, owned by local kids, were propped against the building. I did see a difference, though, between this store and the one in Summerset. In addition to the other signs, this building had a sign advertising fresh minnows, leeches, and fishing equipment sold around back.

When we walked in, I noticed a big community bulletin board. A large poster in the center caught my attention.

Grabbing Abby's arm, I pointed to it. "Look at that. There's going to be a spaghetti dinner tonight at the city park to raise funds for the new Little League field. And look who's sponsoring it."

"I see," she said. "PSI. Rick was right about them contributing to the community. I think that event is one we need to attend."

Nodding my agreement, I followed Abby into the store. I pulled out a cart, Abby took the grocery list from her pocket, and we started wandering down the aisle, making our selections.

I had picked up a bunch of bananas when I felt a trickle of power in the air. Looking away from the fresh fruit, I saw a Native American man standing not ten feet from us, looking at the vegetables.

He was dressed in a faded blue work shirt and jeans and wore a slouched hat that had seen better days. A long gray braid hung in a straight line down his back. In his left hand, he carried a small shopping basket, half full. On his wrist, I could see a wide band made of white, black, red, and yellow beads.

But it was his face that drew me; skin colored a dark copper, round with high cheekbones and a prominent nose. A proud face, and one that had seen hard times.

I didn't realize I was staring until the man looked at me with eyes so dark they were almost black. And in those eyes, I saw a power held tightly in check. A light flared in them, and I smiled, trying to cover my embarrassment at getting caught staring. A frown tugged at the man's mouth and he looked away. I felt like I had been judged and dismissed as unimportant.

Before I could point the man out to Abby, he turned away from the vegetables and started walking toward us, his eyes downcast. As he walked, he passed a group of teenage boys standing in front of the magazine rack.

I'd noticed the group before spotting the man. They'd been standing there, flipping through the magazines and whispering. What they did next surprised me.

As he walked past them, one boy took a step back and extended his foot, tripping him. Another boy mumbled something I couldn't hear.

I felt Abby stiffen beside me.

The man righted himself, and with a single glance at the boys, kept walking. Abby made a move to say something to him, but he ignored her.

I sensed Abby doing a slow burn, so it didn't surprise me when she lifted her chin, drew herself up to her full height, and marched up to the group of boys.

Unaware of her, they stood chuckling, patting the back of the boy who'd tripped the man. As if they were proud of what he'd done.

"Young man," she said in a clear voice that got their attention. "Do you always show such disrespect to adults?"

The boy stepped away from his friends. "What's it to you, old lady?" he asked with a sneer on his face.

I've known my grandmother all my life, and I've heard her called many things. I also knew that anyone who called Abby old did so at their own peril.

With a look that would scorch bark off a tree, Abby

reached out and took the mouthy young man by the arm.

*Oh my God, she's going to zap him.*

I watched the young man's eyelids open wide while he stared at Abby. His friends wisely took a step back as their friend stood mesmerized by her eyes drilling into his.

Suddenly, she released him, her point made. He staggered a bit, but his friends gathered round, steadying him and looking nervously at Abby's retreating back.

When she reached me, I whirled the cart around, away from the group of boys. "Abby," I hissed, "why did you do that?"

"That young man needed to be taught some manners," she said emphatically.

Abby always had been big on manners.

I glanced quickly up and down the aisle. The Native American man stood several feet away, watching with a sour look on his face. He frowned at me, turned, then disappeared around the corner.

"But did you have to be the one to do it?" I muttered in a harsh whisper.

She wiped the hand she'd used to grab the young man on her pant leg before answering me. "You're right. I'm sorry. I shouldn't have done that."

I narrowed my eyes and looked at her. She didn't sound too sorry to me.

"What did you do to him?"

"Oh," she said, finding something fascinating over my right shoulder to stare at, so she wouldn't have to look me in the eye. "Just nudged his conscience a bit with my thoughts. He's really not a bad boy; just trying to impress his friends. I planted a suggestion that, next time, he should find a more positive way."

With that, she grabbed the cart and started down the aisle, leaving me to follow.

I did. Shaking my head all the way.

Maybe if I hadn't been so focused on Abby, I would have noticed that the Native American man hadn't been the only one watching us.

# Seven

When we arrived at the cabin, Lady met us at the door, her tail swishing the air, her need obvious.

"Lady has to go outside. I'll put away the groceries if you want to take her for a walk, Abby," I said, and placed the sack I carried on the counter.

"No," she replied, putting her sack down and handing me Lady's leash. "Why don't you take her?"

I took the leash. "You sure?"

She smiled and nodded. "Yes, I'm sure. I didn't have time last night to put much away in my bedroom, and I'd like to organize the kitchen while I'm at it."

I should've known. When it came to her kitchen, even a temporary one, Abby tended to be picky. She viewed it as the heart of any home, and wouldn't be content until she had everything organized.

"All righty, then," I said, and snapped the leash on Lady's collar.

"Wait," she said, stopping me and crossing to the cupboard. Removing a spray bottle, she handed it to me.

I looked at the unmarked bottle. "What's this?"

"Natural bug spray. I've heard the deer flies are nasty up here."

After spraying my arm, I sniffed. Not bad, lemon. I coated all of my skin left exposed by my shorts and tank top, then sprayed Lady.

Once outside, Lady discreetly took care of business, and we set off down the lane in the opposite direction of the main road. I wanted to see where the road led.

A slight breeze stirred the air, and overhead I heard the cawing of crows. A thick stand of pine grew on either side of the lane, blocking any view of cabins or the lake. It seemed that Lady and I were totally alone.

She ran from side to side, pulling the retractable leash out as far as it would go. Nose pressed to the ground and tail wagging a happy rhythm, she acted like she couldn't inhale all the new smells fast enough. She was so intent on smelling everything that she startled a blue jay pecking in the tall weeds. The angry bird took flight, scolding the intruder all the way. Lady, as startled as the blue jay, plopped down on her haunches, and with her head cocked to one side, stared after the bird.

I laughed at the look on her face. "What's wrong, girl? That mean old bird scares you?"

Laying her ears back, she stood and wiggled her way toward me.

"It's okay." I bent down and scratched her ears. "He's gone."

Reassured, she resumed her hunt for new smells.

The lane narrowed, while the trees encroached closer and closer to its edge. I saw bugs swarming in the air ahead of us, but Abby's spray kept them away. Finally, I saw a steep path off to my left, and through the trees, the lake shimmering in the sunlight.

"Shall we go see what's down by the water?" I said aloud to Lady.

She answered me by bounding down the path. I

followed, trying to keep my footing on the packed dirt as Lady pulled me forward. We came to a stop at the bottom of the hill, and to my surprise, I saw we weren't alone after all.

A young girl, about thirteen or fourteen, sat on a large rock at the lake's shore. From my spot behind her, I saw long blond hair tumbling down her back. Gangly arms, sticking out from the short sleeves of the white top she wore, were braced against the rock. I heard the rhythmic splash of her feet in the water and the clear notes of a song that she sang to herself. A soft, happy, almost wordless song I didn't recognize.

"Hi," I said, my voice breaking into her song.

Her head snapped around, and violet eyes, unlike any I'd ever seen, widened in surprise. She jumped up from her perch on the rock and stared at me, like a wild thing when suddenly confronted. She had a small build, all arms and legs. And her incredible eyes were set in a pale, delicate face.

She reminded me of a wood sprite.

Uncomfortable under the girl's intent gaze, I broke eye contact and looked around, trying to think of something to say to break the silence growing larger with every passing moment. I spied a shiny object hanging from the tree branch between where I stood and the girl. It appeared to be a silver necklace shaped like a spider's web with a bright red stone placed dead center in the web.

"That's pretty," I said, my hand moving toward the necklace.

"Don't touch it!" She scrambled toward the tree, and grabbing the necklace, shoved it in the pocket of her baggy white shorts.

Now that she was over her initial surprise, the girl didn't seem to be intimidated by me at all. She gave me the once-over, then turned to Lady, who'd been sitting at my side with her tail thumping the ground. "Nice dog," she said, glancing at me before returning her attention to Lady. "Is she friendly?"

"Oh yeah. Lady doesn't know the meaning of the word 'stranger.' " I gave the girl a tentative smile.

Ignoring me, she squatted down and began to pet Lady. "Who are you?" she asked abruptly.

"Ophelia—"

"What are you doing here?" she asked, breaking in.

"I'm on vacation with my grandmother," I said, trying to keep my voice patient.

She looked up at me, her eyes suspicious. "Lots of lakes in Minnesota. Why did you come to this one?"

*Great, I'm being interrogated by a kid. Well, two can play that game.*

I ignored her question and asked one of my own. "What's your name?"

She focused again on Lady. "I'm called Tink."

Not "My name is Tink," but "I'm called Tink." It struck me as an odd way to tell someone your name.

"Is that a nickname?"

She answered my question with a shrug and continued to pet the dog.

I tried once more to engage her in conversation. "Do you live around here?" I asked in my most friendly voice.

Another shrug. "Maybe," she replied in a cocky voice.

Friendly didn't work, so I retreated to sarcasm. "You're not real talkative, are you, kid?"

Before she could answer, a man's voice from the top of the hill called out. "Tink, are you down there?"

As she rose to her feet, a look of dismay crossed Tink's pale face. "I'm here," she yelled back.

I turned to see a man, also dressed in white, loose fitting clothes, come down the hill. Thin face, rather aesthetic looking, with dark hair shot with gray. He had a goatee, also dark with gray streaks. But I couldn't see his eyes. They were hidden behind mirrored sunglasses. The sandals he wore on his feet made his progress difficult. He slipped, and halfway down slid until he reached Tink and me.

"Where have you been? We've been looking all over for you," he said, laying a hand on Tink's thin arm. "And where's your necklace?"

With a repentant look, Tink reached in her pocket and pulled out the necklace. She handed the shiny spider's web to the man.

Taking it from her, he slipped the chain over her head. "You know you're not supposed to take the necklace off, don't you?" he said as he straightened the web till it hung straight. He stepped back and looked her over. "You're clothes are dirty, too," he remarked in an even tone, eyeing the grass and mud stains on her once pristine top. "You'll have to change as soon as we get back."

Silently, with her head down, Tink nodded.

Not wanting to hear this guy continue to ream the kid, I cleared my throat.

He looked away from Tink to me. "Oh, I'm sorry. How rude of me to ignore you. It's just . . ." His voice trailed off as he glanced back at Tink. "We were worried about her," he said, his eyes returning to me.

"I understand," I said, holding up a hand.

"I'm Jason Finch," he said, taking my upturned hand

and shaking it. "And you've already met my niece, Tink."

"Ophelia Jensen." So, not a foster child, but a relative, I thought releasing his hand.

"And this is your dog?"

As he said it, he reached out toward Lady, but before he could touch her, she backed away from his outstretched hand.

Embarrassed by Lady's reaction, I gave the leash a small tug and pulled her closer to my side. "Sorry, she acts that way around strangers sometimes," I lied.

Lifting her head at my lie, I saw Tink raise her eyebrows, but she remained silent.

"Staying here at the lake?"

"Yes, just down the lane." I pointed to my left.

"Ahh, one of the rental cabins." He looked over at Tink. "I apologize for rushing off, but I'd better get this young lady home before her aunt calls the sheriff."

"I understand. Nice to meet you, Jason, Tink."

With her eyes downcast, Tink walked past me to follow her uncle. Her shoulders slumped as she climbed the steep path, and around her seemed to hang a feeling of dejection, of defeat.

The wood sprite, the singing girl with a cocky attitude, was gone.

When I returned to the cabin, Abby had everything cleaned and arranged to her liking. She listened intently while I told her of my meeting with Jason and Tink.

"What did you say the necklace looked like?" she asked with a funny expression on her face.

"A spider's web," I said impatiently. Fives times she'd asked me about the stupid necklace. "Now do you think—"

"You said the necklace had a stone in the center?" she broke in.

"Yeah, a red stone. Now what I want to know is, do you think—"

She interrupted me again. "I'm not so sure the necklace isn't important."

"Enough about the dumb necklace. It's not that big of a deal," I informed her in an exasperated tone. "I've seen a lot of teenagers at the library with them on. They seem to be popular. I want to know—" I held up my hand, stopping her when she opened her mouth. "—if you think Jason and Juliet Finch could be mistreating the girl?"

Her mouth closed and she frowned. "I don't know. Did you see any bruises?"

I thought about Tink's pale arms and legs. Any marks would've definitely shown against her fair skin.

"No, but there are many ways to mistreat a child. Often the marks don't show."

Abby nodded sadly. "I wonder if there've been any rumors. Rick would've mentioned them, I think. And wouldn't Brandi have said something to her mother if she'd noticed abuse?"

I sighed. "Maybe, but what if Brandi didn't know about it?"

"I don't know." Abby pursed her lips. "I would think living that closely together, it would be hard to keep the mistreatment a secret."

"Well all I know is the kid changed the instant the uncle showed up."

"And when he placed the spider's web around her neck."

"Oh for Pete's sake," I exclaimed. "Would you forget about the necklace?"

A thoughtful look crossed Abby's face. "No, Ophelia, I don't think we should."

With that, Abby rose and left the room. The discussion was tabled for now.

# *Eight*

We easily found the town park holding the spaghetti dinner. Abby and I pulled in to the parking lot, and after turning the SUV off, we sat and surveyed the park.

A large poster with a graph, tacked to a post, indicated how much money had been raised for the new ball field. Bright balloons hung around the sign, drawing attention to it. Banners advertising a drawing for free gifts donated by local business hung from the trees.

Parents sat in lawn chairs sprinkled across the green grass, while small children played on the merry-go-round and slid down the slide. Older children, spiffed out in baseball uniforms, circulated through the crowd selling chances for the drawing.

I turned and looked at Abby. "Okay, Ace, what do we do now?" I asked.

"We mingle. Get acquainted with people," she replied with a slight shrug.

My lips twisted into a frown. "And I'm *so* good at that," I answered with a note of sarcasm.

"It's not hard."

Easy for her to say. Abby had a grace, a style, that drew people to her. I may have inherited some of her talents, but whatever gene was responsible for Abby's natural charm had definitely passed me by. Crowds made me nervous and ill at ease. When confronted with strangers, words would freeze in my mouth like a warm tongue on a cold pump handle. The only remedy that worked was a fast retreat into sarcasm.

While I thought about my lack of social skills, I continued to watch the groups clustered around the park. Several people were standing in line by the picnic tables. The tables were covered with pots of spaghetti, bowls of salads, and trays of desserts. Behind the table, several people stood serving the food to the waiting line. And they were dressed all in white. They must have been the "shadows," the elusive group members Rick had referred to.

"Abby," I said, motioning toward the tables. "Suppose those are members of PSI?"

"Yes," she said, her eyes narrowing as she watched them.

I shook my head. "How can someone serve spaghetti dressed in white?"

"Very carefully?" she replied, arching an eyebrow.

"Funny." My words were accompanied by a slow roll of my eyes. I pushed the SUV door open. "We're not going to accomplish anything sitting here. Let's go mingle."

"Wait," she said, laying a hand on my arm. "Do you see the man you met in the woods today?"

Scanning the group in white, I shook my head. "No, I don't."

I exited the SUV, and grabbing the lawn chairs out of the back, followed Abby across the park.

Tonight, Abby wore one of her flowing skirts and matching tops. The skirt drifted around her ankles as she walked, and gave her an appearance of almost floating across the grass. Strangers stopped to greet her with a smile and a shake of the hand. Me, I stood at her side, silent, and received nods and half smiles.

Nope, I did *not* inherit the charm gene.

As we walked on, Abby stole a glance my way. "You know, Ophelia, you need to work on your people skills."

"What people skills?"

"Exactly my point," she said in a sardonic tone.

I stopped. "See that shade tree over there?" I said, pointing to an unoccupied space. "You mingle. I'm parking myself over there."

After striding over to the tree, I planted myself in the lawn chair and did what I do best. Watch and observe. It's amazing what you can learn about people if you pay attention.

It didn't take long for my attention to be drawn to a short woman dressed in white. Short and dumpy—no doubt the one Rick said they called Winnie, exactly as he had described her.

And white was definitely not a good color for her. It made her wide hips look even wider. So did the tunic and long pants she wore. They highlighted every roll, every bump. Her dark hair with gray strands was twisted around the top of her head in a tight bun, and straggly strands hung around her plump face. Small eyes peered out from behind heavy black glasses. Her hands flitted nervously about her while she talked to another woman also dressed in white.

The other woman was Winnie's antithesis. She was as tall and rangy as Winnie was short and squat. And on her, the tunic and pants looked good. They complemented her slim frame, and the dark amulet she wore around her neck shone against the all-white background.

Her manner was also the opposite of Winnie's. Where Winnie seemed to vibrate with nervous energy, the other woman radiated calm. She listened with a patient look on her face as Winnie flung her hands about, talking.

I was so busy watching the tall woman that I quit paying attention to Winnie. Big mistake. If I'd been watching her, I might have caught her edgy glances. I didn't, not until it was too late.

When I finally turned my attention from the tall woman back to Winnie, I saw her looking my way with an anxious expression on her face. I watched the tall woman's eyes follow Winnie's. Looking quickly over my shoulder, I checked to see what the two women stared at so intently. Nope, nothing behind me. Crap. Me—they stared at me.

With a quick pat on Winnie's plump arm, the tall woman turned away from her and purposely walked straight toward me.

I lowered my head and slouched in my chair. If I shrank myself small enough, maybe she'd pass me by. I glanced up quickly at the woman. Nope. She still headed my way, her long strides eating up the ground between us. Looking back down, I studied my hand lying passively in my lap. When I felt her presence in my space, I raised my eyes to her face.

"Hi," she said while she bent slightly at the waist and extended a hand, "I'm Juliet Finch."

A striking woman, she possessed an angular face with hazel eyes. Hazel eyes that probed mine.

Standing, I took a deep breath. Juliet seemed to tower over my five-foot-four height, and I needed to tip my head back a bit in order to maintain eye contact. "My pleasure," I replied, shaking her hand. "I'm Ophelia Jensen."

"Are you new to the community, or vacationing here?" she asked in a friendly voice.

That's funny. Evidently her husband didn't tell her about running into me at the lake. I decided not to enlighten Juliet about my meeting with Jason. And Tink.

"Vacationing."

Juliet gave me a brilliant smile. "This is a wonderful place for relaxing. There are so many beautiful lakes around here. Where are you staying?"

"At Gunhammer Lake."

A look of surprise crossed her face. "We live on Gunhammer Lake. You must be renting one of Arnie's cabins?"

Arnie? Arnie who? Rick had neglected to tell me who owned the cabin we were staying in. At a loss how to respond, I smiled like an idiot and wobbled my head in way that could be taken as either a no or a yes.

Taking my wishy-washy nod as an affirmative answer, a bright smile lit Juliet's face. "That Arnie's quite a character. He's lived on the lake forever, but he's a little on the reclusive side."

I thought of the man Abby and I had seen in the twilight last night. He looked pretty reclusive to me. "Does Arnie have red hair?" I asked, giving it a shot.

"Oh no." Juliet's smile faded to a slight frown. "Arnie's about eighty-four and quite bald. Why?"

"Last night we almost ran into a man with red hair. Literally. He was standing in the middle of the road as we neared the cabin."

Her hands, which had been hanging loosely at her sides, clenched, and her frown deepened. "Duane Hobbs."

"Who's Duane Hobbs?"

With effort, she seemed to concentrate on relaxing her fingers. An uncomfortable silence hung in the air while she slowly smoothed imaginary creases from her tunic before she spoke. "Duane's a so-called handyman around the lake, but I wouldn't let him do any work for me if I were you."

A thousand questions bounced around in my head, but only one came rolling off my tongue. "Why?"

"He's . . ." She paused. ". . . strange."

The one word I'd heard so much lately popped into my head. "Spooky?"

"Yes," she said with a sigh. "That's a good word to describe him. He wanders around the woods at all hours, doing God knows what. I guess he wasn't always like this. At one time, he was the pride of the community. A high school hero. But then he went off to Vietnam and has never been the same since."

Hmm. I wondered why Rick hadn't mentioned Duane Hobbs. Had he already checked into the man's background and found nothing? I scuffed the ground in front of my chair with my toe. It would've been nice if Rick had informed of us of some strange guy wandering around.

"Is he dangerous?"

"No. I don't think so. I guess there was a problem a few years ago when some developers were looking into building a public boat ramp on the north side of the lake. Rumors of vandalism, that kind of thing. But no one was hurt and they never proved Duane was the one responsible."

"Did they build the boat ramp?"

"No, it turned out to be too expensive. Since then, the lake has remained untouched by developers."

"And that's the way Duane likes it?"

"Yes, he resents outsiders."

"Like your group?" I asked pointedly.

Juliet looked at me in surprise. "Yes," she replied. As she flipped a strand of hair over her shoulder, her eyes narrowed and her gaze drifted toward the children playing nearby. "Outsiders. Ha. If anyone—"

But before she could finish, a soccer ball careened across the grass toward us, with a small boy following it in fast pursuit, oblivious to everything around him. Both the ball and the boy came to a sudden stop near her foot. Crouching down eye level to the little boy, Juliet picked up the ball and handed it to him. Tousling his hair, she grinned warmly at the child. "Here you are, Matthew. Try and keep it over on the playground."

"Yes, ma'am," he replied, returning her grin with a gap-toothed smile of his own.

Straightening, Juliet watched the little boy scamper back to his playmates.

"Do you have children?" I asked, pretending not to know about Tink. I wanted to see what she'd say.

Still watching the children play, a wistful look crossed Juliet's face before she turned to me.

"In a way. Jason and I are raising my sister's child."

"Oh," I said, scanning the children at play. "Which one is she?"

Once again she ran her hands nervously over her tunic. "Tink, my niece, isn't here. She's . . ." Her voice trailed off while her attention shifted to the children. ". . . rather frail, and these things tend to be too much excitement for her to handle."

Frail? The girl I'd met at the lake didn't seem frail to me. Thin, yes, but not frail. I remembered how she scampered up the hill after Jason. Maybe she had some kind of illness, not evident when one first met her. Maybe that's why they worried about her.

Shifting forward in my chair, I looked up at her with sympathy. "That's too bad. It must be difficult for her not to play with other children."

"Yes, yes, it is," she said abruptly. Looking down at me, she grasped my hand and gave it a quick shake. "It was nice meeting you, Ophelia. I hope you enjoy your stay at Gunhammer."

Before I could reply, she pivoted and walked with long strides back to where Winnie still stood serving spaghetti.

I shook my head in disbelief. Usually, parents were more than happy to talk about their offspring, but the mention of Juliet's niece had brought a sudden end to our conversation. Only one thought came to mind.

Why?

# Nine

The rest of the evening passed uneventfully. I sat calmly under my tree, watching, and left my place only long enough to stand in line with Abby for a plate of spaghetti. While we ate, I filled her in on my conversation with Juliet.

"So does the name Duane Hobbs jangle any psychic bells for you, Abby?" I asked as I reached over and took her empty plate.

Closing her eyes, she took a deep breath. A moment later she opened them. "No, sorry, not even a jingle. What about you? Did you sense anything when Juliet mentioned his name?"

"Nope, but I'm not as good as you are at picking up stuff quickly," I said with a shrug, and stood to dispose of our empty plates. When I returned, Abby sat staring off into space. A light touch on her arm brought her attention back to me.

"Where do we go from here?" I asked.

A frown marred her face while she looked at me. "I don't know, but it's almost as if I can feel a clock ticking."

A similar frown now wrinkled my face. "I know. I feel it, too." Sitting down again in the lawn chair, I watched the crowd as people began to gather up belongings and call for their children. The event at the park had almost ended and we'd learned nothing. Only that Duane Hobbs liked wandering around the woods.

Standing, I folded up my lawn chair and extended a hand to Abby. "Come on, we might as well leave."

Abby grasped my hand and rose gracefully to her feet.

She picked up her lawn chair and folded it, and we began our trek back to the SUV. We were almost to the car when I heard the sound of hurrying feet in the grass behind us. Looking over my shoulder, I saw the woman named Winnie rushing up to us.

"Oh my. I was afraid I wouldn't catch you and I wanted to introduce myself," she said while she gasped for breath and stuck out her hand. "I'm Winnie Donner."

The sound of Winnie's voice startled me. There was no doubt in my mind that the woman had to be at least in her late fifties, but her voice sounded like that of a girl, high-pitched and a little breathless.

Abby stepped forward and took Winnie's hand in hers. "Abigail McDonald and my granddaughter, Ophelia Jensen," she said, waving her other hand in my direction.

"Hi, Ophelia," Winnie replied, releasing Abby's hand and grasping mine. "Juliet told me you're our neighbors, well sort of neighbors. We're right down the lake from your cabin, on the other side, of course. Great to have you at the lake. I hope you enjoy your stay here. So nice of you to come tonight."

Her words ran on and on, and with each one, Winnie

pumped my hand vigorously. My arm felt like it was coming loose in the socket. I gave my hand a slight tug and she released me.

Fighting the urge to rub my shoulder, I gave Winnie a small smile. "Nice to meet you, Winnie."

She took a step closer to me. "I saw you both today in the grocery store," she said, and waved a finger in front of my face.

I took a step back, but she closed the distance with another step of her own, and it set my nerves on edge.

*Hadn't this woman ever heard about personal space?*

I gritted my teeth and held my ground.

Abby, aware of how I felt about strangers standing too close to me, took Winnie's arm and gently turned her around until Winnie faced her, allowing me to take another step back. "Really, I didn't notice you," Abby said.

A sly look crossed Winnie's face. "Well, I noticed you. I was standing down the aisle from you when those boys tripped Walks Quietly—"

"Walks Quietly?" I cut in.

"Yes, the Native American, the one the boys tripped," she repeated. "I noticed they acted rather odd after you spoke to them, Abigail."

Great, this fluttery little woman had witnessed Abby zapping that kid. Eyebrows raised, I looked at Abby. *Okay, how are you going to get yourself out of this one?* I thought.

Seeing my look, Abby lifted her chin a fraction and turned her head back to Winnie. "Oh, the young man only felt embarrassed. I'm sure he didn't expect to be reprimanded for what he did."

I raised my hand to my mouth to cover my sudden

grin. *Reprimand? I guess you could call momentarily jumbling someone's circuits a reprimand.*

Abby noticed my reaction and gave my foot a nudge with the toe of her shoe.

Forcing the grin off my face, I looked back at Winnie. She seemed perplexed. "Really? Embarrassed? I thought something more had happened—"

"Don't be silly," I broke in. "What more could there be? You know how teenage boys are. They don't like being called on bad behavior, especially in front of their friends."

Winnie slowly nodded as she thought about what I'd said. "I guess you're right. It's just—"

"Oh dear, look at the time," Abby said, glancing at her watch. "Didn't you want to be home by eight, Ophelia?"

Again I felt my foot being nudged. "That's right. I don't want to leave Lady shut up in the cabin for too long." Glancing over my shoulder at Winnie, I hurried toward the SUV. "Nice to meet you, Winnie. Umm, stop by some time," I called back to her.

I could've bitten my tongue off. The last thing I wanted was Winnie stopping by for a visit.

After returning to the cabin, Abby and I decided to table any discussion about what had happened at the park, so after Lady's quick run around the yard, we said goodnight.

But I couldn't sleep. The air in the cabin seemed oppressive, stifling. Grabbing a blanket from the bed, I quietly slipped out onto the deck. I made myself comfortable in one of the chairs and stared out over the lake.

Much better, I thought after taking a cleansing

breath. A thousand stars hung above me in the night sky, and below, on the surface of the lake, the reflection of a crescent moon played upon the water. The air felt cool against my skin, and I let the peace I'd felt here earlier wash around me.

Leaning my head back against the chair, I closed my eyes and thought about my impressions of this place. It was a place of magick, as Abby had said. Even now, in the stillness of the night, I could feel the hum of energy around me. A positive energy. Had the lake always been this way? Had the Native American tribes once living along its shores, before the white man came to displace them, felt the same kind of peace? I wished I knew. Maybe Walks Quietly could tell me? Could give me the history of the lake. No, for some reason I knew he wouldn't want to talk to me. The look he gave me at the store told me he wanted nothing to do with Abby or me. And the power I sensed in him. What was that all about? Was he some kind of shaman? A psychic? If so, how did he feel about Jason Finch's group? Who could answer that question? Juliet? Winnie?

A shudder ran up my arm. I didn't want to talk to Winnie again, but I had a feeling I would. Especially since I'd opened my big mouth and invited her to stop by. The sound of my groan bounced across the lake. Something about that woman was intrusive, and it made me uncomfortable. She did like to talk, though, and maybe if I could tamp down my discomfort long enough, I might be able to learn something from her.

And then there was Juliet. I had a feeling she'd be more guarded than Winnie. Questioning her wouldn't be easy. She'd shut down immediately as soon as I mentioned her niece.

Unanswered questions flitted through my brain. I

opened my eyes and scrubbed my face with my hands. Who was I kidding? Although I'd never admit it to him, Henry had been right. Abby and I weren't trained investigators. We didn't know how to question people. And we didn't have any business trying to find Brandi. Our ill-advised blundering might even make the situation worse, if Brandi truly were in danger, like Abby thought.

The peace I'd felt earlier faded like an old song. The melody was still there in the corner of my mind, but I couldn't remember the words anymore. The feeling had been replaced by another, one more disquieting, more sinister.

Giving up, I gathered the blanket and stood to walk back inside the house, and then I saw it. Across the lake, little bursts of light bobbing through the trees. Was it Duane Hobbs, armed with a flashlight, wandering around the woods as Juliet said he did?

I crossed to the edge of the deck and leaned against the railing, while I strained my eyes against the black night to see the lights more clearly.

They seemed to hover near the ground, flickering on and off. Someone with a flashlight wouldn't do that, would they? Unless they were signaling someone. But why would anyone be signaling this time of night, and to whom?

I rubbed my eyes and looked again. The lights were still there, hanging right above the ground. They seemed to pick up speed, and with a movement that made the hair on the back of my neck stand up, they shot up through the trees, paused, and shot back down again.

Dropping the blanket, I ran to Abby's room. "Wake up. Abby, wake up," I said, gently shaking her arm. "There's something odd going on across the lake."

"What . . ." she asked, her voice heavy with sleep. "What's going on?"

"There are strange lights bobbing around across the lake." I tugged at her arm. "Come on, you've got to see this."

I drew back the covers and handed her the robe at the foot of her bed.

Sighing, Abby slipped her arms into her robe. "It's probably just that Duane Hobbs," she grumbled.

"Not unless he climbs trees. The lights shot off the ground and into the upper branches."

"How odd," she said, standing.

"No kidding. Now come on." I propelled her forward. "You need to see these lights."

We walked quickly through the cabin and out onto to the deck. Silently, we stood side by side and stared out over the lake.

"I don't see any lights," she said, not looking at me.

Of course she didn't see any lights. They were gone.

# Ten

The sound of a motor pulled me out of a restless sleep.

*Damn, who would be mowing their yard this time of the morning?*

I forced my eyelids open and found myself staring at a foreign ceiling.

The sound wasn't a lawn motor, but a boat motor. *Oh yeah, we're not in Iowa anymore, Toto. We're in Minnesota. Not quite Oz, but still a place with a lot of crazy stuff going on.*

I threw on an old pair of jeans, a T-shirt that said "If you don't like my attitude, quit talking to me," and slipped my feet into a pair of canvas flats. A quick five minutes devoted to face, teeth, and hair, and I was ready to face the world.

Well, maybe not face it, but at least look at it sideways. After what I'd seen last night, I wouldn't be able to look at the world head on until I had a very large dose of caffeine. Wandering out into the hallway, I went in search of coffee.

In the living room, the bank of windows immediately drew my attention. Queenie lay curled up on the floor in a square of morning sunshine, enjoying a snooze. And through the windows, I saw a cloudless blue sky and water that rippled and shimmered with reflected light. My gaze wandered to a spot across the lake from our cabin, to the thick stand of weeds growing along the shoreline, their feathery tops swaying in the breeze. From there, I noticed the dark green pines interspersed with silvery white birch growing a distance from the shore. Did I really see lights last night? Or had it been an overactive imagination? I closed my eyes and stroked my forehead, trying to recall exactly what I'd seen.

"Do you have a headache, dear?" Abby asked gently.

I tore my attention away from the scene outside and turned to see her standing in the kitchen, a spatula in one hand and a cup of coffee in the other. A cup that she kindly extended toward me.

Without a word I took the cup and wrapped both hands around it. Until I felt the warmth seep through the mug in my hands, I hadn't realized they were cold. I let the heat leak through them and into my body while I slowly sipped.

Smiling, Abby turned back to the stove and poured batter into a waiting pan. "I thought pancakes would be nice for breakfast," she said with her back to me. "Sit down and drink your coffee. They'll be ready in a minute."

Everything needed for breakfast had been laid out on the table, so after crossing the room, I pulled out a chair and sat. The clock above the stove ticked away while I thought of how to bring up a subject I'd rather leave alone. But not talking about what I'd seen last night wouldn't change what happened. And I needed to know if Abby had an explanation.

"Ghost lights," Abby said, still facing the stove.

With my face creased in a puzzled look, I stared at her back. "What?"

With a slick move that spoke of years of practice, Abby flipped the pancakes. "What you saw might have been ghost lights—strange lights that bob and weave. That is what you wanted to ask me, isn't it?"

"How did you know I . . ." My voice trailed off. *Duh, Abby always knew.* "Oh, never mind," I said with a wave of my hand. "Dumb question."

Abby looked over her shoulder and grinned before turning back to the stove.

"You think that's what I saw? Ghost lights?" I asked, gripping my coffee cup tighter.

"You sound surprised. Rick told us about strange lights over dinner."

"Yeah, but I didn't believe him," I scoffed.

After Abby flipped the pancakes onto the waiting plates, she crossed to the table and placed them on the table. Then pulling out her own chair, she joined me. We both seemed lost in our thoughts while we put creamy pats of butter between each fluffy pancake, and then poured thick maple syrup over them.

The only sound was the heavy ticking of the clock and the occasional click of silverware on the china plates.

After eating quietly for a few moments, I finally broke the silence. "You believe me when I say I saw lights, don't you?"

Abby heard the uncertainty in my voice and reached across the table to pat my hand. "Of course I believe you. You are *not* given to hysterics, nor are you susceptible to the power of suggestion. If you say you saw lights, you saw lights."

I gave her a weak smile. "Thanks for the vote of confidence. You know there could be a logical explanation. It could've been a flashlight, a reflection—" I stopped, trying to think of other reasons, other causes for what I saw.

"Marsh gas is always popular." Abby forked the last of her pancake and popped it in her mouth.

"Marsh gas?" I asked, picking up both plates and carrying them to the sink.

"Yes. Marsh gas, swamp gas—whatever name you choose. It was a common explanation for any strange lights that occurred in the mountains when I was a child."

The plates clattered in the sink when I turned in surprise. "You've had experience with this?"

"Yes. Several times mysterious lights were reported seen around our home. I've seen them myself. Mother always said it was because of Aunt Mary and her talent that called lost souls to our home. She was unmarried and lived with us, you know. She—"

"Wait a second." I crossed to the table and looked down at her. "Back up. She called lost souls? What do you mean she 'called lost souls'?" I asked, my voice rising.

Abby shrugged a shoulder "She didn't *call* them or invite them to visit her. They seemed to seek her out."

I plopped down in the chair next to her—my knees suddenly weak. "Why her? Why—"

"It was her talent. It acted like a beacon, so to speak, to those who needed help crossing over."

"You lived in a house with—with—" I stumbled over my words, unable to say the one I needed to.

"Ghosts?" Abby said, filling in the blank. "Yes. And before you ask," she added, holding up a hand, "no,

I've told you I've never seen one, not even as a child, when I would've been most receptive to that kind of visitation. I'd feel odd flares of energy sometimes, or maybe a cold spot or two. But nothing too odd. I think it was because they never were around for very long. Aunt Mary was always able to help them."

This new twist about our shared heritage was almost too much to absorb. In all of Abby's tales about the women in our family and their various gifts, she'd never told me about this.

"You lived in kind of a clearinghouse for ghosts," I said in a shocked tone.

Abby beamed a smile at me. "What a good way to describe it. Very clever of you, my dear," she said, patting my face.

For once, her touch didn't comfort me. What if I had more in common with Great-Aunt Mary than I supposed? What if the lights appeared because of me? What if new talents were beginning to develop? What if—

"Stop it, Ophelia." Abby's voice broke through my thoughts.

I looked at her, confused.

"I know what you're thinking. Even someone who's not psychic could read your thoughts on this one. You're worried you're responsible for those lights across the lake. Listen," she said, her voice stern as she took both my hands in hers. "Don't forget what Rick said—the lights were here before we were. And right now, we don't know if what you saw were ghost lights. Maybe there is some logical explanation for them."

I knew what her response would be before I asked the question, but fool that I am, I asked it anyway. "And how do I find out?"

"You're going to go to the place you saw the lights

and investigate. There's a boat for our use tied at the dock. It's exactly like the fishing boat your grandfather had, so you should have no problem operating it. The trolling motor for the boat and the battery are in the shed next to the dock. I walked down to the lake this morning, before you woke up, and found them." Abby stood, walked to the sink, and started rinsing plates. "You'll be fine. You have your amulet, and I presume you've brought some of your crystals. Be sure to carry some hematite, or maybe some jet, to absorb negativity."

Dang, she had this all figured out. Resigned to the inevitable, I rose and headed toward my bedroom to grab my crystals, but after taking a couple of steps, an idea struck me. She certainly seemed eager to get me out of the cabin. Suddenly suspicious, I turned and studied Abby with narrowed eyes.

"What are you going to do while I'm gone? You're not planning on cooking something up, are you?"

Abby continued to rinse the dishes and kept her back to me. "Umm, not exactly."

"What, exactly?"

"Okay," she said, drying her hands and turning around. "With everything that's happened, I think a little protection might be in order. I'm going to smudge the cabin and put salt around the foundation."

Smudging—the ancient art of purifying a home by walking around and wafting smoke from sage leaves throughout the rooms. And, of course, salt to represent the element of Earth, to contain and hold. Abby's cure-all for psychic nasties. It would place a shield around the cabin. But Abby preferred using sea salt, and I doubted, however well-stocked the cabin might be, that the cupboards would contain any of that particular remedy.

"Ha," I said, my tone sarcastic. "You don't have any of your stuff with you."

"Oh *please*," she said, arching an eyebrow. She turned and began removing things from the cupboard—an abalone shell, a bundle of leaves, and a feathered fan. Last, but not least, she removed a large round container. Turning back to me, she rattled the container and winked. "Sea salt—a good witch never leaves home without it!"

# *Eleven*

The boat, motor, and battery were right where Abby had said they would be. And it was exactly like the boat Grandpa and I had spent many happy hours in fishing. A tug of sadness pulled at my heart.

*Oh, Grandpa, what would you think of all of this? Your beloved wife investigating missing persons and your granddaughter developing a habit of tripping over dead bodies? You always understood about the gifts given to the women of our family, but I think this might have pushed even you over the edge.*

After hooking up the motor and the battery to the boat, I started the motor and cast off. Slowly, I put the propeller in reverse and eased away from the dock. Once away from the shore, the light breeze tossed my hair around my shoulders, while the hot August sun beat down on the top of my head. I lifted my chin toward the sky and took a deep breath. The air carried the aroma of lake water and pine, mixed with the faint odor of gasoline from the exhaust of speedboats. Not since my last time fishing with Grandpa had I smelled that particular combination of scents. Looking over the side as the boat glided across the water, I saw submerged weeds weaving back and forth, pushed by unseen currents.

I exhaled slowly, and the tension I didn't know I carried seemed to release knot by knot.

God, I'd forgotten how much I loved being out on the water.

All too soon I neared the opposite side of the lake. Cutting the motor and raising the prop, I allowed the small boat to glide into shore. Barefoot, and with my pant legs rolled up, I jumped out. Soft sand squished around my feet while cool water lapped against my ankles as I waded to the shore, tugging the boat with me. I secured it to the nearest tree with the rope attached to the bow. Satisfied the boat would stay put, I slipped on my shoes and clambered up the hill, away from the lake and into the pines. All the time praying I didn't run into any poison ivy.

The hill leveled off and I headed east toward the area where I had seen the ghost light. As I walked, sunlight filtered through the braches of the pine trees, and their soft needles littering the ground muted my steps. The only sound I heard was the rattling of the birch leaves.

I stopped, closed my eyes, and turned on my radar.

I probably look like a dog sniffing the air, I thought. *A dog?*

Once, I'd used the analogy of a dog's heightened sense of smell to describe my psychic talent to Henry. My lips tightened in a frown. I hadn't thought of Henry since he stormed out of my house. So much had happened that I'd blanked him from my mind. Why had Henry suddenly popped into my head now?

I shoved the question away and continued walking. Out of the corner of my eye, light glinting off metal caught my attention. I took off toward it.

A high woven-wire fence stretched between metal poles wound its way through the trees. It must have been the fence Rick mentioned, the one that created the boundary of the old Butler estate. I thought it was much farther down the lake. Had I walked that far? Looking over my shoulder, I tried to judge my distance from the lake, but the trees blocked any glimpse of water. Turning back, I noticed a section of the woven wire had been pulled back away from one of the poles, leaving a hole.

A hole big enough for someone to wiggle through. Someone about my size. I took a step forward.

*Don't do it,* said my common sense.

*Hey, it's not like I haven't trespassed before,* I argued back.

*Right—and got shot in the process,* the little voice pointed out.

*Oh, yeah. Maybe I should listen this time.*

I turned away from the fence and began to retrace my steps, when a chattering squirrel drew my attention.

He sat high in the tree, watching me and prattling, as if scolding me for contemplating trespassing.

"Enough already," I said aloud, stopping under the tree. "I'm leaving."

The squirrel paused as if he were out of breath from his prattling.

And when he did, I heard it—a whimper. Or thought I'd heard a whimper. I cocked my head, straining to hear a sound. Nothing. Looking back up at the tree, I saw the squirrel had disappeared, and on the same bough, a hawk now sat.

Motionless, the hawk stared down at me. A second later, with unbelievable grace, he launched himself airborne. He circled twice above my head and then flew in the direction of the fence. The hawk circled again. This time directly over the hole in the fence.

I couldn't shake the impression he wanted me to follow—through the fence. Without a second thought, I did—I squirmed right through the break. *So much for common sense.*

I walked deeper into the woods, occasionally glancing up at the hawk flying in the sky above me. The trees grew thicker together in this section of the forest, blocking more and more of the sun the farther I walked. The air seemed to thicken, too, and the birch trees no longer rattled. Again I glanced up, looking for the hawk, but he'd vanished.

Thanks a lot. You lead me here, and then you disappear, I thought while my eyes scanned the branches above me for a sign of the hawk.

Head tilted back, I walked along, still searching the branches for the bird. A shock, as if I'd touched an electric fence, stopped me. Jerking around, I looked for what I'd touched, but nothing was in sight. Only an old, abandoned cabin, sitting in a clearing about fifty feet from where I stood.

I remembered Rick's map of the Butler estate. Had he drawn a cabin this far away from the main house? I didn't think so. And all the cabins he'd drawn were inhabited. Eyeing the cabin, I didn't think anyone could be living in it. Sections of rafters peeked out from holes in the roof. The main door hung crookedly from rusted hinges, and on either side of it, windows, their panes broken, stared out toward the clearing. Two steps, with the treads half gone, led to a sagging front porch. And along the porch ran a wooden railing with several posts missing. It reminded me of a smiling mouth with several teeth missing.

Ghost lights. Abandoned cabin. Was this where Fred Albert, Violet's brother, spent his last days?

I took another step forward, only to be shocked again. But by what?

Perplexed, I tucked a strand of hair behind my ear, while I studied the ground at my feet. Could there be some kind of invisible fencing buried in the ground? Like the ones people used to keep their dogs in their yards? No, an invisible fence only worked with a collar that acted like a receiver. But maybe my psychic talent acted the same way.

Kneeling, I picked up a stick and dug at the ground, but the hard-packed dirt snapped the stick in two. When the stick broke, the smell of cedar filled the air. I sat back on my heels and examined the broken end. I took a deep breath.

Yup, definitely cedar.

My eyes skimmed the clearing, but I didn't see any cedar trees. Examining the ground around me, I saw another stick to my right, then another to my left. The sticks seemed to be in a pattern. Standing, I followed the trail of cedar sticks. They ringed the cabin. And with the sticks, in regular intervals, lay bundles of leaves, tied in the middle with rough string.

I didn't need to smell the bundles. I recognized the leaves by their silver-gray color. Sage. One of Abby's favorite herbs.

*No way. This couldn't be a piece of Abby's work. She hadn't been at the lake long enough to do something like this. But if not Abby, then who? And why?*

I stood and took a calming breath. Opening my mind, I sent a tentative finger of energy toward the circle of cedar. I felt a shock, but not as strong. I tried again, only instead of a finger of energy, I pushed with both hands against what felt like an invisible wall.

The wall seemed to bend inward against my hands while the scent of cedar grew stronger.

I shoved harder this time, and felt the wall crack.

Warmth seeped out and enfolded me with soft, gentle hands. The cedar smell that had been so strong only a moment ago was replaced with the aroma of apples and cinnamon, reminding me of childhood days spent in Abby's kitchen. I relaxed, and as I did, I thought I heard a muted voice in my ear.

*"Let me take care of you. Everything you desire will be yours,"* said the sibilant tones.

*Take care of me?* I tugged against the invisible hands that held me, but their grip strengthened. *I don't want to be taken care of. And everything I desire might not be good for me.* I tugged harder. *Without need, want, and struggle, you don't learn, you don't grow.* In my mind, I saw myself prying grasping fingers from my wrists.

As I did, the air around me changed with a sudden surge of cold. The cloying scent of something rotting replaced the comforting smell of apples and cinnamon. And the soft, warm hands? The flesh melted away until nothing was left but bone. Bone that poked and pinched as if trying to find a point of entry into my body, into my soul.

As I struggled, I looked at the cabin, with its broken windows and crooked door, and it appeared to take on a malevolent look. Black dots feathered the edges of my consciousness while I stared at the leering facade. My last thought before the dots merged into total darkness came out of my mouth in a rough whisper.

"Abby."

# *Twelve*

*Cold—I'm so cold.*

A tiny bit of heat sparked somewhere inside of me as a warm cloth wiped my face. With it, the darkness in my mind faded. Opening my eye, I saw Abby's face, filled with concern, hovering over me. A gasp of relief escaped me—I was back in the cabin, in my bedroom. I'd survived whatever had happened in the woods.

After struggling to sit up, I threw my arms around Abby and hugged her close, and the smell of the baby powder she always wore chased away the rotten smell that still lingered in my senses. I squeezed my eyes shut to hold back the sudden tears that filled them.

Abby's arms tightened around me and she murmured soft words in my ear while my body trembled with a cold deep inside me.

What had I stumbled onto in those woods?

Opening my eyes, I noticed Walks Quietly standing silently at my bedroom door. Our eyes met for only a moment, and then, without a word, he turned and left.

Releasing Abby, I scooted back toward the headboard, while she reached around behind me and plumped the pillows. When I settled back against them, a cool hand stroked my face while the other hand tucked the blankets tightly around me.

"Better?" Abby asked, her face still pinched with worry.

Wordlessly, I nodded.

"Good. Here, drink this," she said, handing me a cup from the nightstand.

While I held the warm cup, its heat soaked into my very soul, chasing the last of the cold away, and its fragrant aroma cleared my mind. I took a cautious sip, but didn't recognize the taste.

"What the hell happened?" I asked, passing a hand over my eyes.

"I don't know," Abby said. "I'd just finished smudging the cabin when Walks Quietly appeared at the door, with you in his arms—unconscious. He went straight to your room and put you on the bed. Then he gave me a packet of herbs from his pocket and told me to make tea with it—"

"You don't know what this is?" I interrupted, eyeing the cup with suspicion.

"No," Abby replied calmly.

I felt a look of horror on my face. "What if he's trying to poison me?" I shoved the cup toward her. "I get the distinct impression he doesn't like us."

"Nonsense, he wouldn't poison you," Abby said, refusing to take the cup. "If he'd wanted to get rid of you, he wouldn't have hauled you clear across the lake. He would have left you where he found you. He was trying to help you. When I came back in with the tea, he was muttering words in a native tongue and rubbing something on your forehead."

My hand flew to my brow. Feeling an oily smudge, I rubbed at the spot, transferring some of the substance to my fingers. I held them under my nose and inhaled. "What is this?" I asked, extending my hand.

Abby sniffed at the stuff on my fingers and shook her head. "I don't know." Taking my hand in hers, she glanced out the window, then back at me. "I need to know what happened."

With a sigh, I relaxed against the pillows and quickly related my story.

". . . and another thing," I continued, "the cabin wasn't on Rick's map."

"Maybe he didn't know it was there."

"Well, somebody did. And they laid some kind of protective spell around it, using the cedar and sage. I messed with it when I tried to feel what lurked on the other side." I shuddered at the memory. "Abby, whatever's in there isn't just bad, it's the total absence of good—it's absolute evil."

"Hmm, I see," she said thoughtfully. "I imagine Walks Quietly had something to do with the spell, with the magick."

"Did he say anything?"

"No. He didn't offer any explanation. You were so pale and cold, I didn't take the time to ask questions. I simply did what he told me." Abby looked over her shoulder. "I'd hoped to talk to him after we took care of you, but I see he's gone."

"Yup, gone like a puff of smoke." Now hot, I wiggled out from underneath the covers. "Do you think the cabin had anything to do with Brandi's disappearance?"

"Maybe. Since it's obvious Walks Quietly doesn't want to tell us about the cabin, I think we should take another look at it."

I jumped out of the bed, sloshing the tea I still had in my hand. "Are you crazy? I told you whatever's there is evil." I shook my head until I almost felt my brain rattle. "No way am I going back there. And absolutely, positively, I'm not letting you go!"

Abby arched an eyebrow as if to say, *Oh yeah?*

I shoved my hands in my pockets and started pacing the small room. "Nope, not going to happen, we're not going to do it—"

Abby's voiced stopped my pacing. "Ophelia, what if Brandi *is* in that cabin?" she asked softly. "Don't her parents have the right to know what happened to her?"

An image of a pile of bleached bones in an empty field flashed through my mind. I wasn't able to bring closure to the missing man's family in Iowa, but maybe . . .

Taking my hands from my pockets, I looked down at Abby, sitting on the bed, her hands calmly folded in her lap. "It's dangerous."

She nodded wisely. "I know, and it would be foolish to go rushing back to the cabin. But there are ways, things we can do to protect ourselves."

"Yeah? Like what?" I asked skeptically.

Abby cocked her head. "Well, we can—"

A knock at the cabin door interrupted her.

"That may be Walks Quietly," she said, rising from the bed and hurrying from the room.

I went to the window overlooking the lake and stared across the water. What crept around in those woods? In the cabin? Was it the ghost of Violet Butler's crazy brother, Fred Albert? Did I want to get up close and personal with whatever it was again? A shudder shook my shoulders. Not really. And I didn't want to drag my grandmother into it, either.

Abby's excited voice broke into my thoughts.

"What a surprise! What are you doing in Minnesota?" I heard her exclaim.

She sounded happy to see whoever it was. Leaving the bedroom, I rounded the corner of the kitchen to take a look at our surprise guest. I stopped dead.

Darci stood in the middle of the kitchen, hugging Abby. And right behind her, a mound of luggage.

My face screwed up in a frown, but before I could voice what I thought, Darci took charge of the situation.

"Hi, Ophelia. Surprise!" she squealed, rushing at me and throwing her arms around me.

Awkwardly, I hugged her back. "Yeah, what a surprise," I said, my voice tinged with sarcasm. "How did you manage to finagle this one, Darci?"

She released me and took a step back. A wounded look crossed her face, but I wasn't buying it.

"What do you mean?" she asked, her voice full of innocence.

I gave her a knowing look. "Let's go for a walk, shall we?" I grabbed Darci's arm and tugged her toward the door.

"But Ophelia . . ." A whiny tone crept into her voice. "I just got here."

"A walk will be good for you after your long trip," I said, motioning her out the door.

By now it was late afternoon, and the trees cast long shadows across the road. I saw a flash of red in the leaves above us as a cardinal flitted from branch to branch. Darci walked beside me without speaking, waiting for me to speak first.

She didn't have to wait long.

I got straight to the point. "I don't mean to be rude,

but what are you doing here? And who's running the library?"

"Nobody—it's closed. The day after you left, the air conditioner went on the fritz—"

"Great. How long will it take for them to fix it?" I asked, breaking in.

"At least a week. The thing's so old, they had to order the part from Chicago. Since the library's closed, the library board decided it would be a good time to fumigate the library. The building will have to air out for a couple of days after they spray."

"I guess that's good, then," I said, and picked up a branch lying across the road. "The bugs were taking over."

Darci gave me a big smile. "I saw it as a sign."

Stopping, I looked over at her. "The bugs taking over were a sign?" I asked.

"No, silly. The library closing was a sign. A sign I was supposed to help you out on this latest caper." Her eyes sparkled as she said it. "I mean, it's not like I had anything else to do."

"Darci," I groaned, and threw the branch into the woods. "You've been reading too many detective novels. This isn't a 'caper,' this is serious. There's a young woman missing, and we haven't got a clue why."

Walking away from her, I decided now was not the time to tell Darci about my experience at the abandoned cabin. Not if I intended to try and convince her to go back to Iowa. If she learned about what had happened that morning, she'd be on it like flies on . . . well, it wouldn't be something she'd leave alone.

"I can help you. You know I can," she pleaded while she hurried to catch up with me. "I've helped you before—"

"You're right, you have helped me," I said, interrupting. "But I don't see how you can this time."

She stopped and tossed her head indignantly. "Humph, I can help in a lot of ways. I may not be psychic, like you and Abby, but I'm very good at worming information out of people."

I stopped, too, and snorted. She had that right. I'd seen her in action. People, especially men, always focused on the way Darci looked. They never suspected that behind the naive, "I'm so helpless" act, she was busy learning all kinds of information about them. Information that would be committed to her incredible memory and called forth at any time she wanted.

"Well?" she said, crossing her arms.

I gave a quick nod. "Yes, you're very good at getting people to tell you things."

"Thank you. So I can stay?"

"No."

Darci's eyes filled with tears. "Why not?"

*Crap, now I'd hurt her feelings.*

I reached over and patted her arm. "Darci, it's not because you aren't a very talented woman, and it's not because I don't want your help—"

"Then why?" she asked before I could continue.

"Because, like I told you before, the situation could be *dangerous*," I said, trying to place as much emphasis on the word "dangerous" as possible. Maybe I could scare her.

She sniffed again. "I can take care of myself."

"I know you can," I replied, my voice placating. "But we've only been here a couple of days and already there have been incidents."

"What kind of incidents?" Her eyes shimmered with unshed tears.

"Ahh, well . . ." My voice trailed off.

*Dang, now Darci was worming information out of me.* I watched her face while I tried to think of a way out of the corner I'd put myself in. How much could I tell her without giving away what had really happened that morning? As I thought about what to say, I saw that her tear-filled eyes weren't quite as "teary" as they had been. The tears seemed to be drying up.

*Why, the little trickster!*

Placing my hands on my hips, I suddenly smiled. "Okay, knock it off. I'm wise to you—you're running a con. If you make me feel guilty enough, I'll agree to let you stay with Abby and me. Right?"

She lifted one shoulder carelessly. "Hey, it was worth a shot. Almost worked, too, didn't it?" she asked with a grin, the tears completely gone now.

My smile broadened. "Yeah, it did."

Linking my arm with hers, she pulled me back toward the cabin. "Look at it this way, Ophelia, if I can almost fool you into doing what I want—and you know me—just think what I can accomplish with people who *don't* know me."

"You don't have to prove anything to me, Darce," I said, matching my stride to hers.

"Okay, then let me help you and Abby find this girl. I promise I'll stay out of the hocus-pocus stuff. All I'll do is ask questions. See what I can find out from the people who live here."

If Darci worked the community angle, and Abby and I worked on Jason and his crew, we might learn more, and faster.

The image of a ticking clock flashed through my mind.

I skidded to a stop, pulling Darci around. "Okay, do

you promise," I said, shaking my finger at her, "and I mean promise, that you'll only ask questions? And at the first sign of trouble, you'll back off?"

"Of course," she replied with a toss of her head.

I put my hands on my hips and stared at her. "Darci?"

"Oh all right. I promise." She lifted a hand to her chest. "Cross my heart and hope to—"

I held up my hand to stop her. "Don't—"

"—die."

"—say it," I finished in a whisper.

# *Thirteen*

Darci and I were about a hundred yards from the cabin when a figure in fatigues crashed out of the woods to our right. Surprised, Darci grabbed my arm.

Duane Hobbs. His orange hair stuck up all over his head, with little pieces of wood and leaves caught in the tangles. He whipped his head from side to side, searching up and down the lane for something. Spying us, he zeroed in. "Where is she?" he yelled.

I took a deep breath and tried to stay calm. "Who?"

"That snot-nosed kid, the one that lives with the groupies across the lake. The one that's friends with the Indian."

Tink, he obviously meant Tink. So she was a friend of Walks Quietly? Interesting.

"Why do you want to know?"

From the corner of my eye I saw Darci glare at me as she gripped my arm tighter.

Duane took a step closer to us. "You know where she is?"

Simultaneously, Darci and I stepped back. "No, no we don't," she said, rushing into the conversation. "We don't know where she is." She shook my arm. "Do we, Ophelia?"

Ignoring her, my eyes never left Duane Hobbs. "You didn't answer my question," I said, sounding braver than I felt. "Why do you want to find her? And what will you do to her if you do?"

A nasty grin, showing yellow teeth, spread across his face. With a practiced move, he spit a stream of tobacco at our feet. "I just want to tell her to quit spying on me."

"She spies on you?"

Darci's fingers pinched my arm.

"Yeah, she spies on me. It's not nice to spy on people. Bad things can happen."

I stepped forward, dragging Darci with me. "Are you threatening to harm her?"

His voice cackled with a rusty laugh. " 'Course not. But look what happened to that other girl." He turned back toward the woods. "The one with the red hair. She was spying, too," he said over his shoulder as he loped off into the brush.

"Hey, wait a second." I made a move to follow him, but Darci pulled me back.

"Are you crazy? You can't follow that guy—"

I shook her hand off my arm. "But he knows something about Brandi."

"He's not going to tell you anything. The guy's creepy. If you really want to find out what he knows, ask Rick to come up here and talk to him. It's safer." She shook her head in disgust. "You're so worried about keeping everyone else out of danger, but from what I see, I think you'd better start worrying about yourself."

Before I could reply, Darci let go of my arm and marched ahead of me to the cabin.

Since Abby's room had twin beds, she decided Darci would share it with her. Where Abby intended to put Darci's mountain of clothes, I had no idea, but hey, not my problem. I just wanted to go to bed.

I felt exhausted. So exhausted that I didn't do justice to the great meal Abby had prepared for dinner. Cold pasta salad with tiny bits of green pepper and cheese marinated in Abby's homemade dressing, hamburgers cooked on the grill, and ice cream with chocolate sauce for dessert. Instead of enjoying the meal, I fought to keep my eyes open and my head from dropping face first into my bowl of ice cream. The conversation between Abby and Darci flowed around me without any contribution on my part. When I finally finished my ice cream, I glanced up from the empty bowl to see them watching me.

"What?" I asked, raising my hand to my face. "Do I have chocolate sauce dripping off my chin or something?"

Abby smiled. "No, dear, I just asked you if you were tired."

Sliding the bowl away, I rested my elbows on the table. "Yes, I am. Too much has happened today, and I can't seem to process all of it."

"I'm sure you're still suffering some effects of what happened to you at the cabin across the lake," she said, rising and picking up the empty bowls.

Looking at her, I narrowed my eyes and shook my head slightly. The last thing I wanted to do right now was play interrogation with Darci.

Too late. Darci's eyes widened and she wiggled closer to the table. "What happened this morning?"

I let out a long sigh and waved her question away. "I'm not up to talking about it now—"

The ringing of the telephone interrupted me. Yes, saved by the bell. Stumbling to my feet, I rushed to the living room to answer it.

I picked up the cordless phone. "Hello."

"Hi, Ophelia," said a warm voice on the other end of the line.

"Hey Rick," I answered, and walked out onto the deck.

"I wanted to call and let you know what I've learned. The estate is still owned by the Butler family."

"Really? The Finches are renting it?"

"I don't know. The Butler place wouldn't come cheap, so I've got a forensic accountant looking into PSI's finances. I want to know exactly what the connection is, and more information on how they're financing their lifestyle."

"Follow the money, right?" I asked, smiling

Rick laughed. "You got it. So how's it going? Are you enjoying yourself?"

Looking out over the quiet lake, I thought about it. The lake was one of the most beautiful places I'd ever seen, but enjoying myself? Not really.

"I didn't think we were here to have a good time; I thought we were here to find Brandi."

"You're right. Have you met any of the group yet?"

"Yes. Both Juliet and Jason, Winnie, and the girl, Tink."

"What were your impressions of them?"

"Juliet seems nice, devoted to the girl. Winnie is

annoying. And Tink? She reminds me of a wood sprite."

"What about Jason?"

"Him, I can't quite figure out yet," I said, leaning against the wooden railing of the deck. "But there's something unusual going on."

Rick chuckled. "No kidding. That's why I wanted you and Abby to go up there."

"No, I didn't mean whatever's happening has anything to do with Brandi's disappearance." I paused. "It might. I don't know right now. As for Jason, I met him down by the lake where I'd been talking to Tink. I'd found her there by herself. Then he showed up."

"That's interesting. In all the time I spent up there, I never saw her," Rick replied, his voice thoughtful.

"It doesn't surprise me. I think they must keep a tight rein on her and don't let her go many places."

"I heard she's sickly, so that would explain maintaining a close watch on her."

"And I think they try, but I got the impression she likes to slip away. But I wouldn't describe her as 'sickly.' She's thin, but she doesn't strike me as someone with a chronic illness." I walked over to the corner of the deck. "Even though when I met Juliet, she alluded to that fact the kid wasn't well."

"You didn't believe her?"

"I don't know. It didn't fit with my impression." I rubbed my tired eyes with one hand. "I'm sorry. I know I'm not making much sense."

"That's okay. Don't worry about it," Rick said in a kind voice. "You've only been at the lake for about a day and a half. I was up there for weeks. But already you've accomplished more than I was able to."

I decided to tackle the question that was really bothering me.

"Did you hear of any rumors of the Finches abusing Tink?" I asked abruptly.

"What?" He sounded perplexed at my question.

"Abuse. When I was with Tink at the lake and Jason showed up, her attitude changed completely. She'd been cocky, almost mouthy, but when he appeared, it was like a switch had been thrown. She turned into this meek, submissive little thing."

"Maybe because she got busted running off?"

"Maybe." I blew out a breath. "I don't know. The whole experience seemed odd."

"In answer to your question—no. I didn't hear any rumors that the girl's being abused. I think someone would've hinted at it. The community may appreciate what PSI is doing for them, but I don't think they'd turn away from a young girl being mistreated. Any abuse would've been reported."

"If they knew about it. A lot of secrets can be hidden behind closed doors."

Rick didn't speak for a moment. "If so, I've got a feeling you'll uncover them."

Suddenly, I remembered Duane Hobbs. "Speaking of secrets—why didn't you tell me about Duane Hobbs?"

"What's there to tell?" Rick's voice carried a note of surprise. "What happened to Duane is an old story, and one that happened to a lot of soldiers. A young man goes off to war and returns seriously messed up. He's harmless." He sounded very sure of himself.

"I think he knows something about Brandi. He said she was spying on him."

"Right. Duane thinks everyone is spying on him. Did he also mention he knows who killed JFK, where Jimmy Hoffa is buried, and what the lights over Roswell are?"

I felt my bubble burst. I'd been so convinced questioning Duane would help solve the mystery.

"So he's paranoid and believes in conspiracies?" I asked, not keeping the disappointment from my voice.

"Yeah."

"Shoot. Another dead end?"

"Yup."

"What about Walks Quietly? Someone else you neglected to tell me about."

I could almost hear the wheels in Rick's head spin as he went over what he knew about the man. The knowledge came out in concise words.

"Lives down the lake from where you're staying— back in the woods where the lane narrows. He's also a Vietnam vet, like Duane. He served with honors. His Native American heritage is Dakota Sioux—"

I broke in before he could finish. "I thought the tribes around here were Ojibwa?"

"Most are, but there are still some Sioux in the area. Ojibwa are ancestral enemies of the Sioux, so maybe he feels he doesn't have much in common with the other Native Americans living around the area."

"Is he married? Does he have children?" I asked, breaking in again.

"I heard he has a daughter in Nebraska. But he keeps to himself, and I heard he isn't overly fond of white people."

"Is there a specific reason?"

"I couldn't find out. People clammed up about him, like they did when I asked them about PSI. But for a different reason. I got the impression they not only don't trust him, they're afraid of him, too."

Rick paused, and over the phone I heard a door open

and shut, followed by the sound of a female voice calling out. Rick had company.

I thought of a long-ago kiss in front of a warm fire, and felt a tug at my heart. So much for Abby's remark about life's patterns changing. Rick wasn't for me nine months ago and he wasn't for me now. Had I really expected he'd been pining for me all these months? Not likely. Rick wasn't the kind of guy to pine.

I heard a muffled "Just a minute," as if he'd covered the phone with his hand.

His voice came out clear when he spoke again. "Sorry about that. Back to my story—some people even made a funny sign whenever I mentioned his name."

"Great," I mumbled into the receiver.

"What? I didn't hear you," Rick said. "Do you know what the funny sign might mean?"

Clearing my throat, I spoke louder. "It's protection against the evil eye."

# *Fourteen*

After a restless night, haunted by half-remembered dreams that left me feeling on edge, I rose shortly before dawn. Quietly leaving my room, I peeked into Abby's room. Both she and Darci lay curled up on their separate beds, sleeping deeply. With Queenie following me, I went to the kitchen and made coffee. When the last of the coffee had dripped into the pot, I poured a cup and took a cautious sip of the strong, hot liquid. Its warmth seemed to ease away the lingering malaise of dreams I couldn't recall.

With cup in hand, I wandered through the living area and out onto the deck. I leaned against the railing and stared out at the lake. In the gray light, early morning mist wafted across the still water, and from a distance I heard the cawing crows. My gaze traveled around the shore of the lake to the spot where the abandoned cabin lay hidden in the trees.

I didn't doubt Walks Quietly's tie to the cabin. From the moment I met him, I sensed the power that he carried deep inside. And the cabin? A great deal of power lay there, too. A great deal of evil. And strong magick surrounded it. But had the magick been used to contain the evil or create it? I didn't know.

*But I bet Walks Quietly does. Where did Rick say he lived?*

My decision made, I swilled down my now lukewarm coffee and headed back to my room. I changed quickly from the sweats I'd worn to jeans, a light sweatshirt, and tennis shoes. Tying my shoes, I prayed I could get out of the house without waking Abby and Darci. I had a feeling Abby wouldn't approve of my idea.

Hurrying to the door, I found Lady watching me with hope in her eyes.

"No," I whispered. "You have to stay home this time. Abby will let you out when she gets up."

Her tail sagged and she gave me a dejected look, but went back to her spot by the windows and lay down.

Shutting the door as silently as I could, I took off down the lane toward the path Rick had mentioned.

So far so good. At least as long as I didn't run into Duane Hobbs skulking around the woods.

An old pickup marked the spot where the lane narrowed to a simple path. And straight ahead I could see wisps of smoke hanging above the treetops. As I rushed forward, the path in front of me curved, and after rounding a bend, I found myself in the front yard of a cabin, a well-maintained cabin.

Stopping, I scanned the clearing where the cabin sat. The cabin itself had siding weathered to a muted shade of gray, but the tin roof looked shiny and new. A wide porch covered the front of the house. From the chimney, what had been only wisps from a distance were now puffs of smoke that bellowed into the morning air.

A shed that had seen better days sat away from the

house, and cords of wood were stacked against the side of the building. Near the shed, an axe, with the blade partially buried in a chopping block, awaited its owner's use. To the right of the shed I noticed a bundle wrapped in white cloth, hanging from a tree branch. My eyes traveled across the front of the cabin to the other side. Another bundle, this one red, hung from a different tree. Looking up at the tree next to me, I saw a third bundle, but instead of white or red, this one was yellow.

What were they? I made a move to touch the yellow bundle when I heard a creak. Whipping back toward the house, I saw the door slowly swinging open, and ducked behind the tree that held the yellow bundle.

From my hiding place I watched Walks Quietly stride into the center of the clearing around his cabin. Taking a pouch from his shirt pocket, he opened it and placed a pinch of something in his right hand.

Light from the morning sun illuminated the spot where he stood, and the sky above him was shot with pink and gold. He extended his right hand, palm up, toward the sky and began to chant in words I didn't know. He turned to his right, to the south, still chanting.

The words made no sense to me, but I felt their sound vibrate in my soul. A sound that mingled with the morning call of the birds in an age-old song. I watched while Walks Quietly continued his circle, facing west, north, and then back to the east. I don't know how long his ceremony took. Time had lost meaning as I felt myself swept up in the rhythm of his chant.

His voice dropped to a whisper as he closed his right palm and sprinkled whatever he held on the ground. A sense of reverence filled the clearing, and for a moment even the birds were quiet.

"You can come out from behind the tree now," he said clearly.

Sheepishly, I slunk out from behind it.

"Didn't you see the No Trespassing sign?" Brown eyes stared at me in a way that made me squirm.

"Yeah," I answered like a petulant child. "Are you going to have me arrested?"

His face tightened and his hands clenched and unclenched at his sides. "It wouldn't do any good. What do you want?"

"I'd like to ask you a question." I chewed on my lip, nervously waiting for his reply.

For a second he seemed to think about it, but then he turned and over his shoulder said, "I don't answer questions from whites."

I rushed after him and caught up. "Please." I placed my hand on his arm. All became still and my brain hummed with the power I felt inside this man. I dropped my hand and took a step back. Shoving my hands in the pockets of my sweatshirt, I stared at the ground.

Seconds ticked by while I felt the weight of his stare. Finally his voice broke the silence.

"What's your question?"

Tamping down my nerves, I looked at him. "I've been told you're Tink's friend. Is she being mistreated?"

His eyes narrowed in suspicion. "The child is nothing to you," he replied.

Offended, I tilted my chin. "If you mean I don't know her, you're right. But it doesn't mean I'd stand by and do nothing if I knew the girl was being mistreated."

"And what would you do?" he scoffed. "Go to your authorities?"

"Well, yes, I would." My tone strident. "I'd find

someone to get her out of the situation she's in, to help her."

"But if no one would? Would you? And how far would you go with your help?" He stopped and looked past me into the woods. "Would you be responsible for her? Care for her?" he asked, looking back at me.

"I don't know." I shuffled my feet and thought about Tink's violet eyes and happy song. "Yes, yes I would." I met his stare straight on. "I'd do whatever I could for her."

Walks Quietly nodded, and I felt like I had passed some kind of test.

"No," he said softly. "She isn't being mistreated, but her spirit isn't free. You've asked your question. Now go, Ophelia Jensen." He turned and walked toward the cabin.

"Wait," I called out. "What about Duane Hobbs and the girl, Brandi?"

He faced me. "The red-haired girl from across the lake? What about her?"

"She's missing."

A light flickered in his eyes and disappeared. "I know nothing. Let your authorities find her."

"But they've tried." I sounded desperate. "They can't find her."

"I can't help you," he said abruptly.

I wasn't about to back down. I'd seen a spark of something in his eyes when I told him that Brandi was missing.

Standing straight, I glared at him. "Can't or won't?"

"Either way. It doesn't make a difference," he said in a hard voice. "I won't be involved with the problems of the whites." He turned away, dismissing me.

"Okay," I called out again. "What about the cabin across the lake. The one you—"

He spun around. "You silly, foolish woman! You don't know what you're dealing with—stay away from there." He took a step toward me.

My eyes wide with fright, I turned and flew down the path, so intent on getting away from Walks Quietly that I missed the flash of white skittering through the woods.

# *Fifteen*

When I arrived back at the cabin, the only ones to greet me were Queenie and Lady. A note from Abby on the refrigerator said she and Darci had gone into Melcher for breakfast. A postscript, with a happy face beneath Abby's elegant handwriting, hoped I had a nice walk. Lots of exclamation points followed the statement. Darci.

I moped around the cabin, playing with Lady, petting Queenie, but nothing seemed to hold my attention for long. The sun, high in the sky now, shone down on the lake, making the water look cool and inviting.

Changing into a bathing suit and throwing a shirt and shorts over it, I slid my feet into flip-flops, grabbed the sunscreen, and headed down the hill to the lake. Maybe relaxing on the dock would quiet the unease I felt.

Once on the dock, I peeled off my shirt, lathered on the sunscreen, and let the warm sun beat down on my back and arms. My unprotected back might get a little red, but the heat felt so good, I didn't care. Sitting down on the edge of the dock, I let my feet dangle in the cool lake.

In the clear water beneath the dock I saw flashes of

silver as tiny fish swam along the sandy bottom. Several lurked close to the pilings, hiding from the larger fish that saw them as a tasty meal. The motors of ski boats rumbled in the distance, and the sound of waves lapped the shore. A breeze stirred the pines growing behind me, and finally I felt my body begin to relax.

I lay back on the dock and stared at the trails of white clouds moving slowly across the sky. As a child, I'd played the game all children do and tried to see what shapes the clouds made. I did it now.

What did I see? One cloud looked like a dragon. A plump cloud formed the body and wisps trailing away made wings and a long arched neck. The shape shifted and, to my eyes, formed a face, a smiling face. My eyelids closed with the image of the face locked in my mind.

While I lay there, I felt the air suddenly cool, as if one of the clouds blocked the sun. Unwilling to open my eyes, I waited for the cloud to move on, but the temperature continued to drop and my skin prickled at the unexpected chill. I thought I heard a voice in my ear. With eyes still closed, I strained to hear the words, but they whispered and hissed like a snake. My stomach cramped.

A scene unfolded in my mind. A book with a black cover sat on a table surrounded by candles. The cover flipped open, moved by unseen hands, to show pages yellowed with age. And as the flame of the candles wavered madly, a huge spider with dark hairy legs crawled across the table and onto the book. The voice turned from a whisper to a growl. Frightened, I jerked up right and opened my eyes. Dizziness and nausea swamped me and I closed them again.

The growl grew louder and louder, but now, over the

sound, I heard someone calling my name. Forcing the nausea away, I opened my eyes again and looked out over the lake.

A small fishing boat approached with a figure waving an arm in the air and calling to me. I didn't recognize the man, but I did the voice.

Rick. How did he sneak up here?

I lowered my head and inhaled deeply through my nose. The last of the dizziness faded, but left me shaking inside. Lifting my head, I stood and gave him a weak wave.

When I saw the way Rick was dressed, I would've laughed if I hadn't felt like crap. His clean-cut, kind of preppy look was gone. He wore a sweat-stained T-shirt and ripped cutoffs. A baseball cap, worn with the bill in back, covered his dark brown hair. And beneath his dark sunglasses, the three-day shadow of a beard covered his face.

*So he hadn't shaved for his hot date last night.*

Rick cut the motor and the boat slid alongside the dock. He threw me a line and I tied the rope to a piling. He pulled his dark sunglasses off and bewilderment crossed his face.

"Hey, you don't look good—"

"Thanks," I said shortly. "Nice to see you, too. How did you—"

"I meant you're pale," he interrupted as he stepped onto the dock. "Are you sick?"

I thought about the stomach cramps. No need to tell him, so I lied. "No, I'm fine."

"How long have you been in the sun?" he asked, his eyes mirroring his disbelief. "You might be dehydrated."

Reaching into the boat, he grabbed a jug and

handed it to me. "Go ahead—it's water. And I haven't touched it."

After the scene I saw in my head, catching germs from Rick was the least of my worries.

Gratefully, I took a sip. The cold water slipped down my throat and I felt better. Maybe he was right, I thought. Maybe what I'd seen was some kind of peculiar reaction to heat stroke.

*Yeah, right.*

Lowering the jug, I handed it back to him.

"Better?"

I nodded, unable to find my voice.

Rick's gaze shifted away from me, and he stared out over the lake. The minutes ticked by and the silence remained unbroken. Like neither one of us wanted to be the first to speak.

"Where are Abby and Darci?" he asked, ending the standoff.

"They went to Melcher for breakfast."

He turned toward me. "Why didn't you go with them?"

I wasn't ready to tell him about the visions.

"I had things to do," I said tersely.

A typical reporter, Rick persisted. "Like what?"

He wouldn't cut me any slack until I told him everything. My stomach cramped again and I knew I wasn't up to playing any games.

Throwing up my hands and taking a deep breath, I let the words spill out. I told him everything—the cabin, the strange lights, the unusual dreams.

He listened without expression until I'd finished.

"What do you think?" I asked, hoping for his approval.

"That's it?" he asked, his face still a mask.

My expression fell. "For now," I replied defensively. "I've found more clues than you did."

"We've got suppositions, visions, not clues. I don't see how any of this can help find Brandi." He shook his head. "There's a logical explanation for all of your 'clues.'"

I crossed my arms. "Yeah? Like what?"

Rick looked up at the sky and shook his head again. "Duane Hobbs is a nutcase who thinks he sees the boogeyman; Walks Quietly resents being spied on by you; and the Finches are a couple worried about their sick child."

"I told you, I don't think she's sick," I said in a stubborn voice.

"And your medical degree is from where?" he shot back.

I ignored his sarcasm.

"What about the abandoned cabin?" I asked. "How do you explain *logically* what happened to me there?" Irritated, I narrowed my eyes and glared at him.

He lifted one shoulder and settled his sunglasses back on his face. "An overactive imagination? You were alone, in a strange place, maybe a little spooked, and you started seeing things that weren't there."

My irritation boiled over into anger. "I know what I know," I said, my voice rising.

"Which isn't much." His jaw clenched while he continued to stare out over the lake. "We've got to find her, Ophelia."

My anger faded to frustration. I slapped my hand against one of the pilings. How could I explain that underneath all this beauty, something evil was lurking? The truth was I couldn't. As he'd said, visions and suppositions weren't proof. We were no closer to finding Brandi today than we were yesterday.

Defeated, I looked over at him. "What are you doing here?"

He shrugged again. "I felt so helpless after I finished talking to you on the phone that I threw some stuff together and drove up here in the middle of the night. I'm staying in Brainerd. It's a big enough town, no one will recognize me." He turned and looked at me, his eyes mirroring his impatience. "I don't like feeling helpless."

"You don't want to feel helpless? Find out why, of all places, the Finches are renting the Butler estate." I picked up my shirt lying on the dock and turned away. Walking toward the steps leading to our cabin, I called over my shoulder, "See you later, Rick."

"Wait a second," he exclaimed. "Where are you going?"

"To pursue my overactive imagination," I said loud enough that he could hear me, and kept walking. "Right now, it's all we've got."

By the time I'd reached the top of the stairs and crossed the deck, I heard voices from inside the cabin. Abby and Darci were back.

Darci ran over to me before I'd finished sliding the door shut. "Where did you go on your walk this morning?" she asked, grabbing my arm and pulling me to the kitchen table. "Did you go back to that cabin? I saw you on the dock with Rick. What did he say?" Pausing for a breath, she jerked out a chair from the table and gently shoved me into it. "I've got so much to tell you, but you go first."

Abby's eyes met mine from where she stood over by

the counter. She smiled and shook her head before joining us at the table.

After a deep sigh, I quickly related all that had happened from the time I left the cabin until now.

Darci seemed a little deflated when she learned I hadn't returned to the cabin by myself. But it was Abby's reaction I cared about the most. "So what I saw on the dock—a dream or a vision?" I asked her.

She leaned forward, crossing her arms on the table. "I don't know. Have you been dreaming at night?"

"No . . . yes . . . maybe . . ." I said, hesitating while I tried to remember, but all I could recall were vague impressions and the same feeling of growing uneasiness that had been troubling me. Maybe Rick was right; my imagination had gone into overdrive.

I rubbed the knotted muscles in the back of my neck. "One thing I do know—Walks Quietly does not like whites or cops," I said emphatically. "I don't understand why—"

"I do, I do," Darci said, squirming forward in her chair. "Duane Hobbs killed Walks Quietly's wife and got away with it."

*"What?"* My hand dropped away from my neck and I stared at her.

Abby turned to Darci. "You'd better explain, dear, before Ophelia goes into shock."

"Okay," Darci said, her eyes wide as she scooted her chair closer to the table. "Fifteen years ago the body of a woman was found by the side of the road. She'd been a victim of a hit and run driver."

"Walks Quietly's wife?"

"Yes."

"That's really sad, Darci, but what's the connection to Duane Hobbs?" I asked.

"He was driving the truck that hit her."

I was confused. "I thought you said the accident was a hit and run?"

Darci nodded once. "I did. There were no witnesses—no evidence."

"But Duane was a suspect?" I asked.

"Yup."

"Why him?" I still didn't get it.

"Fifteen years ago Duane was just wild, not crazy. He had a job, did pretty well during the week, but on the weekends he cut loose. At the time of the accident, there had been several complaints about his driving."

"But he was never arrested?"

"No." Darci gave me a sly look. "Did I tell you, at the time of the hit and run, his cousin was the sheriff?"

Finally, I got it.

Leaning back in my chair, I massaged the back of my neck again. "A cover-up."

Satisfied that I finally understood, Darci straightened and hooked her arm across the back of her chair. "In a way. Everyone thinks that since the cousin couldn't prove Duane was the driver, he did the next best thing. Threatened him enough that Duane never drove again. He sold the truck right after the investigation closed. Walks Quietly tried to get the sheriff to dig a little deeper, leave the investigation open, but he refused."

"Why didn't Rick know about this?" I asked, my eyebrows coming together. "He's a trained investigator, and people froze whenever he brought up Walks Quietly. He said they acted scared and wouldn't talk to him."

*"Please,"* Darci said, drawing the word out. "A bunch of old fishermen sitting at the counter in the coffee shop told me about Duane and Walks Quietly.

You really think they'd be as talkative with Rick as they were with me?"

I looked Darci over—halter top, shorts, clouds of blond hair falling around her shoulders. I smiled. No, I didn't suppose they would've been as anxious to talk to Rick. But with Darci? They would have wanted to impress her with their insider's gossip.

My smile disappeared. "Did anyone speak out? Did anyone agree with Walks Quietly?"

"No." Darci shook her head. "Everyone approved of the cousin's solutions."

"Everyone except Walks Quietly," Abby said, breaking her silence. "And I don't blame him. No one was brought to justice for his wife's death. It would—"

A knock on the door stopped her from finishing, and our three heads turned simultaneously to the door.

Crap—Winnie dressed in her white tunic uniform.

After pushing back her chair, Abby crossed the kitchen and opened the door.

"Winnie, how nice of you to stop by," she said in a gracious voice.

My jaw clenched. I'd had a rough day, and those knots in the back of my neck were sending currents of pain up to the base of my skull. I didn't feel like being social, but as Abby held the door wide and Winnie stepped in, I knew I had no choice.

Abby quickly introduced Darci, while Winnie joined us at the table.

"Thank you, thank you," she said, her hands fluttering.

What she was thanking us for, I had no idea. My expression must've mirrored my thoughts—Darci shot me a quick, questioning look. I gave my head a slight shake and turned my attention back to Winnie.

"I'm sorry for dropping in unannounced," Winnie said in her high, girlish voice. "But Juliet and Jason would like to invite you to the compound for dinner tomorrow night." Her hands flapped at the air. "Jason feels he made a poor impression on you when he met you, Ophelia, and he wants to correct it."

Puzzled, I sat back in my chair. "Why would he think that?"

"Well, he was in a hurry to get Tink home, and he feels he was short with you." She picked up a napkin and started pleating it like a fan.

"Not at all," I said, sitting forward. "I understand Tink isn't very strong?"

Winnie unfolded the napkin and smoothed out the creases. "No, she isn't."

"What's wrong with her?" Darci piped in.

"She isn't . . ." Winnie's voice trailed off while she studied the napkin lying on the table. ". . . healthy."

Darci leaned closer to Winnie. "What do you mean—Ouch."

"Oh Darci," I said. "I'm sorry. Was that your leg? I thought it was the table."

Darci turned to me with her eyes narrowed in a frown, but before she could open her mouth, Abby took charge of the conversation.

"Winnie, it's lovely Jason and Juliet thought of us, but Darci and I have already made plans."

Darci looked at Abby in surprise, but Abby ignored her.

"But Ophelia would love to join you, wouldn't you, dear?" Abby said with a sweet smile.

Trapped by my darling grandmother, I had to agree, and nodded my head silently.

"Oh that's wonderful." Winnie discarded the napkin

and hurried to her feet. "Juliet will be so pleased. And Tink," she said, her voice rising a few decibels. "She'll be so excited. She loved meeting you, and the poor child . . ."

Her attention shifted from me to Queenie, who had strolled into the kitchen to check out all the commotion.

"What a lovely cat!" Winnie exclaimed, bending over to pet Queenie.

But before Winnie's hand touched her, Queenie's eyes scrunched into narrow slits and her back arched in a high curve. Her fur fluffed out like porcupine quills, and from deep in her throat came a low, unrelenting hiss.

Startled, Darci, Abby, and I watched the scene in surprise.

Winnie straightened and stared at Queenie, her eyes round with astonishment.

Queenie gave Winnie one last glowering look, turned and marched out of the kitchen. Our last sight was her tail, held high and still puffed out in a cloud of black fur, disappearing around the corner.

# *Sixteen*

It was becoming a morning ritual to drink my first cup of coffee out on the deck. I enjoyed the quiet and the feeling of being alone. My only companions were my own thoughts and whatever wildlife wandered by. Today, from my spot on the deck, I watched a mother duck with half-grown youngsters moving stately along the shoreline. Every now and again one would pause and stick its bill in the water, capturing a juicy bug. And as they did each morning, the crows cawed in the distance.

Greeted each morning by crows and sung to sleep each night by the loons. I knew from now on I would never hear their calls without remembering this place.

Scratching on the glass doors interrupted my musings. Looking over my shoulder, I saw Lady with her nose pressed against the glass. Her tail waved while she looked at me with anticipation.

"You want to go for a walk, don't you?"

Her head cocked and her tail wagged faster, as if she'd understood me.

"Okay," I said, walking to the door and sliding it open.

She let out a short bark and ran to the kitchen door. I followed her.

"Shush," I said, and snapped the leash on her collar. "If you wake everybody up, you won't get to go. Darci will want to go detecting and Abby will want to mix up some potion. And we'll be busy trying to keep them both out of trouble."

Grabbing a sweatshirt from the hook by the door, I threw it on over my T-shirt and sweatpants and off we went.

I wanted to avoid the path to Walks Quietly's cabin, so we went in the other direction. Soon we came to another path leading down to the lake. Maybe from there I could get a closer look at the ducks I'd watched from the deck. I whistled for Lady to follow and headed toward the path. But when I rounded the corner, I saw we weren't alone.

Walks Quietly sat on a boulder at the edge of the lake. Tink sat at his feet on a blanket. His hands rested lightly on his knees and his head was bent toward the girl.

Tink's face wore a rapt expression as she stared up at him.

His deep voice carried up from the lake and he appeared to be telling Tink a story.

Wordlessly, I motioned for Lady to sit, and I listened.

Many years ago when the earth was young and the stars were new, there were two brother eagles. Elder Brother was thoughtful and respected others. Younger Brother was arrogant and thought of no one but himself. Younger Brother wished always to best Elder Brother.

One day as the morning sun greeted the world, Elder Brother decided to fly as high as the clouds. Up and up he flew, his strong wings beating against the wind.

From his lofty place in the blue sky, he saw the mountains with white peaks below. Rivers snaked through lush green valleys carrying water to all the villages. Forests of great pines, white birch, and red maples stretched across the world beneath him. The beauty he saw swelled his heart and made him glad.

Happy in his flight, he slowly returned to earth and told Younger Brother of all the wonders he had seen.

Younger Brother asked, "Why did you stop? Why didn't you fly higher and higher?"

"I am satisfied with the wonders I have seen and wished to return to continue in the ways of our father," Elder Brother answered simply.

The next day Younger Brother thought about what Elder Brother had accomplished. "I can do better," he thought. "I am stronger, I can fly higher, and I can see more wonders than my brother."

Younger Brother took flight. He flew over the white-peaked mountains, the lush valleys, and the great forests, but he didn't see their beauty. All he wanted was to fly higher and higher.

And while he did, the sun grew hotter and hotter. But Younger Brother didn't care. All he thought of was beating his brother. He glanced down once and saw the earth, a small round ball below.

"I am higher than any eagle has ever flown. From here, I could rule the world," he said. He flew higher still.

The sun beat down so hot on his head feathers that they began to smoke. Still he did not stop his upward flight. Finally he could stand the heat no longer and he swiftly returned to earth to cool his burning head and neck.

Once he'd safely landed on the shore of a great lake,

Younger Brother saw his reflection in the quiet water. All the beautiful feathers on his head and neck were gone. He was bald and ugly. No longer a handsome eagle who could rule the world.

"Younger Brother, you will rule the world, as you wished for in your arrogance and rudeness." The voice of the Great Spirit drifted across the lake. "But not as a mighty eagle. You will rule as one who cleans the earth of dead things, of carrion. None will admire you and all will shun you."

That is how the bird known as the vulture came to be.

Tink smiled up at Walks Quietly. "And the lesson of the story is, 'Be careful what you wish for, you might get more than you expected.' "

Walks Quietly patted her head. "That's right, little one," he said, smiling.

I didn't think the man knew how to smile.

Tink's head suddenly whipped in my direction and violet eyes glared at me.

Lady, remembering her new friend, Tink, gave a happy bark and headed down the hill.

I had no choice but to follow.

Lady ran up to Tink and planted wet, doggy kisses all over the girl's face. Laughing, Tink threw her arms around Lady's neck and gave her a hug, while Walks Quietly watched the scene with a fond expression on his face. But when he turned toward me, his expression changed and hard brown eyes stared at me.

Embarrassed at being caught eavesdropping, I hung my head.

"Do you spy on people every day?" His tone seemed soft, but it carried a reproach.

Refusing to be intimidated, I stood straighter. "No, I don't spy on people—" I stopped, remembering yesterday. "Okay, so yesterday I watched you uninvited—"

"That's the definition for spying, isn't it?" Walks Quietly cut in.

"All right, I was spying. There, I confessed." I fisted my hands on my hips.

A slight smile played at the corner of his mouth.

"But I wasn't spying today," I said defensively. "Lady wanted to go for a walk."

Walks Quietly reached out and patted Lady's head. "So this is Lady. Tink told me about her. Nice dog."

Lady turned her attention from Tink to him, and with one swipe of a pink tongue licked his hand.

He gave her a genuine smile.

"Look, I'm sorry I interrupted you," I said. "I really didn't mean to overhear your story, but I kind of got engrossed in the tale."

Walks Quietly stood slowly, as if his joints ached. "It's an old tale, but one people would do well to remember." He reached down to Tink and pulled her to her feet. "You'd better get home, little one, before they miss you," he said in a kind voice.

"Do I have to?" she pleaded.

"Yes," he replied.

She gave Lady a hug and me a frown, before scurrying up the hill.

Walks Quietly followed her, passing me without speaking.

On the way back to the cabin, my mind felt like it was twisted in knots. So many things had happened; so many things didn't make sense.

"Where have you been?" a voice from behind me said.

I skidded to a stop and whirled around. "Rick. What are you doing here?" I glared at him. "And what are you doing jumping out of the trees, scaring me like that?"

He chuckled. "I didn't jump out of the trees, but I'm sorry if I startled you." He fell into step beside me. "What are you doing out here so early in the morning?"

"Lady wanted to go for a walk." I gestured toward the lake. "I ran into Walks Quietly and Tink down there. Neither one seemed happy to see us. Wait—let me re-phrase that," I said with a wry grin. "They were happy to see Lady, but the same can't be said for me."

"Not winning any popularity contests?"

"Nope."

Rick gave me a playful nudge in the ribs. "Hey, Jensen, I still like you."

"Right," I said in a sarcastic voice.

"No." Rick placed a hand over his heart. "I really do like you, Jensen. I—"

"Will you stop?" I lifted a hand, halting the stream of words. "It's too early in the morning for joking around."

He kicked a small stone across the lane. "Okay. I heard from the forensic accountant," he said, changing the subject.

"What did he find out?"

A smug look crossed Rick's face. "You're not going to believe it. After what he learned, I stayed up past midnight surfing the Web for more information."

My curiosity poked its little head out. "Well, tell me."

"Juliet Finch is Violet Butler's great-niece," he said with a flourish.

"No sh—er, no kidding?" I caught Rick's sudden grin out of the corner of my eye. "So they own the place?"

"No, it's held in a trust, but Juliet has lifetime rights."

"The Butlers never had any children?"

"No, they raised Violet's niece, Mona, as their own. She was a devoted daughter to them. Even took care of Violet after Victor Butler died." Rick paused and gave me a sideways look. "In fact Mona and Violet died together in a house fire back in 1995. Seems Violet liked smoking in bed."

"Any other family?"

"Not that I could find. There was a sister, must've been Tink's mother. She died a couple of years after Violet and Mona."

"Of an illness?"

"No, some kind of accident, but I couldn't find out what."

I felt a breeze prickle my skin. "None of these women died of natural causes?"

"Nope. Seems the women in the Butler family don't die of natural causes."

"That's strange." I rubbed my arms, chilled again by the breeze.

"I think so. I also think it's strange all these deaths occurred *after* Juliet married Jason."

# Seventeen

Standing in front of the bathroom mirror, I put my hair in a twist and held the strands in place with long bobby pins. While I did, my gaze slid to Abby, sitting on the edge of the tub, watching me.

"Okay, so tell me again why you aren't going to this dinner tonight?" I said, fastening the last pin in place.

Abby gave me long, patient look. "I don't think it would be wise to take Darci. I'm afraid her curiosity might give more away at this point in time than we want. Winnie might be easily fooled, but I don't think Juliet and Jason Finch would be."

"So you're staying home to babysit her." My mouth turned down in a frown. "And sending me, alone, into the lion's den."

Abby's chuckle echoed off the tiled walls. "Don't you think you're being a tad overdramatic, my dear?"

"These people could be kidnappers. What if I don't come back?"

"I'll send Rick to storm the gates," Abby said, still smiling.

My frown deepened. "No thanks. I'll rescue myself if I need to."

"I thought as much." Abby rose and came to stand behind me, our reflections joined in the mirror.

Her eyes were twinkling with humor, but mine narrowed with worry.

Her expression changed as the humor slipped away. "Is your head still bothering you?"

"Yes," I said, opening the medicine cabinet and grabbing the aspirin. "I think I've taken a ton of these today." I shot the pills to the back of my throat and chased them down with a long drink of water. "Yuck," I said, and wiped my mouth with a towel. "I think they're starting to upset my stomach."

Abby studied my face in the mirror. "Drink some chamomile tea when you get home. It will relieve the stress you're feeling and help you sleep." She placed a hand on my shoulder. "Let the leaves steep for five minutes, okay?"

"Okay." I patted her hand and plastered an encouraging smile on my face. "I'll be fine. I don't want you to worry. That's my job, remember?"

Abby's reflection smiled back at me in the mirror. "Ophelia, I've worried about you since the day you were born, and will till the day they lay me in my grave. That's *my* job."

When Abby said the word "grave," a shiver ran up my back and I felt tears tease at the corner of my eyes. "I don't like it when you use words like that."

Her eyebrows lifted. "What words?"

I looked down. I didn't want to meet her gaze in the mirror. "You know—'grave,' " I said softly.

Both hands squeezed my shoulders. "Oh my dear," she said, her voice full of love, and a smile playing at the corner of her mouth. "Everyone must die someday."

"But not for a long time, right?" I heard the desperation in my words. A world without Abby was unthinkable to me.

She nodded. "Right." Studying my face again, her smile faded. "Maybe you shouldn't go tonight. You're awfully pale."

"I can fix that," I said with bravado, and picked up the makeup brush Darci had insisted I buy.

I swirled the brush around in the blush, another item she'd convinced me that I needed, and with heavy strokes applied it to my face. "There, how's that?" I asked, eyeing myself in the mirror.

Abby cocked her head and winced. "I think you should soften the color a bit. Right now you resemble a Kewpie doll."

She was right—my cheekbones wore two bright pink circles.

"Dang it, I'm never going to get the hang of all this *stuff,*" I said, waving my hand at the makeup that littered the back of the sink.

"Here, try this," she said, and handed me one of those funny triangle-shaped sponges. "Blend everything in with this."

I wiped the sponge across my cheeks. "Humph, not bad," I said, turning my head this way and that. "It almost looks natural."

Abby laughed. "That's the point, Ophelia. You're not supposed to look like you have makeup on."

"Now that's stupid. Why wear it, then?"

Abby rolled her eyes. "I give up." She paused and looked me up and down. "You look very nice. The outfit flatters you."

I glanced down at my clothes. We'd decided my jeans and funky T-shirts wouldn't cut it for a dinner with the Finches, so Darci and Abby had picked my clothes for the evening. The outfit they'd come up with was a strange mix of pieces from both their wardrobes. The skirt belonged to Abby, as did the shirt I wore open over the sparkly little number Darci insisted I borrow. I didn't fill the knit top out as well as Darci did, but it looked okay.

Twenty minutes later I was walking up the graveled path to the door of the main cabin at the compound.

I stopped for a minute and gaped. Cabin—ha. The structure, made of weathered logs, was two stories high. A balcony ran all the way around the second story. Above the balcony a pitched roof, shingled in cedar shakes, pointed toward the night sky. Standing there, gazing at the house, it seemed that the roof's sharp peak aimed straight at the waxing moon.

A rectangle of light suddenly stretched across the ground and ended at my feet. My eyes followed the path of light to where Juliet stood in the open doorway.

Swinging the door wide, she motioned for me to come in. "Ophelia, I'm so glad you could join us tonight," she said when I reached her.

"Thank you for inviting me," I replied.

"There will only be five of us tonight. We eat our main meal together at noon, so the rest of the group won't be joining us," she said over her shoulder as we walked into the main room.

The cavernous room was two stories high, with the second floor balcony running around three sides. Walls made of white pine logs stretched toward the peaked ceiling overhead. And windows, overlooking the lake, ran from the planked floor to the uppermost point of the peak. Hallways on both sides led away from the main part of the house.

A kitchen, separated from the rest of the room by a long counter, sat to my right. I saw Winnie buzzing back and forth from the stove to the cabinets, removing bowls from the cupboards. Noticing me, she gave me a quick nod and resumed her tasks.

The smell of beeswax filled the room from the dozens of candles glowing everywhere. Candles on a table next to heavy pottery plates and chunky glasses; on a stand in the corner, next to a loom with a half-finished piece of fabric attached to the frame.

Spying the loom, I turned to Juliet. "Do you mind if I look at your work?"

"Of course not. Do you weave?" she asked, leading me toward the windows and the loom.

"No, I don't," I said, admiring the brightly colored threads.

She ran her hand across the piece. "I love weaving." Her face took on a faraway look. "To me, it represents life. All the threads form a pattern in the fabric, just the way events form the pattern of our lives. Pull one thread, and the whole piece unravels." She shook her head, snapping out of her mood. "Sorry, I didn't mean to be so philosophical."

"That's okay. It's wonderful you enjoy it so much." I examined the unfinished piece. "And you do beautiful work."

"Thank you," she said shyly. "But it's more than just creating something useful. The act calms me, lets me get in touch with my inner self, and opens my mind to another dimension."

"You're psychic," I blurted out before I could stop myself.

"You mean like your grandmother?" she asked, smiling.

My mouth dropped open. "How—How . . ." I stuttered.

Juliet laughed. "Don't be concerned, Ophelia. We don't broadcast what we learn here. Winnie saw what happened the other day in the grocery store between your grandmother and that group of boys. She's trained to see what others miss." She paused. "Your grandmother must be very talented."

"We don't talk about it," I mumbled.

She laid a hand gently on my arm. "You have no need to fear; you'll find acceptance with us. We've learned everyone has a certain amount of talent." Her face tightened in a frown. "But our narrowed-minded society refuses to let individuals explore their potential. And without that, there—" She stopped abruptly and her face brightened. "Jason."

I turned and saw Jason, walking into the room with Tink by his side. One hand rested lightly on the girl's narrow shoulders, but when he saw Juliet, the hand dropped. He hurried across the room. Tink stopped and stood rooted in the center of the room.

Without a glance toward me, he reached out to Juliet and took her hands in his. Leaning down, he kissed her on both cheeks while murmuring words I couldn't hear.

Juliet's face flushed with pleasure.

Stepping back, he slipped one arm around his wife's waist and turned to me.

When I met Jason at the lake, he'd worn sunglasses and I didn't see his eyes. Now I did. Dark and deep-set in his narrow face, they blazed as he looked into mine. They seemed to probe, penetrate, as if he was attempting to see inside my head. I felt mesmerized. Unnerved, I took a step back and broke eye contact.

When I returned my eyes to his face, the impression I had was gone. All I saw was a pair of dark brown eyes looking at me companionably.

"Ophelia, welcome," he said, smiling.

"Thank you."

He glanced over at Tink. "Come over here, darling," he said, extending his arm toward her, "and say hello to Ophelia."

Tink crossed the room with her blond head down. Dressed in an outfit identical to the ones the adults wore, she took her place next to Jason.

Up close, I saw she wore her spider's necklace. The fragile silver web sparkled against the white of her tunic. And the bloodred stone in the center glowed in the candlelight.

"Hello," she said in a small voice.

"Hi, Tink. Nice to see you again," I replied pleasantly.

When she didn't answer, Juliet's smile faded, replaced with a look of concern.

Jason covered the moment by laying a hand on Tink's shoulder. "Darling, why don't you give Ophelia the gift you made for her?"

Without a word, and with her eyes still downcast, Tink walked like a puppet to the table and picked up a small package, wrapped in homemade paper. Returning, she handed me the gift. As she did, she finally looked up at me.

I almost dropped the small parcel. Her violet eyes were vacant. *Nobody home.* The thought jumped into my head, but lucky for me, not out my mouth.

"Ahh, thank you, Tink," I stuttered, trying to recover myself. "Very nice of you to think of me."

Juliet watched Tink proudly while I unwrapped the

gift. Once free of its paper, the scent of roses and lavender crept up from the small, square muslin pouch I held in my hand.

"A sachet?" I asked.

"Yes," Jason said with satisfaction. "Tink makes them all by herself and we sell them at craft shows. Don't we, darling?" he asked Tink.

Wordlessly, she nodded, her eyes once again fixed on the floor in front of her.

Before I could reply, Winnie's high voice called from the kitchen. "Dinner is served."

## *Eighteen*

We ate a simple but delicious meal of vegetarian lasagna, fresh salad, and whole grain bread. Jason and Juliet carried most of the conversation, asking questions about my life in Summerset, my job at the library, what I liked to read, and so on. Jason told amusing stories, but he played to an audience of one—Juliet. Even when speaking directly to me, he would cast quick glances her way to gauge her reaction. But all during the conversation over dinner, the subject of psychics and the paranormal *did not* come up.

Winnie tried to join in with her high fluty voice when given the opportunity. Juliet acknowledged her remarks with tolerant looks, but Jason's face pinched with annoyance. And every time his expression changed, Winnie's level of exuberance drooped like a wilted flower.

Tink ignored everyone. With her head down and her eyes fixed firmly on the table in front of her, she moved her fork from her plate to her mouth with all the emotion of a robot. Several times during the meal I caught Juliet watching her with a worried look on her face.

What was wrong with this kid? I was not an expert

on children, but I'd been around enough kids at the library to know Tink's behavior was anything but normal.

The meal finished, Winnie went to the kitchen and came back with a teapot and three cups.

Juliet moved around the table to Tink's chair. Stroking her bent head, she gazed down at her. "It's time for your studies now, dear. Say good-night to everyone and I'll be in later to check on you."

Tink rose without comment, mumbled a quick good-night, and wandered off down the hall.

Juliet, her hands clasped tightly in front of her, watched Tink's retreating back. Sadness hovered around her like a fog.

Jason stood and crossed to stand behind his wife. He placed both hands on her shoulders and kissed the top of her head. She responded by leaning back against her husband.

It seemed Juliet drew strength from Jason's touch, and the air of sadness lifted. Turning to me, she smiled. "Why don't you and Jason enjoy your tea on the deck? I'll join you after we're finished cleaning up."

I stood quickly. "No, please, let me help."

She waved my request away with one hand. "No, you're our guest. It won't take Winnie and me long."

Winnie bustled toward me with cup in hand, so I had no choice but to do what Juliet requested. I followed Jason out onto the deck.

The moon I'd noticed when I arrived was high above the pine trees now, hanging in a sky littered with stars. We couldn't see the lake from where we sat—too many trees blocked the view—but I could hear the gentle lapping of the water on the rocks along the shore.

I looked over my shoulder toward the cabin I knew lay hidden in a clearing, past the pines that ringed the Finches' house. A chill crept up my spine.

"Did someone step on your grave?"

Startled, I whipped my head around to look at Jason sitting in one of the deck chairs. "What did you say?"

Light shining from the interior of the house cast his strong face in half shadow, but I could still see his smile.

"You shivered. It made me think of the old saying about when someone shivers; it means their grave has been stepped on." He leaned forward. "It's just an old saying. I'm sorry if it upset you."

"No, I'm not upset," I said, sitting on the deck chair next to him. "I was so wrapped up in the beauty here, your voice startled me."

Jason tilted his head back to look at the stars. "It is beautiful here, isn't it?" he said in a contented voice. "I love this place. Founding this community—it's a dream come true for me. When the world spins out of control, this place is my island of peace."

I tapped the side of my cup. "I don't mean to be snoopy . . ." Yeah, right, Jensen, I thought, pausing. ". . . but what exactly do you do here?"

Jason chuckled. "You're direct, aren't you?" Not waiting for me to answer, he continued. "We're studying the innate intuitiveness everyone is gifted with and to what degree."

"Psychic research?" I took a sip of the hot tea.

"Yes." Jason's white teeth gleamed in the half-light. "Psychic talent is so misunderstood."

*Try living with it, buster.* I kept that thought to myself.

"Now it's my turn to be direct," Jason said, turning his head to look at me. "Winnie believes your grandmother is a psychic. Is she?"

Until that night, no one had ever asked me straight up about Abby, and now both Juliet and Jason wanted to know about her. "Ahh, well," I hedged, "let's just say she has certain talents."

"Do you share those talents? Are you a psychic?"

"Are you?" I shot the question back at him.

He chuckled again. "You're not going to confide in me, are you? I don't blame you. As I said, psychics are misunderstood, at times even feared." He stopped and framed his answer. "No, I'm not a psychic, but I *am* working on developing what intuitiveness I do possess. It's a goal all of us have dedicated our lives to. That and spiritual growth."

"That's it?" I asked, perplexed. "That's all you're doing here?"

"Yes," Jason said, amused. "You sound like you don't believe me."

"I've heard stories." I stopped, trying to organize my thoughts. "Séances, things disappearing."

Jason's laugh echoed across the lake. "You caught me."

I leaned forward in surprise.

*Could it really be this easy to worm a confession out of him?*

Jason noticed my shocked expression and laughed again. "Ophelia, in the past, in what seems a lifetime ago, I was a stage magician."

"What?"

"Magic, prestidigitation, sleight of hand, pulling rabbits out of a hat."

"I know about magic," I said, trying to absorb what his past might mean.

"Do you?" He leaned forward and watched me intently. "Do you really?"

"Of course," I said, not wanting to look in his eyes.

He and Juliet had asked pointed questions about whether Abby and I were psychics, but now he was crossing over into a subject I had no intention of discussing.

Jason slid back in his chair, breaking the moment. "Before I met Juliet, I played clubs on the East Coast. I suppose someone learned of my past, and from there, the rumors started."

I cocked my head. "So you don't hold séances?"

"Heavens, no." He shook his head emphatically.

"Nothing disappears?"

"Only my socks. I seem to be good at that, but I haven't figured out how to make them reappear." He grinned. "Not a very good magician, am I?" His grin slid away. "Meeting Juliet changed my life. She opened my eyes to real magic, the magic of discovering our own potential. Once I'd learned that what I did on stage seemed like such a sham—"

"You quit?" I asked, breaking in.

"I prefer the word 'retired,' " he said in a wry voice. "But yes, I stopped performing and devoted my life to self-discovery and—"

Before he could finish, the door opened and Juliet stepped out onto the deck, holding the teapot.

"Would you like more tea?" she asked.

I covered my cup with my hand. "No thank you, but it's very good."

"I'm glad you enjoyed it. A friend of ours sends it

from England. I'd be happy to make a packet of the tea for you to take home," Juliet said graciously.

"That's very generous of you," I replied.

Jason stood and looked down at me. "If you'll excuse me, Ophelia, I always help Tink with her studies before she goes to bed. And I'm sure she's waiting for me." He smiled and shook my hand. "I enjoyed our conversation. Please come back."

I nodded my agreement.

Jason gave Juliet a quick kiss and left. She watched him leave with a look of concern on her face.

It was time for me to go. When I rose, Juliet turned to me.

"You're not leaving, are you?"

I glanced at my watch, but couldn't see the time in the dim light. "It must be getting late, and I should go."

"Please stay. This is such a treat, for me to entertain someone. Jason doesn't like a lot of company, so we don't have visitors often." She sighed. "I love our group, but it's nice to talk to someone from the outside for a change."

"All right. If you're sure?" I said, sitting.

"I'm sure," she replied, placed the teapot down on a table and sat in Jason's chair, casting a nervous glance back toward the door.

Light from the windows spilled across Juliet's face, and I saw lines of worry creasing her brow. Turning her head toward me, I watched her struggle to relax.

Again she glanced at the door. "I hope Jason is able to convince Tink to go to bed."

"She has trouble sleeping?"

"Yes."

I was surprised. The girl seemed barely awake during dinner.

"I don't mean to pry, but what are Tink's health problems?" I asked.

Juliet gave a long sigh. "Her problems are more emotional than physical. Tink has always been difficult, but since her mother died . . ." Her voice trailed off.

"How did her mother die?"

Juliet rubbed her arms as if suddenly cold. "My sister fell down a flight of stairs, breaking her neck." She stopped rubbing her arms and hugged herself. "We don't know for sure how the accident happened. The only other person in the house at the time was Tink."

My eyes widened. "How terrible. How old was Tink?"

"Five," she said in a small voice.

Now I felt a chill. I crossed my arms and sat back in my chair. "You said Tink has always been difficult? In what way?"

Juliet's eyes took on a faraway look. "Temper tantrums. Even as a toddler, she'd fly into a rage and break toys. Miranda, my sister, tried to hide them from the family, but we knew."

"Where was the father?"

Juliet made a derisive noise. "He took off when Miranda got pregnant. Good riddance, as far as I was concerned. I'd always suspected that he abused Miranda, but she would never admit it." She took a sip of cold tea from the cup Jason had left on the table. "My sister liked her secrets, but she did hint that there'd been a history of family violence in his background."

I thought for a moment before I spoke. "It's none of my business, but is Tink seeing anyone?"

"You mean a psychiatrist?"

I nodded.

Juliet shook her head in disgust. "We've been to so many doctors—psychiatrists, psychologists." Her hands clenched the arms of the chair. "And they all had a different diagnosis. Right now, in order to control her, we have her on so much medication, she's a zombie."

Her frustration was so strong, I could feel it. At a loss for words, I plucked at my skirt and tried to think of something encouraging to say to her.

Juliet, fidgeting with her hands, didn't notice my discomfort, and continued. "But someday we won't have to rely on the doctors or the medication." She gripped her chair tighter. "Our research into the mind is going to help Tink and others like her. I know it will."

Impressed by her passion, I laid a comforting hand on her knee. "I'm so sorry, Juliet."

She relaxed her hands and gave me a small smile. "Thank you. I'm sorry, too. I shouldn't have dumped all of this on you. You barely know me."

"Don't worry about it," I said, sitting back. "Everyone needs to vent once in a while."

"If you only knew," she said, staring down at her lap. A tear slipped from the corner of her eye and slid down her face. "Tink has no memory of the day her mother died, and I hope she never does."

"Wouldn't it be better for her to remember?" I asked gently. "Then she could deal with it."

Juliet wiped the tear away and sniffed. "No, no. You see, I was the one who found Miranda." She hesitated. "And Tink, huddled at the top of the stairs where her mother had fallen. She was in shock and she didn't speak for two weeks. And when she did, that day was blanked from her mind."

"She *saw* her mother fall?"

But Juliet was lost in the past and didn't hear my question.

The words tumbled out of her mouth in a rush. "She didn't mean to. I know she didn't. She was angry, upset. She was a child," Juliet said, her voice pleading. "She didn't understand the consequences of her actions. She did what she always did when she was angry—she pushed at her mother." She lifted her face and looked at me. "Only this time it happened at the top of the stairs."

I closed my eyes at the pain I saw written on her face.

Juliet believed that Tink had caused her mother's death.

# Nineteen

*Too much information. Too much information.*

My hand gripped the steering wheel so tightly, my knuckles turned white. I longed for the good old days. When I'd had the nice, strong wall built around my emotional life. When all I had to worry about was Abby, Lady, and Queenie. I hadn't even had to worry about my parents. Margaret Mary and Will were safely tucked away in Florida—happily retired.

But now? I'm skulking around, trying to find a missing girl and hearing heartwrenching stories about children who accidentally kill their parents. It sucked.

It also sucked being shut up in my vehicle with the flighty Winnie while I drove down the lane to the compound gate. Seems one of Winnie's many jobs was to shut and lock the gate every night. So here I was, after Juliet's tearful good-byes and apologies for letting her emotions get the best of her, listening with one ear as Winnie prattled on about nothing in particular.

"Jason's a magician?" I broke in on whatever it was Winnie was talking about.

"*Was* a magician—he isn't now. Oh, he still does parlor tricks to amuse Tink and the rest of the group. But they're only for fun," Winnie said, squirming around in her seat. "He sure reads about magic and magicians, though."

"Really?" I stole a glance at Winnie. "Who?"

"Houdini, Blackstone, some guy named Von Schuler," she replied, tapping her hand on the door panel.

"Von Schuler? I've never heard of him."

"Me, either," she said, and giggled. "I think Jason really likes him. He has a lot of things about him lying around in his office. Even a big framed poster of Von Schuler on the wall." She shivered slightly. "I don't like the poster. Whenever I'm cleaning Jason's office, the eyes seem to follow you around the room. It's spooky."

Dang, there was that word again.

Winnie grabbed the dashboard. "Oh, here's the gate. You can let me out here," she said.

When the SUV rolled to a stop, Winnie hopped out, gave a quick wave, and hurried over to the gate. I drove through and proceeded on my way back to the cabin.

Once inside, Lady greeted me at the door, prancing. I checked the clock on the kitchen wall: 11:00 P.M. Snapping Lady's leash on her collar, I let her rush through the door with me following. Maybe a quick run around the yard would help us both sleep.

Lady did her thing, and then set about sniffing around the yard, her leash stretched out to its full length.

I stood and watched her while I thought about my evening. Jason and Juliet Finch seemed to be caring parents to a troubled girl. At least now I knew why the kid walked around in a daze. She was zoned out on drugs ninety percent of the time. But what I knew about Tink did nothing to explain Brandi's connection to the group. The Finches' activities seemed pretty harmless to me, and after spending time with them, they didn't strike me as kidnappers.

So where was Brandi? And what had happened to her? Were we wasting time looking for her here at the lake?

Lost in my thoughts, I didn't notice that Lady had stopped her patrol around the yard until I heard the deep rumble coming from her throat. Tiny hairs on the back of my neck stood at attention, and it felt like eyes were staring at me from the woods beyond the cabin.

Lady lifted her head and sniffed the air. The rumble turned into a full-fledged growl.

I felt the adrenaline kick in. Fight or flight. I chose flight. "Okay, that's it. We're going inside," I said, and gave her leash a pull.

She looked at me over her shoulder, then turned back to watching the woods.

"I mean it." My heart began to thump in my chest, and I gave the leash another tug. "Let's go."

After a short warning bark at whatever she thought lurked behind the trees, Lady ran past me and onto the porch.

Me? I couldn't follow her fast enough. I stumbled up the steps and through the door. With my heart still doing a staccato beat, I dropped the leash and locked the door. Hurrying over to the sliding glass doors in the living room, I checked those, too. All secure.

I breathed a sigh of relief, while my heart slowed to its normal rhythm.

After unhooking Lady's leash, I wandered down the hall to my bedroom. As if she didn't want to let me out of her sight, Lady walked beside me, glued to my leg.

I stopped for a moment and listened at the door of

Abby's room. The sound of even breathing was all I heard.

Entering my room, I flicked on the lights and got ready for bed, while Lady curled up over by the windows. But as I took off my skirt, I felt something in the pocket.

Oh yeah, the sachet Tink had given me.

Removing the small pouch, I tossed it on the nightstand next to my runes and finished undressing. And while I did, I felt the headache I'd been fighting all day make its presence known again.

I knew I should make the tea Abby had suggested, but aspirin would be easier. My stomach did a slow roll and queasiness burned my throat. Nope, I'd had too many aspirin today—sleep was what I needed. I shut off the light and tumbled into bed.

I had just begun to feel myself glide off into sleep when I heard it. A faint buzzing coming from somewhere in the room.

I sat up in bed and peered around. Probably a dang bug trapped in either the light shade or between the windows. Plumping my pillow, I lay down and tried to ignore the sound.

But it got louder.

Irritated, I turned the light back on and got out of bed to investigate. I checked the windows, the lamp shade, but couldn't find anything that would make that sound.

I shoved my hands on my hips in frustration and took a deep breath. The strong scent of lavender and roses made my stomach lurch.

Yuck, I'd never sleep with that smell around me all night.

Grabbing the sachet, I crossed the room and shoved

it in an empty dresser drawer. With a quick push, I closed the drawer. The scent was gone.

And so was the buzzing.

Long streams of toilet paper hanging from bare branches swayed in the October wind. Dead leaves, hurried along by the wind, rattled like bones as they rolled down the street. Sounds of childish laughter rang out as little ghosts and goblins rushed from door to door, filling their bags with candy.

All Hallow's Eve. Halloween.

In my dream, I walked up the path leading to the haunted mansion alone. Once a year, the old Johnson mansion became the site of chills and thrills as the Summerset Chamber of Commerce sponsored a haunted house for the local children. Jack the Ripper, Freddy from *Nightmare on Elm Street,* the Phantom of the Opera—all could be seen lurking in the corridors of the old house.

I brushed aside the fake cobwebs draped around the door and pushed it open. The house was strangely silent. At this time of the night there should have been the screams and shrieks of the terrified reverberating off the walls of the faded rooms. But I heard nothing.

Something tickled my cheek and I brushed it away. Looking up, I saw hundreds of tiny plastic spiders suspended by thin wires hanging from the ceiling. Dodging as many as I could, I went down the hall and into the room that would've been used as a parlor.

Velvet ropes blocked off most of the room. And from behind them I saw a figure of a man bound in chains. A small man with dark wavy hair, his well-developed muscles straining against the links that held him. I'd seen his face before on an old vaudeville poster: Harry Houdini. Looking like he came straight out of Madame Tussaud. A wax figure. The Chamber had gone all out this year.

Across the hall, in the room that had been the dining room, a different wax figure stood in the center of the room. A dignified figure with thick white hair that circled his head like a halo. His hands were frozen in place above a lit lightbulb that seemed to float before him. The famous Blackstone.

Turning away, I continued down the hallway to the staircase. The carved banister curved majestically toward the second storey, where pale light spilled onto the polished floor from one of the rooms above. Grabbing the banister, I climbed toward the light.

The room I viewed from the hallway was not roped off as the others had been. More spiders on invisible strings hung around the door. Sweeping them away, I shuddered and made a move to take a step forward, but something held me back.

Standing in the center of the room, behind a long table, was a figure dressed in a black robe, a hood obscuring his face. In the light of the fire, the shadow he cast loomed like a huge bat on a wall covered in peeling paper. He had one arm outstretched as if in supplication, while in the crook of his other arm he held a book. A black book with strange gold writing on its cover.

To his right and to his left, tall, smoking braziers filled the air with an almost noxious odor. In front of the braziers, dark brown candles burned on the table. The candles were carved with the same strange writing as on the book.

But the black figure wasn't alone. Another wax figure lay prone on the table before him. This one dressed in white.

My eyes traveled up the body and stopped at the head. The hood covered most of the features, and I couldn't make out the face of the reclining figure. But from beneath the hood a strand of carrot-orange hair peeked out.

My heart slammed against my ribs and my mouth went dry.

Brandi?

I made a move to enter the room, but the man in the dark robe suddenly came to life and swung his outstretched arm toward me. Bony fingers pointed at me and unknown words poured out of the void where the face should've been.

I jumped back. He wasn't a wax figure after all.

With his words, the evil I'd felt at the abandoned cabin in the woods rushed at me in a surge. My knees gave way and I crumpled to the floor. With my forehead pressed against the cold wood floor, I felt the evil wash over me, its pressure threatening to crush me.

*It's a dream, it's a dream,* I repeated in my mind. *And dreams can't kill you.*

But I felt like the life was being squeezed out of me.

I lifted my head, and when I did, the prone figure turned its face. I saw Brandi's eyes, round with terror, staring into mine.

She turned her head forward, and as she did, slowly pulled up into a sitting position as if controlled by hidden strings. Sitting there, she seemed to shrink, grow smaller. The hood fell back and the carrot-colored hair changed, growing lighter.

Her head rotated toward me again. Her mouth was pulled back in a feral grin. And the eyes of a hunter met mine from across the room. Hungry eyes. Violet eyes.

*Oh my God! Tink.*

# *Twenty*

Slowly I surfaced from my dream. My head felt heavy, so heavy that I had to struggle to lift it. Inside my mouth, my tongue seemed thick. I tried swallowing but my throat was too dry.

Was it a dream or a vision? A prophecy or the circuits of my subconscious twisting reality into bizarre pictures? I didn't know. Sitting up in bed, I turned on the light and pulled a notebook and pen from the drawer in the nightstand.

Okay, what was the setting of the dream? A haunted house at Halloween. Ghosts and witches, given my heritage—go figure. Spiders? The library had been infested with them when I'd left Iowa, and the problem had been unresolved. Maybe my brain was still stewing about the situation.

The cast of characters? The three magicians? Winnie had planted them in my head. Houdini and Blackstone were known to me, so they had faces in my dream. But Von Schuler? I'd never heard of him. Understandable that his face would be hidden—my subconscious had no point of reference. That left Tink and Brandi.

I had started out this trip concerned about the missing Brandi, but now, after what Juliet had told me about Tink, my concern extended to her, too. The poor kid. In a way, even though she was surrounded by people, she was as lost as Brandi.

I snapped the notebook shut. There, I'd explained away the dream. That's all it was—a dream.

One little detail niggled at me. The book. Where had that element come from? *It's a book; I'm a librarian?* Nope, that explanation didn't feel right.

I chewed at my lip while my eyes skimmed the room. They stopped when my runes caught my attention. I hadn't used them since the night before we'd left for Minnesota. The question had been, "What would we find in Minnesota?" The runes had answered, "Pertho"—mystery and magic.

I snorted. They'd been right.

What would they tell me now? I blew out a breath. I wasn't up to doing a reading. *But wait, what about a quick check? Stick my hand in the bag, draw a rune, and see what it means?* Worth a shot.

Picking up the pouch, I imagined a white light surrounding me and peace flowing through me. As a sense of calm settled in my heart, I opened the bag and touched the stones. I felt each rune, waiting for that one special stone to give me a familiar tingle, to speak to me. Nothing happened.

I tried again. The runes felt cool and smooth against my palm. But nothing else. Not even a trickle of energy pricked at my fingertips.

The runes were silent.

Frustrated, I withdrew my hand and returned the pouch to the nightstand. I rubbed my forehead; my headache was back. And this time aspirin wouldn't cut it.

I threw on my robe and went to the kitchen to brew the tea Abby had recommended earlier. After putting the kettle on to boil, I stood at the stove waiting. A soft touch on my arm had me whirling around in surprise.

"Dang it, Abby," I said, clutching my chest. "You almost gave me a heart attack."

Dressed in her flannel robe with her thick silver hair hanging in a braid over her shoulder, she looked concerned. "You're pale." She placed her hands on either side of my face. "Sit down. I'll finish the tea."

Pulling out a chair, I sat at the table. Before long Abby set a steaming cup of tea in front of me.

She joined me on the other side of the table and waited to speak until I'd finished most of the hot tea.

"Better?"

"Yeah." I reached across the table and took her hand. "Thanks."

She gave my hand a quick squeeze. "You're welcome. Now what's going on?"

I withdrew my hand and scrubbed my face. "Oh," I said with a long sigh. "I don't know. I don't know—"

"Why don't you start at the beginning, dear?" Abby asked gently.

Quickly I related all that had happened since I'd left for dinner with the Finches.

"So do you think my dream was simply something out of my subconscious, too?" I asked.

A thoughtful look crossed Abby's face. "Could be."

I let out another sigh. A sigh of relief. "I'm so glad you agree with me."

"But . . ."

*Crap, why does there always have to be a "but"?*

"What about the book? What would trigger that appearing in your dreams?" she asked.

I shook my head. "I don't know."

"Do you remember what the symbols were?"

"I think so," I said, trying to picture the book in my mind. "If you have a piece of paper, I think I could draw them."

A look of fear crossed Abby's face. "No," she said emphatically. "We don't know what they are or what they mean. To draw them could invoke something we don't know how to deal with."

"Oh come, Abby," I scoffed. "Whatever they are, they're just a bunch of lines put together."

"No," she said with a quick shake of her head. "They're symbols, and symbols have power."

My eyes narrowed as I watched her. "What kind of power?"

"I don't know. I suspect, based on what's been happening to you, nothing good."

The weariness I'd been fighting overcame me, and I felt my body sag against the back of my chair.

"Come on," she said, standing. "Let's get you to bed. We're not going to solve anything tonight. Tomorrow's soon enough."

She pulled me to my feet, and throwing an arm around my shoulders, escorted me to my room. Once there, she tucked me in as if I were a child. With a quick kiss on my forehead, she turned out the lights and left.

I stared at the dark ceiling while I felt my eyelids grow heavy. Finally, my body relaxed and sleep called to me.

Unfortunately, the last memory I had before my mind went into free fall was a pair of violet eyes.

Dressed, but not quite ready to be sociable, I wandered to the kitchen and found Abby puttering around.

Seeing me, she smiled and handed me a fresh cup of coffee. "Feeling better?"

"Yeah, a little," I said, taking a sip. "Where's Darci?"

"She had an errand to run, but should be back—" She stopped and cocked her head, listening.

The sound of a boat motor rumbled from the lake below. A sound very close to the cabin.

Abby opened the cabinet door and took out a small cooler. "Go put on your swimsuit while I get this ready," she said, walking over to the refrigerator.

"What's going on?" I asked, shoving my hands in the pockets of my shorts.

"Never mind. Get your suit on, and then take this down to the dock," she said, pointing to the cooler.

Quickly, I did what Abby had told me. And when I returned to the kitchen, she handed me the cooler without explanation.

I opened my mouth, but she interrupted.

"Go," she said, shooing me toward the sliding glass doors.

"Okay, okay," I said over my shoulder, and left the cabin.

Arriving at the top of the steps leading down to the lake, I saw a pontoon boat, tied to the dock. A woman stood on the deck, her hand shading her eyes, looking up at me.

Blond hair, bikini top, wearing shorts—really short shorts. Darci.

"Where did you get this?" I asked when I reached the dock.

"I rented it. Come on, let's go for a ride." She moved behind the steering console and sat on the bench seat located at the rear of the boat. "I see Abby gave you the cooler," she said as I stepped aboard.

"You two have been plotting, haven't you?" I asked.

At the same time, Darci gunned the motor. With one hand to her ear, she shook her head, pretending she couldn't hear me.

Giving up, I set the cooler down and cast off the line. Slowly, the pontoon pulled away. Once the boat cleared the end of the dock, Darci swung the nose around and headed away from the shore.

Without speaking, I sat on one of the bench seats and enjoyed the ride.

The pontoon Darci had rented was about sixteen feet long and about twenty feet wide. Two bench seats stretched along both sides. In front, the deck extended out over the points of the aluminum pontoons, creating a swim platform, perfect for sunbathing.

The pontoon rode the wakes created by the ski boats that whizzed by gracefully. Adjusting my steps to the rolling motion of the deck, I crossed to the back and took a place next to Darci.

*Couldn't pretend not to hear me now.*

"I suppose you want to know about yesterday?" I asked.

"No," she replied without looking at me.

"Last night?" I asked, my voice confused.

"No." She turned and looked at me. "Ophelia, sit back and relax."

"What's in the cooler?"

"Never mind. You'll find out when we get there." She didn't take her eyes off the water.

"Where's that?"

*"Ophelia,"* she said, lowering her sunglasses and staring at me. *"Relax."*

"I don't know how anymore," I muttered.

"Try and remember." She shoved her glasses

higher up on her nose and put an end to conversation.

A few minutes later an island appeared in the center of the lake. Darci turned the wheel and headed toward it. When we were about fifteen feet from the island, she cut the motor and the pontoon drifted to shore. She stood and threw the anchor overboard.

"May I talk now?" I asked sarcastically.

She smiled. "Yes. As long as it isn't about spiders, books, magicians, or missing girls."

My eyes widened in surprise. "You *really* don't want to know about yesterday?"

"No, I don't," she said with emphasis. "Abby filled me in this morning." Darci removed a bottle of suntan lotion from her bag, poured a generous amount in her hand, then tossed the bottle to me.

I dumped some of the lotion in my palm and rubbed it on my legs. "Darci, this isn't like you. You're usually full of questions. What's up?"

She whirled, and taking off her sunglasses, gave me a fierce glare. "Have you taken a good look at yourself lately?"

"Well, yeah," I said, squirming on the seat. "Last night, when I was getting ready to go."

She put one hand on her hip. "And what did you see?"

I lifted my shoulders in a shrug. "I don't know. Same stuff as usual—two eyes, a nose, and a mouth."

"Not funny," she said with a toss of her head. "Did you see the dark circles under your eyes? Did you notice how pale you are?"

"Abby might have mentioned it," I replied grudgingly.

"You're so worried about everyone else that you're not taking care of yourself." She eyed me critically.

"I've got to tell you, Ophelia, you're starting to look positively haggard."

"Thanks a lot," I sputtered.

"Well you are. We're worried about you." Darci stomped her bare foot. "You've been here, what four, maybe five days? And look at everything that's happened to you. Dreams, evil cabins, threats from some crazy guy It's getting to you. You're even losing weight."

"Hey, a few pounds wouldn't hurt," I said with a smile, trying to defuse the apprehension I felt pouring off of her.

"That's not funny, either."

"Look, Darce, I appreciate your concern, but maybe I'm coming down with a summer cold or something."

"I don't think so. And neither does Abby." Darci flounced over to the swim deck. "I brought you out here to get away from the cabin for a while and from all the stress." She spread out a beach towel and dropped down on her knees. "And you're going to relax, gosh darn it," she said, shaking her finger at me.

I chuckled. "Yes ma'am." I saluted.

Darci rolled her eyes, and without a word stretched out facedown on the beach towel.

Still smiling, I walked over to the starboard bench, sat, propped my legs up, and stared down into the water.

The water below the pontoon was deep, but clear enough that I could see the lacy fronds of weeds growing on the bottom. The waves hitting the shore rocked the boat gently. I tipped my head back and closed my eyes.

They shot open. Remembering what had happened the day on the dock when I'd closed my eyes, I decided maybe I should keep them open.

I returned to watching the underwater plants sway in rhythm with the waves. A turtle glided by, his dark shape almost hidden in the vegetation. Out of the corner of my eye I spotted a flash of orange among the weeds. Turning my head, I looked hard at the place where I'd first seen the flash. Nothing. Probably a fish trying to hide from the turtle.

The roar of a speedboat caught my attention. Over the sound of its engine, I heard whistling and yelling. Looking toward the sound, I saw the boat zooming close to where we were anchored. One guy drove, while two guys stood straight up in the boat, waving their arms, yelling and smiling.

Ahh, yes. Darci in her bikini.

She lifted her head, gave them a passing glance, then ignored them.

The driver of the boat, seeing Darci's reaction, cut hard to the left, away from us, and went back the way they'd come.

The wake created by the sharp turn stirred the water around the pontoon forcefully. I looked over the side and saw the weeds whip back and forth. Again I caught a glimpse of something orange. It appeared to be orange fibers weaving in and out of the fronds. The fibers glided upward, freed by the churning water. And as they did, they grew in quantity. More strands emerged out of the depths of the lake. They undulated in the current and were attached to something white and pasty. The pale belly of what looked like a dead fish rose with the strands.

The fish grew bigger as it approached the surface. Only as it came into sight, I could see it wasn't a fish. No fins, no gills, no tail.

Instead of a fish head attached to the end of the cracked, bloated flesh, a hand drifted in the water, its fingers flopping in a macabre wave.

I'd found a body.

# Twenty-one

I sat bundled on the couch in a blanket that Abby had found in the closet. And in spite of the hot August day, my shoulders shook with trembling and my muscles tightened with tension. Dressed in jeans and a T-shirt now, I clenched a steaming mug of tea in my hands

Darci, also wearing jeans and a shirt, fared a little better than I did. She didn't have the shakes, but her normally tan face was three shades whiter than milk. Her hands also gripped a large mug of Abby's tea.

Peppermint tea could settle the stomach; spearmint tea would help with colds and flu; chamomile tea could provide a good night's sleep. But I didn't know if Abby had a specific tea to help someone who kept finding bodies.

If she did, I hoped I was drinking it now.

We had returned to the cabin immediately after our discovery and reported what we'd found to the sheriff. Darci had done well, kind of, for finding her first body. She hadn't screamed, cried, or jumped up and down. She did almost pick off two skiers with the pontoon in her haste to get back to the cabin. But after achieving a spectacular wipe-out and uttering a few profanities and remarks concerning blondes, the skiers survived.

Not like the person we found floating by the island. Who was it and how did they die? *Okay, Jensen, face it,* said a voice in my head. *Orange hair, been missing for two months. Who do you think it is?*

Brandi.

I hadn't told the sheriff when he took my statement about my suspicions. It was up to the law to figure out the who, the how, and the when. Rick had asked us to find her, and we did. Our job was done.

Poor Rick. We'd called him after the sheriff. He'd shown up at the same time and, using his job as a journalist as an excuse, had talked the sheriff into allowing him to witness the divers retrieve the body. Tough job—observing the body of a young woman he'd watched grow up as it was hauled out of the lake.

But something was off and I couldn't put my finger on it. My mind circled back to my original question while I sipped my tea. *Who did I think it was?*

My answer had been Brandi. The answer explained where she was now, but where had she been for the last two months? I didn't know much about forensics, but I assumed that a body left in the water for two months wouldn't look like what I'd seen.

I looked at Abby standing by the sliding glass doors and watching out over the lake.

"Abby, do you think she's been dead all this time?" I asked.

She continued to stare out the doors.

"Abby," I said louder.

Slowly she turned her head toward me. "What?"

"I asked if you thought Brandi's been dead all this time."

"I don't know," she said, passing a hand over her eyes.

Her action concerned me. "Abby, are you all right?" I made a move to leave my cocoon on the couch.

"Sit down," she said, waving me back to my place. "I'm fine, but I'm confused. I would've sworn the girl was still alive."

"For a couple of psychics, there's sure a lot we don't know," I said ruefully.

Darci frowned. "What do you mean?"

I crawled out from underneath the blanket. "Except for some eerie dreams and the freaky experience at the cabin, I haven't picked up anything. It's like I'm blocked. The runes aren't even talking to me."

"What about you?" Darci asked, turning to Abby.

Abby didn't speak for a moment. She simply stood by the door rubbing her arms. I thought she'd missed the question.

"Let's go out on the deck," she said abruptly, and slid the door open.

Queenie had been lurking around Abby's feet, and when the door opened, she made a break for the great outdoors. Lady was right on her heels.

"Queenie!" I shrieked. "Get back in here. Lady, stop."

Abby tried grabbing Lady's collar but missed. She hurried out the door after the animals.

Darci and I followed.

Lady had stopped at the end of the deck, but Queenie had made it as far as the trees. She stopped, and with a look at me that said "Leave me alone," calmly sat down and began to clean her fur.

I made a move to go fetch her, but Abby's hand on my arm stopped me.

"Let her be. She'll be fine. I'll keep an eye on her so she doesn't wander off," Abby said.

At the sound of Abby's voice, Lady cocked her head, and Abby scratched her ears. Reassured she wouldn't have to return inside, she picked out a corner of the deck and lay down.

Each of us found our own spot, Darci on one of the chaise lounges, and Abby and me in chairs. The sun chased away the last bit of my trembling, and my tension melted away.

I noticed Abby seemed more relaxed, too.

I repeated the question Darci had asked. "Abby, are you sensing anything?"

She tucked a stray strand back into the braid circled around the top of her head. "Yes. No. Maybe," she said, her tone uncertain.

"That's pretty noncommittal," I said with a smile.

Abby shrugged slightly. "I know." She stared at the trees across the lake. "There's something at work here, but I can't put my finger on it. It's elusive, it plays in the shadows. What's more, it's intentional. Whatever it is, it knows we're here and it's teasing us."

"Do you think it's a ghost?" Darci asked in a hushed voice.

I glanced at Abby. She raised her eyebrows but didn't speak.

"Let's forget about ghosts and things that go bump in the night, shall we?" I watched both of them. "The problem at hand is, where has Brandi been for the last two months, and did she drown, or was it murder?"

There. I'd laid the question eating at all of us on the line.

"Abby, what do you think?" I asked.

She lifted her shoulder and shook her head.

"Darci, what about you?"

"Me?" she asked, surprised.

"Yeah, you. You're a smart woman. What do you think?"

"Hmm—well, I don't think the body has been in the water for two months. That means either she's been here at the lake the whole time and hiding, or left and came back. Both case scenarios are suspicious."

"I agree," I said. "Next question—do we stick around and find out what happened, or do we leave and let the sheriff figure it out?"

"I think, before you decide to leave, you should take Abby and pay a visit to the Finches," Darci said with a thoughtful expression on her face.

"Why?" I leaned forward. "I was there last night and didn't pick up on anything. Juliet explained away my concerns about Tink—the changes in her personality aren't due to abuse. It's because the kid's zoned out on meds most of the time. The Finches are only a couple trying to do their best to raise a child with some serious problems." I shook my head. "And Jason isn't the Rasputin Rick seems to think he is."

Darci gave a little pout. "I still think you should go."

Giving up on her, I turned to Abby. "Do you think we should talk to the Finches?"

"I suppose," she said, her voice sounding troubled.

Watching her, I frowned. "Abby, what's with you today?"

Her face cleared and she smiled. "Nothing, dear. I'm sorry if my behavior is worrying you. I'm puzzled, that's all."

I narrowed my eyes. "Are you sure?"

Her smile widened. "Yes, I'm sure. Come on, let's

go," she said, rising. Her smile left her face and she reached in her pocket and pulled something out. "Darci, I want you to carry this."

Abby handed her a small crystal.

Darci turned the rock over in her hand. "What is it?"

"A piece of hematite. You've had a bad experience today. The hematite will help absorb the negativity."

"Okay," Darci said, her tone bright. She stuck the crystal in her pocket and smiled up at Abby.

Abby returned her smile.

I crossed to the door and slid it open, but before I could step into the cabin, Abby called out.

"Wait, Ophelia. Let's go around through the yard."

I looked over my shoulder at her standing by the steps leading down to the side of the cabin. "But I don't have my keys to the SUV."

"I have mine." She jingled a set of keys in the air.

With a shake of my head, I closed the door and followed Abby. "Hey Darci, keep an eye on the cat, will you?" I called over my shoulder.

"No problem," she answered distractedly.

Taking a quick look, I saw Darci wasn't paying attention to our departure. She had the crystal in her hand, studying it.

After we were out of Darci's hearing, I shot a look at Abby. "Why did you give Darci a crystal?"

"She needed it," she replied, climbing the hill to the SUV.

"To disperse the negativity?" I asked.

"Among other things," she said, outdistancing me.

I scrambled to catch up with her. "What other things?"

"Protection."

* * *

All the way over to the Finches, I tried to get Abby to explain to me what she meant by "protection," but she waved my questions aside. We also decided not to be the ones to mention the body found in the lake. If Juliet knew, we'd let her bring it up first. Arriving at the compound, we found the gate open and drove through.

It had been dark when I'd arrived last night, but now I could see how the compound was laid out. To our left there was a large vegetable garden. Two men worked in it, hoeing weeds. Beyond the garden, a distance away, I made out the white tops of bee supers.

Juliet answered the door when I knocked.

"Ophelia, nice to see you again," she said with a questioning look.

A look that said, "What are you doing here?" Dang, I hadn't thought of an excuse for suddenly appearing at the Finches' door.

"Ahh, hi Juliet. Ahh, I thought—" My mind scrambled for a reason to explain our presence.

Abby took charge and stepped forward, extending her hand. "Juliet, I'm Abigail McDonald, Ophelia's grandmother," she said easily. "Sorry to drop in unannounced like this, but I wanted to meet you."

*Smooth, Abby. Give her the truth, but not the whole truth.*

Juliet took Abby's hand in both of hers. "Oh, Mrs. McDonald—"

Abby broke in. "Please, call me Abby."

"All right, Abby." Juliet flushed with pleasure. "I'd hoped I would meet you. Please come in." She released Abby's hand and motioned us into the main room. "I don't know what Ophelia has told you about our little group, but we're conducting psychic research. And I know you're very gifted," she said, her face shining with admiration. "Winnie told us how you handled the boy in the grocery store. I'd love to ask you some questions." She followed us.

Abby turned to Juliet. "Oh, dear," she exclaimed. "I'm afraid that's a subject I don't discuss. The way I was raised, you know. My mother believed talking about one's talent, especially to those outside your family, diminished it." She smiled. "Probably just an old mountain superstition, but . . ." She let her voice fade as her eyes darted to mine.

I dropped my gaze and stared at a spot by my foot. Boy, Abby was good. I'd never heard of that "old mountain" superstition.

Juliet blushed. "I understand. Maybe after you get to know us better."

Abby smiled vaguely.

A slight figure appeared from the hallway. I froze while violet eyes stared into mine. The same violet eyes that had haunted my dream.

"Tink, come over here, darling, and meet Ophelia's grandmother," Juliet said, holding out her arm to the girl.

Tink walked slowly over and took her place at Juliet's side. As Juliet made the introductions, Tink slowly raised her head to face Abby. Their eyes locked, and for a moment wordless communication passed between them.

An uncomfortable silence seemed to fill the space separating Tink and Abby. Finally, Abby, with her eyes never leaving Tink's face, cocked her head and arched an eyebrow. The moment was gone.

"If you'll excuse me," Juliet said to Abby and me. "Tink, let me get your medication." She crossed to the kitchen and brought back a pill bottle and a glass of water. Shaking out a couple of pills, she gave them to Tink along with the water.

I watched while the girl popped the pills in her mouth and followed them with a long drink of water. With an innocent smile, she handed the glass back to Juliet.

A frown crossed Juliet's face. "Tink, where's your necklace?"

Tink's closed hand moved swiftly to her chest. "I forgot to put it on."

"Tink," she said reproachfully.

"I'm sorry. I'll go put it on." She looked up at Juliet. "After I do, may I go down to the lake?"

Juliet looked at her watch. "Yes, but only for an hour. Then you have to do your chores."

"Okay." Tink stuck both hands in her pockets and grinned. She glanced over at me watching her. The grin disappeared and her eyes narrowed as if daring me to speak. She knew I knew.

The kid had palmed the pills.

# Twenty-two

Tink beat a hasty retreat down the hall without saying another word.

"I apologize for Tink's manners," Juliet said with a frown. She pointed to the couch. "Let's sit down. May I get you anything?"

"No," Abby said, taking a place next to me on the couch and smoothing her hands over her lap. "I'm afraid we haven't been completely honest with you, Juliet."

Perplexed, Juliet's eyes traveled from Abby's face to mine. "In what way?" she asked as she sat in a chair across from us.

"We're at the lake investigating the disappearance of a young woman you know, Brandi Peters."

Juliet's eyes widened and her face went pale. "You're private investigators?"

Abby leaned forward. "Oh my no," she said in a soft voice. "We're only here to help a friend. Maybe you remember him? Rick Delaney?"

Juliet's hands plucked at the hem of her tunic. "The reporter? Yes, I remember him." Her eyes moved to a spot over our shoulders. "I told the sheriff everything I know. I don't know what more I can tell you."

Oh, yes you do, I thought. I turned to Abby and watched while her eyelids drooped and she placed two fingers on her forehead. In a second they flew open and she fixed her stare on Juliet.

Dismay played across Juliet's face while she witnessed Abby's performance. She exhaled a deep breath. "All right. I wasn't completely honest with the sheriff. But I had my reasons."

"And they were?" Abby asked in a gentle voice.

Juliet clasped her hands tightly in her lap. "You both live in a small town. You know how rumors can get started." She gazed down at her hands. "We've worked so hard building a good reputation with the people who live here. And if word got out—"

"What word?" I interrupted.

Juliet flipped her hair over her shoulder. "There are so many misconceptions whenever people choose to live together in a group like we do," she said, not answering my question.

Abby's eyes slid to mine and she gave her head a slight shake. "What kind of misconceptions?" she asked.

"They assume we're a cult, and with that, all their preconceived opinions come into play."

Abby watched Juliet closely. "Such as?"

She plucked at her tunic again. "You know, sex, illicit drugs, mind control, those kinds of things . . ." Her voice grew faint and she tugged on her bottom lip. "Brandi is a very troubled young woman . . ." She hesitated. "Her behavior forced us into asking her to leave."

"What kind of behavior?" Abby asked.

Juliet abruptly leaned forward, and her eyes searched Abby's face. "She tried to seduce my husband." Her voice was hushed.

Well, *that* put a new spin on things. I opened my mouth to speak, but Abby placed her hand on my leg, silencing me.

Abby's eyes never left Juliet's face. "What happened?"

Sitting back and wrapping her arms around herself, Juliet hugged herself tightly. "One afternoon, Jason found Brandi naked in our bed." Her eyes flared for a moment. "Brandi could be very brazen sexually. Prior to the incident with Jason, several times we caught her trying to sneak off the compound at night."

"And you don't allow that?"

"Of course not." Juliet uncrossed her arms and leaned forward. "That's not what this place is about. We're here for spiritual growth, not running naked through the pines. Things of the flesh are within the sanctity of marriage. I had qualms about Brandi when she first came. But I ignored them—she seemed so lost, so in need of our help—I went against my better judgment."

Abby nodded sympathetically. "She left after you confronted her?"

"I never saw her. Jason was here by himself when it happened. He said the scene got ugly when he rebuffed her, so he left. When he returned, she was gone." Her voice sounded flat and repetitive, like she was retelling a story.

"You believe him?" I asked.

Her eyes narrowed in a flash of temper. "Yes, I believe him. Jason adores me. And I adore him. The girl was a troublemaker from the start."

"A bad influence on Tink, no doubt, too," I said.

She nodded her head vehemently. "Yes, she was. As you know, Ophelia, after what I told you last night, we have enough problems with Tink. I didn't need Brandi encouraging disobedience." Juliet relaxed against the back of her chair. "We thought she'd returned home to her parents until the sheriff stopped by asking question."

"Don't you think you should've told him about the scene with Jason?" I asked.

"What would that serve? She was gone and we didn't know where. Telling the sheriff about what she tried to pull with Jason wouldn't help him find her." She crossed her legs. "Jason wanted to, but I discouraged him. He doesn't get out among the community as much as I do. He's too busy with his studies, so he has no idea how tenuous our acceptance is."

"You really think if it got out about Brandi's behavior, it would affect your standing with the town?" Abby chimed in.

"Yes. I'm not some idealistic New Ager that believes all is peace and love in the outside world. I understand human nature. People always think the worst, whether it's proven or not. Can you imagine what one whiff of scandal about an alleged affair between my husband and a girl young enough to be his daughter would do?" Her head turned and she gazed out at the trees growing around the deck. "We'd have to leave this beautiful place," she said wistfully.

I looked at Abby to try and detect what she thought, but her face was expressionless.

She stood and smiled down at Juliet. "Thank you for being honest with us," she said, laying a hand on Juliet's shoulder.

Juliet reached up and grabbed Abby's hand. "You won't tell anyone, will you?" Her face was etched with concern.

"However painful it might be for them, Brandi's

parents have a right to know what was going on, but we'll leave it up to Rick," Abby said gently.

"But—"

Abby patted her hand. "It will be all right. Don't worry."

Juliet stood and followed us out the door and to the edge of the porch steps.

As we drove away, I saw her in the rearview mirror as she wrapped an arm around one of the posts and sagged against it. The men working in the garden earlier were gone.

"I feel kind of bad about Juliet, Abby," I said, returning my eyes to the lane ahead. "You really pried the story out of her."

"I know. She assumed since I'm a psychic, I'd read her mind and know the truth anyway."

I gave a small grin. "Yeah, that 'I think I see, I think I see' routine really worked."

Abby smiled and turned toward the window. "I saw someone do that on TV once."

"Darci would've been really proud of you for the way you handled Juliet."

Abby chuckled. "Oh, I'll never be as good as Darci."

My face grew serious. "Do you think she was telling the truth?"

"About the failed attempt at seduction? Yes. You spent time with them last night; what do you think? Is Jason a cheater?"

"No," I said with conviction. "She was right when she said he adores her. You could feel the chemistry two feet away. And I sensed he's very protective of her. No, he wouldn't do anything that might hurt her."

"How about Brandi? Would he hurt her?" Abby asked.

I thought about the body in the lake. Could Jason be responsible? Had the scene been so ugly, it ended in Brandi's death? And he'd disposed of the body in the lake? No, we'd agreed the body wasn't decomposed enough. Last night Jason seemed personable and charming, not a killer.

"Did you hear me, Ophelia?" Abby asked when I didn't answer.

"Yeah, I was thinking about it. No, he's different, but I can't see him provoked enough to kill. He's too cerebral, if you know what I mean."

"Meaning he's too smart to kill?" Abby asked with a grin.

"No." I stopped and tried to think of the best way to describe Jason. "I don't think he's passionate enough to kill. The only things I think he truly cares about are his studies and Juliet."

"But if he thought Brandi represented a threat to his marriage?"

"Not even then. I got the feeling last night that both Juliet and Jason are very secure in their marriage. He would know Juliet wouldn't believe anything Brandi might tell her."

"What about Juliet? She's determined to protect the reputation of their group. Would it be enough of a motive for murder?"

"No, I think she's too dedicated to truth and enlightenment for murder. Someone like that usually doesn't see killing as a solution to their problems."

By now we'd reached the cabin. I put the SUV in park and started to open my door.

"Wait," Abby said, laying a hand on my arm. "What do you think about Tink?"

"Tink? What about her?" I looked at Abby in surprise.

"What's your impression?" she asked.

"I think she's a mixed-up kid who's had some tough breaks." I turned my head and gazed out the windshield. "She likes to play games with people. She ditched her meds, you know." I returned my eyes to Abby.

"Yes, I saw that, too."

"And I'd just bet," I said, with a quick nod of my head like I knew what I was talking about, "as soon as she was out of sight of the main house, she made her escape. She's probably running loose in the woods right now, and Jason will be out looking for her before nightfall."

Abby's mouth twisted in a small grin. "You're probably right. The child has spirit." Her expression turned serious. "That's all you saw?"

"Yeah," I said, wondering what she was getting at.

She shook her head and got out of the SUV. With brisk strides she headed toward the cabin.

"What?" I said, and scrambled out. "What did you see?" I ran to catch up to her.

Abby shot me a look from over her shoulder. "Ophelia, that child's an extremely powerful psychic."

# Twenty-three

Instead of going into the cabin, Abby detoured around the building and went through the side yard to the deck. By the time I reached her, she was sitting calmly in a chair talking to Darci.

"Hey, wait a second," I said, bursting in on the conversation. "What do you mean the kid is a psychic?"

"What?" Darci's eyes traveled first to me and then to Abby.

I threw myself down on a chair next to Darci. "Abby says Tink is a psychic."

Darci leaned forward in interest. "Really? I thought you said the kid was just spooky . . ." Her voice dropped away and she cocked her head and eyed me with speculation. "But I can see where having psychic talent would lead—"

I drew myself up and broke in. "Are you insinuating that I'm spooky?"

Darci smiled broadly. "Come on, Ophelia, you're not exactly 'normal.' That's why you're so much fun to hang around with. I never know what's going to happen next." She wiggled around on the chaise. "Besides, normal's boring."

Frowning, I didn't know if I'd been paid a compliment or not. With everything that had happened in such a short space of time, normal didn't sound half bad right now. Boring, maybe, but at least safe.

I turned my attention to Abby. "Okay, so Tink is a psychic—"

"A very powerful psychic," Abby said, talking over me. "I can't believe you didn't feel it or see it, Ophelia. All you have to do is look at her. It's right there in her eyes."

"Well, I didn't see it," I said emphatically, "or feel it."

Abby shook her head. "Her talent is very uncontrolled. Her energy was all over the place. And as soon as she walked into the room, I felt her trying to read me."

"Wow," Darci said, amazed. "When can I meet her?"

I gave her a quelling look and turned my attention back to Abby. "Do you think the Finches know?"

"They are doing research into psychic phenomena," Abby said, lifting a shoulder, "so one would assume they do."

"You know," I said, snapping my fingers, "Juliet did say they're hoping their research will help Tink. But I thought she meant they hope to learn something to help Tink control her rages."

Abby gave an unladylike snort. "Nonsense. That child doesn't have rages."

"But Juliet said—"

She stopped me with a look. "I don't care what she said. As a small child Tink may have had her share of temper tantrums. A lot of children pitch fits—"

"But Tink might have pushed her mother down the stairs during one," I blurted out.

"Humph, I don't believe that one either." Abby settled back in her chair and crossed her arms.

I was getting more confused by the minute.

"Then what do you believe?" I asked.

Abby ignored my question. "Tell me more about the necklace."

I groaned. "We're not back on that dumb necklace, are we? I swear you're as obsessed with it as the Finches."

Darci perked up. "What necklace?"

Great, now Darci would make a big deal about Tink's amulet, too.

"The kid wears this necklace that looks like a silver spider's web, and it has a red stone in the center. Evidently she's supposed to wear it all the time, because whenever they catch her without it on, Juliet and Jason get all bent out of shape," I said.

Darci sank back, disappointed. "That's it? I've seen a ton of kids at the library wearing necklaces in the shape of a spider's web."

With a quick nod, I glanced over at Abby. "See? All the kids wear them."

"You said the stone was red," Abby said, ignoring my remark. "Could it be a ruby?"

"I suppose," I mumbled, and gave up trying to get her attention off the necklace.

"I wonder when Tink was born?" she said to herself.

"Abby, *what* are you getting at?" My voice was tinged with frustration.

She gave me a stern look. "When we get home, I'm giving you all the family's journals, and you're going to read every last one of them."

Now I was more confused than ever.

"What do our family's journals have to do with Tink's necklace?"

"The journals contain spells—binding spells—spells that use spiders' webs."

The light clicked on.

"Someone is trying to bind Tink's powers using that necklace?"

Satisfied that I finally understood, Abby smiled. "Yes. It's my guess the crystal is Tink's birthstone—"

"And the stone fixes the spell specifically on her?" I interrupted.

"Yes. And the spider's web binds whatever the person who cast the spell stated in their intentions."

"In this case, Tink's psychic abilities?"

Abby nodded. "I think so."

"The spell must work." I stared off into space, thinking. "Whenever I was around Tink, the necklace was somewhere nearby. Either hanging on a branch or in her pocket. That's why I never picked up on her talent."

"Maybe. The necklace would definitely work better if it was worn around her neck, but if she was close enough to it, it would still exert some power over her."

"So someone is dabbling in magick?" My eyes drifted back to Abby's face.

"Juliet would be my guess," Abby said.

"But what about Jason? He was a stage magician at one time."

"Ophelia," she chided, "you know stage magic has nothing to do with real magick."

"I know, but what if his interest in fake magic led him to explore real magick?" I remembered my conversation with Jason. "He said meeting Juliet opened his eyes to real magic, but I thought he meant it a different way. That she opened his eyes to the potential that lies within . . ." My voice trailed off while I put two and two together in my mind. "Crap, they're practicing witchcraft, aren't they?"

"Oh my gosh! It's not a commune, it's a coven." Darci's face glowed. "There's a coven across the lake. How cool is that?"

"Slow down, Darce. We're making a lot of assumptions here." I chewed on my bottom lip, thinking.

I thought about the clearing with the abandoned cabin.

"Abby, do you think Juliet or Jason laid down some kind of protective spell around that cabin?"

"If Juliet and Jason are dabbling," she said, "the spell could be theirs. But the day you found the cabin, I assumed Walks Quietly was responsible."

Oh yeah, I'd forgotten about him.

Abby continued. "I don't know exactly what Walks Quietly is—I don't know very much about Native American beliefs—but he's some kind of medicine man."

I rubbed my forehead with the heels of my hands. I felt my headache coming back.

Abby leaned toward me and touched my arm. "Headache again?"

"Yeah." I exhaled slowly.

A look of uncertainty shadowed Abby's face. She pursed her lips before speaking. "There's something else, Ophelia. Earlier I told you something or someone is toying with us, but there is a purpose behind the game, and—"

A voice called out from inside the cabin, "Is anyone here?"

Rick.

"We're on the deck," I called out.

The doors slid open and Rick stepped out. His beard

was thicker now, and his self-confident air was gone. He looked tired, worn down.

Abby stood, shaking her head in sympathy.

Rising, I crossed to Rick and took his hands in mine. "Rick, I'm so sorry. Did you call Brandi's parents?"

"No," he said shortly.

"I know calling her parents will be hard, but putting it off won't make it easier," I said gently.

"It's not Brandi," he said in a low voice.

I released his hands and stepped back. "But who—"

"Duane Hobbs," he replied, cutting me off.

"Duane Hobbs drowned?"

Before he could answer, Abby broke in. "Let the man sit down, Ophelia."

Rick shot Abby a grateful look and sat on the nearest chair.

Abby laid a hand on his shoulder. "Do you want something to drink, Rick?"

"That would be great."

Abby went back into the cabin, while I turned to Rick. "What about Duane?"

He held up a hand. "I'll explain when Abby gets back."

I crossed my arms and tapped my foot. My mind was racing. How did Duane Hobbs wind up dead?

"Rick—"

"I don't want to tell the story twice, okay?" he said, his voice weary.

I took pity on him and kept my mouth shut. Crossing over to my chair, I plopped down and waited.

Abby returned a few moments later with a tray holding a pitcher of lemonade and four glasses. She poured one for each of us, then sat next to me. After passing a hand over her eyes, she took a tiny sip.

Disturbed, I touched her arm. "Abby?"

She reached over and patted my hand, smiling. "Let's hear what Rick has to say."

Rick drained his glass in one long drink. Setting the empty glass on the deck, he leaned forward. "I was in the boat with the sheriff and the medical examiner when the divers brought the body to the surface. I even helped get it into the boat. It was obvious—he didn't drown." Rick winced. "When they turned him over, we saw a deep gash on the left side of his skull. Deep enough to kill him. He also had a piece of cord tied around his foot."

"Oh, my gosh," Darci exclaimed. "Someone killed him and dumped him in the lake?"

"Yes."

"What about the cord?" I asked.

"The end was frayed, like the cord had been rubbing against something repeatedly until the friction wore it through and it snapped. They think his foot had been tied to some kind of weight. The sheriff asked the divers to go down and try and recover it."

I studied Rick's face. "Did they find it?"

"I don't know," he said with a slight shrug. "We left and brought the body back to shore, where the medical examiner's van was waiting to take it to the hospital morgue." His mouth twisted in a wry grin. "The sheriff wants the part about the rope kept quiet. He *strongly* suggested that I not mention it in any report I send to the newspaper."

Abby had listened to Rick's story without comment. Finally she spoke. "Rick, I think it would be best if we went back to Iowa."

He dropped his head for a moment. Raising it, he met Abby's eyes. "I know. I promised there wouldn't be any danger, and now there's a murder."

Abby shook her head. "No, Rick, it's not the murder. I'm sorry Mr. Hobbs met an unfortunate end, but right now I'm more concerned about protecting my granddaughter."

*Me? Why did I need protection?*

I stared at her in confusion. "Abby? What are you talking about?"

Abby watched me, her face full of love. "You asked me earlier about what I sensed—"

I broke in. "Yeah, but you said you didn't know."

"I don't know. At least I'm not certain about what I'm picking up, but we've both felt things. I don't know if what we've felt is human in origin or not." Her eyebrows knitted together in a frown. "I'm not sure if what I feel is tied to Brandi's disappearance or Duane Hobbs's murder. But whatever it is, whatever is hiding in the shadows, is waiting. Waiting for an opening to attach itself to someone . . ."

When she hesitated, my gaze traveled from Abby to Rick to Darci. They all had the same worried look on their face.

"And, my dearest granddaughter, that someone is you."

# *Twenty-four*

I held up my hand. "Whoa—time out. What do you mean 'it' wants to attach itself to me? What's 'it'?"

Abby pursed her lips, thinking. "Some kind of energy, and that energy is centered on you."

I gave a nervous laugh. "You make it sound like I've got a bull's-eye painted on my back, or something."

"You do," Abby said in a no-nonsense voice.

Jumping to my feet, I paced the deck. "Well, that's just peachy, isn't it?" My hand went to the talisman amulet I wore around my neck. "What about this?" I said, drawing the necklace out. "Doesn't my amulet protect me?"

"To a degree, but the fire agate is more for danger coming from a human source."

I skidded to a stop. "*Human source* as opposed to *nonhuman* source?"

Abby nodded. "I think so."

"A ghost?"

She chewed her bottom lip while she thought. "No. What little I'm picking up isn't tied to an earthly plane."

I fisted my hands on my hips. "What's that supposed to mean?"

"It means an entity that's never lived on earth," she said calmly.

"A psychic nasty?"

"A what?" Darci broke in.

"Negative energy that exists outside of the realm we live in. A disembodied spirit." I glanced at her quickly before turning my attention back to Abby. "How could this happen?" I resumed my pacing. "You smudged the cabin, put salt around the outside. We've always been careful, been prepared before opening up to any energy. I don't understand."

"Were you prepared before you tried breaking the field you felt around the cabin?"

"No," I mumbled. "Whatever's around that cabin took me off guard. The energy felt warm and safe, almost seductive—"

"So you relaxed?" Abby interjected.

I stopped and crossed my arms. "Yeah, I did." I hesitated. "Great," I said, throwing my hands in the air. "You're telling me whatever I encountered decided to follow me home."

"Yes."

Goose bumps prickled my arms. "That means it's already attached itself to me."

"No, not yet," she replied.

I stared at Abby, confused. "But you just said—"

She held up her hand to stop me. "It's circling around you. The energy isn't strong enough yet to firmly attach to you."

"But it's looking for a chink in my psychic armor to slip through?"

"Exactly." She appeared relieved that I finally understood. "And it's draining your energy in the process.

I think that's why you've been having headaches and a queasy stomach."

I shuddered. "It's feeding off me. Like a vampire."

"Um-hm. A psychic vampire."

*Oh brother!* I crossed to the railing and looked out over the water. So peaceful, so lovely. What had I done? What had I, in my stupidity, released to create havoc among all this beauty? Talk about a Pandora's box.

I shifted sideways and leaned a hip against the railing. "Abby, have you ever dealt with anything like this before?"

Her eyes took on a faraway look. "A long time ago, in the mountains, before I married your grandfather." She directed her attention back to me. "But my mother and grandmother were the ones who handled the problem. I only helped."

Rick cleared his throat. "Abby, I don't understand half of what you've said, but if you think Ophelia is in any danger, normal or paranormal, I think she should leave."

I whirled around. "No."

*"No?"* Rick jumped to his feet. "Have you been listening to your grandmother? If I've got what she said straight, some kind of evil entity is after you. Aren't you scared?"

I shrugged. "A little . . ."

"A little?" Rick exclaimed. "If I were you, I'd be scared sh—" He glanced at Abby. "Ah, spitless."

"Okay." I looked down and scuffed the deck with my foot. "Maybe I am more than a little scared." Raising my head, my eyes met Rick's. "But whatever's creeping about, I helped release it." I turned back to Abby and gave her a determined look. "How do we send that sucker back where it belongs?"

Abby's face glowed with pride. Standing, she rubbed her hands together. "First of all, I need to do some reading."

"You have your journals?"

"You bet I do—several of them," she said emphatically. "I didn't know what we were going to find when we got here. Only a foolish person would go into a battle without their weapons."

I smiled and put my arms around her. "And no one would dare call you foolish," I said, giving her a hug.

She stepped back, her face stern, but a spark gleamed in her eyes. "Not if they knew what was good for them," she said with a wink. Turning away from me, she marched over to the door, took a deep breath, and walked inside.

"Well," Darci said, rubbing her hands on her legs. "I need some bright lights and music. Anyone want to go into Melcher?"

I rolled my eyes. How many bright lights were there in a town of four hundred? But I understood her need to get away from what we'd witnessed that day.

"Thanks, but no thanks. I'll stay here with Abby. I still think she's acting a bit strange."

Darci glanced at Rick. "You?"

He held up his hand. "I'm beat. I'm going to hang around here for a while, and then head back to Brainerd."

Darci swung her legs off the chaise lounge and stood. "I noticed a decent bar this morning. Maybe I'll run into some of my friends from the coffee shop." She moved to the door.

"Hey, Darci," I called after her. "Be careful."

She flipped me a thumbs-up and glided through the door.

"She's something else, isn't she?" Rick said with a wry grin.

"You bet she is." I returned his grin and sat on the chaise Darci had vacated.

We sat in silence watching the sun drop below the pines. The evening star shone bright in the deepening twilight.

*Wow, Rick Delaney and starlight. Talk about romance.*

I smiled to myself at the thought.

Rick's voice broke the quiet. "What's so funny?"

I leaned my head back and watched the darkening sky. "Nothing. You probably wouldn't see the humor."

"I've got a sense of humor," he said defensively. "I . . ." His voice trailed off as the call of a loon sounded in the distance.

I glanced over at him. "Their call has to be one of the most haunting sounds I've ever heard." Thinking about what I said, I made a face. "Maybe 'haunting' isn't the best word to use right now."

Rick laughed softly. "Not after what Abby said."

"Do you believe in all of this?" I asked suddenly.

"Believe in all of what?"

"Disembodied spirits, ghost lights, you know," I said, wiggling my fingers at him. "Woo-woo stuff."

"I don't know." A smile tickled the corner of his mouth. "By hanging with you, Jensen, I've seen some pretty uncanny stuff. Why?"

I exhaled slowly and stared at the sky. "It would be nice to think someone believed, because my gift's real." I thought of Henry. "And not only when it suited their purpose and they had something to gain. To understand my talent for my sake."

"Unless they're a psychic, I don't know if anyone

really can understand what you and Abby can do."

"Maybe if they cared enough," I replied.

"You've changed, Jensen," Rick said abruptly, changing the subject.

Puzzled, I stole a glance his way. "What do you mean?"

He turned and studied me in the fading light. "You seem more comfortable, more at ease with who you are." A quick grin flashed across his face. "You're still a little prickly, and I think you worry too much—"

"Thanks," I said, and grimaced.

"But you don't have that wall around you anymore," he finished.

I thought about his observations. "You're right. I don't, and I suppose I owe you for that. If you hadn't pulled me into the deal with Adam Hoffman, I'd probably still be hiding from who and what I am."

"Are you happy?" he asked.

"Yes—most of the time. I'm more at peace. There's still so much I have to learn about myself. I get frustrated . . ." My voice faded while I thought of all those years I'd wasted because I was too stubborn, too afraid of my talent, to listen to Abby. "I have a lot of catching up to do," I said, smiling. "What about you? Has your life changed in the last six months?"

"Ahh, I need to explain something to you, Ophelia." Rick fidgeted in his chair. "Last fall, in Iowa, we came close to dying. That brings people together . . ."

"But?" I asked, arching an eyebrow.

What Rick was about to say came to me in a flash. And I wasn't surprised. What did surprise me was how I felt. Okay. I felt okay about what he was going to tell me. No remorse, no regrets, no heart twinges.

But instead of telling him my thoughts, I decided to

let him squirm a bit. Make up for all those times he teased me relentlessly.

"You see, there's this, ahh . . ."

I filled in the blank for him. "Woman?"

"Yeah, and—"

"You're engaged." I broke in again.

"Yeah." He sounded bewildered. "How did you know?"

"Psychic, remember?" I said smugly.

He shook his head. "I hate it when you do that."

I chuckled. "Sorry." I reached over and gave him a friendly punch in the arm. "Quit worrying about it. We're friends."

"We are, aren't we?" he said, his face serious.

"Yes, we are." I smiled. "Are you happy?"

"Yeah."

"What's her name?"

"Gina."

Rick wasn't exactly waxing poetic about his beloved. I felt like a prosecutor going after a hostile witness. I gave it one more shot.

"What does she do?"

"Well, ahh . . ." His voice trailed off.

*Oh, no.* I remembered the first day I'd met Rick. I'd told him he probably dated models, cheerleader types.

I narrowed my eyes in amusement. "No, don't tell me, she's a model, right?"

I watched his head bob up and down in agreement.

My laughter reverberated across the water.

Boy, did it feel good.

# Twenty-five

The next day my morning ritual changed—Abby was up and in my spot on the deck. I had to make a choice. Do I announce the news of Rick's engagement or not? Not, I decided. The news was his to tell, and with so much going on, I didn't want to be in a position where I had to reassure both Abby and Darci that my heart wasn't broken.

I plastered a smile on my face. "What are you doing up so early?" I asked, sliding the doors closed and joining her on the deck.

The shirt she wore over her jeans looked rumpled, and her hair was haphazardly twisted in a loose coil at the back of her head. When she glanced over her shoulder, I saw the effects of a troubled sleep on her face.

"Abby," I said, crossing swiftly to where she stood. "What's wrong?"

"Nothing." She gave me a weak smile. "I stayed up too late reading about psychic attacks."

"That's in your journals?" I was surprised; some of those journals were over sixty years old, and I didn't think they covered such things.

"The journals refer to what's happening to you as

hauntings, evil spirits, and demon possession, that kind of thing."

Demon possession? Wonderful.

Abby noticed my expression and grinned. "Don't worry; the journals contain arts and remedies to deal with the problem."

I'd read some of those old remedies, and some recommended burnt feathers and chicken feet.

I gave her a skeptical look. "We're not going to do anything bizarre, are we? No chicken feathers?"

"No, dear," she said, her voice reassuring. "No animal parts. Just the usual—herbs, candles, and crystals. Maybe a few intentions written on a piece of paper." She sighed. "I wish I knew the origin of what's going on."

I scowled. "We're back to that 'human versus nonhuman' thing, aren't we?"

"We could be dealing with both. It could be someone is using the negative energy, the negative entity, around the cabin and directing it toward you—"

I cut her off, "Someone ill-wishing and using the bad energy to give the spell a little extra punch?"

She nodded slowly. "Yes, and if that's the case, it would be helpful if I knew who's responsible."

"I know," Darci said, stepping out onto the deck.

Abby and I turned in unison and said at the same time, "Who?"

Still dressed in pajamas covered with big red hearts, Darci strolled over to a chaise lounge and flopped down. "Walks Quietly."

I rolled my eyes. "Okay, Sherlock, how'd you come up with that?"

Darci studied her bright red nails. "Easy. He hated Duane Hobbs, he doesn't like you, he knows magick, and according to both of you, he's got the juice."

"Got the juice?" I said, my tone bewildered.

She pulled her knees to her chest and wrapped her arms around them. "Yeah, you know the juice, the jazz, the power . . ." Her voice trailed away.

"Oh, you think he's psychic?" I said, nodding.

Darci tossed her head. "Yeah."

My eyes met Abby's, my question written on my face.

Abby shook her head. "I don't know. We all agree he's very powerful, but whether or not he's psychic?" She shrugged.

I exhaled slowly. "Darci, during all your deducing, did you recall what Abby said yesterday about the Finches? About practicing magick?"

"Yes," she said, with a defensive ring to her voice.

"Maybe they're involved. The abandoned cabin is on their property. Their niece is wearing a necklace that probably has some kind of spell on it. They're involved in psychic research. *And*," I said, emphasizing the word, "they were the last ones to see Brandi."

"Oh pooh." Darci's lip came out in a pout. "So maybe it isn't Walks Quietly."

My right eye twitched. "And maybe it isn't the Finches. And maybe Brandi is cozied up somewhere with a guy she met at a bar. And maybe," my voice rose, "maybe what happened to me at the abandoned cabin was my imagination, maybe—" I stopped abruptly.

Frustration laced with anger slammed through me. To my ears, I sounded as if I was beginning to doubt my own sanity. Doubt Abby.

"I'm tired of this," I said. "We've been wringing our hands and worrying. We haven't accomplished a thing." I strode over to the doors. "I'm getting some answers and I'm getting them now."

"Wait, Ophelia," Abby called out. "Where are you going?"

"Walks Quietly's. And he's going to tell me what he knows," I said in a determined voice. "And when I'm done with him, I'm talking to the Finches."

Darci jumped up and grabbed my arm. "Wait a second, he doesn't like you. You can't go barging up there and force him to talk to you."

I shook off her hand. "Oh yeah? Just watch me."

She tugged on my sleeve. "What if he *is* behind all of this? You won't be safe."

"If I'm not back in thirty minutes, send the cops." I shoved open the doors. "I'm going to see just how much 'juice' this guy's got."

I made a quick stop in my room and loaded up with crystals, shoving every rock I owned in my pockets. I may have been mad, but there was no sense in being foolish. I didn't know what kind of tricks Walks Quietly might have up his sleeve, so I'd take all of mine with me.

With the stones rattling all the way, I reached Walks Quietly's little house in five minutes. I found him in his yard, standing by his woodshed.

He whirled around at my footsteps. "Young woman, what are you doing here?"

"I've got some questions and I think you've got some answers," I said, my eyes narrowed.

"I told you I know nothing." He turned away.

"Oh yes you do." I moved around in front of him. "Someone or something is targeting me. And I don't like it."

He blew out a breath in disgust. "You've brought it on yourself by interfering with things you don't understand."

"Yeah, well, make me understand." I stood my ground.

He glared at me for a moment, then turned and walked away. "I'm not concerned with your problems."

"Wait," I called after him. "Just what and who are you?"

Spinning around, his eyes bore into mine. "I could ask the same of you?"

Standing tall, my eyes never left his. "I'm a psychic and *I* am one of the chosen. I belong to a line of wise women, healers." I paused. "Witches." Squinting my eyes, I took a step toward him. "So don't mess with me."

Emotions played across his face during my little speech—anger, disbelief, and finally humor.

His sudden laughter startled me, and I took a step back.

"You're either very brave or very foolish to confront me this way."

I refused to back down. "I'm not worried. If I'm not back in thirty minutes, those authorities that you're so fond of, they'll be showing up." Crossing my arms over my chest, I continued to stare at him. "You'd better start talking."

Walks Quietly looked down at the ground and shook his head. With heavy steps he walked to the chopping block and sat.

I heard him mutter something about disrespectful women as he did.

Pacing over to where he sat, I stood in front of him. "I don't have time to be respectful. A young woman is missing and a man is dead. I—"

"What man?" he asked, looking up at me.

"Duane Hobbs."

A look of bitterness crossed his face. "I have nothing to say." He rose slowly.

"Wait a second." I laid a hand on his arm, stopping him.

Two eyes as hard as stone drilled into mine, and the air around us seemed to sizzle with energy. I felt the power inside the man push against me.

I focused and pushed back.

Silence dropped over the clearing around his cabin, while we stood engaged in our mental shoving match. Our combined energy churned around us, but neither one of us gave an inch.

I felt myself starting to weaken against the constant force pressing against me.

*No, I would not let him win.*

With a deep breath, I concentrated all my energy against his in one final push.

Walks Quietly took a step back, and the power around us trickled away like water slowly running down a drain.

"You have courage, Ophelia Jensen," he said in a tired voice, and returned to his seat on the block.

Pressing a hand to my forehead, I inhaled long and slow. "You pack quite a wallop, too." Sinking to the ground at his feet, I drew up my knees and rested my head for a moment. Lifting it, I looked at him. "Who are you? Or should I say, what are you?"

His mouth twisted in a humorless smile. "There's no word in your language for what I am." His chin rose and he stared at the trees behind me. "I am Dakota Sioux," he said with pride. "My father, and his father before him, guided our people on their spiritual path. When I was a young man, your government asked me to fight. And I did, but when I came home, there was no warrior's welcome for me. There was no respect. People called us names and heaped dishonor on us." He looked down at me. "I became lost in the white man's world, so when my daughter was grown, my wife and I came to this place. I returned to the ways of my people." His eyes softened at the mention of his wife. "Life was good . . ." His jaw clenched and his eyes lost their softness. "Until my wife was found dead, lying on the shoulder of the road like some dead animal."

I glanced down at my hands, clutched tightly in my lap. I had memories of Brian and how he, too, had been cast away in death, his body found among the garbage in a Dumpster. I understood Walks Quietly's bitterness.

"I'm sorry for your loss," I said gently, and raised my eyes to meet his.

"What do you know of loss?" he asked harshly.

"I know the sorrow from losing someone you love can drive you inside yourself, so far inside you don't know if you can ever find your way out." Unshed tears blurred my vision. I swiped both eyes, wiping them away.

He looked at the ground in front of him.

I cleared my voice. "What do you know about Brandi Peters?"

"Nothing. And I speak the truth," he said in a soft voice. "I'd overheard people talking about her wildness, but I didn't know she left the lake until you told me."

Her wildness, huh? That confirmed what Juliet had told us about Brandi sneaking off the compound.

"What about Juliet and Jason Finch? What about Tink? You know she's psychic, don't you?"

"Yes." His voice was terse.

"Does Tink know?"

He rubbed a hand over his knee, like his joint ached. "She knows she's different, but she doesn't understand why. They keep her isolated and seek to control her through their medicine."

I had a feeling he wasn't talking about the pills.

"The necklace?"

He nodded. "I do what I can to help her, but her gift is something I don't understand."

"The cabin in the woods—"

Walks Quietly surged to his feet. "That is an evil place. Stay away from it."

"No kidding." I jumped up. "Did you lay a spell around it?"

"We don't call them spells." He took a step away from me. "But yes, I put medicine around the cabin."

"I know some places hold ancient evil. Is the clearing one of those places? Have there been legends about that spot?"

"No." He moved toward his cabin, and I followed. "The stories say a white man died in the cabin, a man possessed by bad spirits."

The ghost lights.

I hurried around him to stand in front of him. "Violet Butler's brother?"

"I don't know who the man was." He stepped to the side to go by me.

"Have you ever looked inside the cabin?"

His eyes shot wide. "No," he replied, his voice hard. "It is not safe. Only someone with very strong medicine would be able to go there unharmed."

"Isn't that funny? I happen to know someone who has strong medicine." I turned and walked away from him. "About a hundred years' worth of medicine," I called over my shoulder as I headed down the path and back to Abby.

I was almost to the cabin when a streak of white

came flying out of the woods and stopped on the path.

Tink.

Standing in front of me, she shifted her weight from foot to foot, and every line of her body echoed her distress.

I hurried over to her. "Tink, what's wrong?" I asked, laying a hand on her shoulder.

She turned her face up to me, and I saw her violet eyes wide with fear.

"Ophelia, I need your help."

"What? What is it?"

"I killed Duane Hobbs."

# Twenty-six

"You what?" I gave her shoulder a small shake.

"I killed Duane Hobbs. I—I didn't mean to. It . . . just happened." Her eyes filled with tears. "He tried to hurt me."

I released Tink and pulled both hands through my hair.

I didn't know how to handle this admission. Do I march her back to the Finches and call the sheriff, or what? I was in over my head.

"Come on." I grabbed her arm and pulled her toward the cabin.

Once there, I flung the door open and yelled, "Abby?"

"Out here," she replied from the deck.

I hurried Tink across the room, out the doors, and onto the deck.

Abby sat at the patio table with several old books spread before her. Her reading glasses were perched on her nose. She took one look at Tink and shoved the books aside. "Tink. What is it, my dear?" she asked, her face alarmed.

"Where's Darci?" I asked, propelling Tink toward the table.

Abby's eyes traveled to me. "Melcher. She went to the grocery store."

I pulled out a chair. "Sit," I said to Tink, pointing at it. Turning my attention to Abby, I joined them at the table. "Abby, Tink has a confession." My eyes slid over to the girl. "Go ahead; tell Abby what you told me."

Tink looked first at Abby and then at me. "I killed Duane Hobbs," she said in a small voice.

Abby's hand flew to her face. "Oh, my dear," she exclaimed. "I think you'd better start at the beginning."

Tink's gaze fell to her lap. "I was down by the lake when Duane found me. He started yelling at me, told me I'd better quit spying on him." Fear flitted across her face. "I was so scared. He grabbed me and shook me . . ." Her voice became hushed. "And then I killed him."

Oh brother, I thought, sitting back in my chair. This kid was lying through her teeth. But why?

Crossing my arms, I fixed my eyes on her. "How did you kill him?"

She looked up quickly. "I don't remember," she said as she raised her hand to her mouth and began to chew on her thumbnail.

"Tink, how can you not remember how you killed someone?" I asked.

She dropped her hand and glared at me. "I can't, okay? I must have gone kind of crazy when he started shaking me. Next thing I know, he's dead."

"What did you do after that?"

She lowered her eyes. "I pushed him in the water."

Cocking my head, I watched her. "That's it? You killed him and dumped him in the lake?"

"Yeah," she replied, her voice defiant. "Now are you going to turn me in, or what?"

I leaned forward in surprise. "You want us to call the sheriff?"

"Yes," she whispered.

"Did you tell Jason or Juliet about Duane?" I asked.

"No." She picked at her thumbnail. "They would try and hide it. But that's not right. I deserve to be punished."

My eyes met Abby's from across the table.

Tink lifted her head and saw the look. She shoved back the chair and sprang to her feet. "You don't believe me, do you?"

I shook my head. "No, I don't."

"I don't know why not." She hugged herself tightly. "If I said I killed him, I killed him."

"No, Tink." I let out a long breath. "The sheriff is going to want to know where, how, and why. And you say you don't remember."

"I don't remember." She paced away from the table. "I don't remember killing my mother, either, but everyone believes that I did, so—"

"Wait a second," I broke in. "Did someone tell you that you killed your mother?"

She clenched her hands at her side. "No. But I'm not stupid. I've heard them talking about my mother. I know what they think."

"Who did you hear talking?"

She gave me an angry look. "Everybody. Jason, Juliet, Winnie. They all think I'm crazy."

"Come over here, Tink," Abby said, holding out her hand.

Silently, Tink went to Abby and took her hand.

"Now please sit down, and let's talk about this,"

she said without releasing Tink's hand as the girl sat next to her. She leaned forward, her eyes never leaving Tink's face. "We don't think you're crazy, Tink. We think you're a remarkable young lady, and a very brave one," she added gently. "You're so brave that you're willing to take the blame for something you didn't do. You're trying to protect someone." She paused. "Who is it, Tink?"

Tink dropped her head and studied Abby's hand, holding hers. Tears rolled down her face. "Walks Quietly," she said in a hushed voice. "I know he didn't kill Duane, but the sheriff's going to think he did." She lifted her head. "I heard Winnie talking to Juliet about it. Everybody knows he hated Duane 'cause Duane killed his wife."

Abby reached over and wiped Tink's tears away. "But if Walks Quietly is innocent?"

Tink sniffed. "It won't matter. They're all scared of him and they're going to use this to send him away."

"So you thought if you confessed, you could save him?" Abby reached in her pocket and handed Tink a handkerchief.

"Yeah. I figured I'm a kid," she said, taking the handkerchief and wiping her face. "And if the sheriff thought it was in self-defense, they wouldn't send me to prison, or anything."

"But Tink, if your plan worked, it would mean a killer would go free." Abby squeezed her hand.

Tink shook her head. "I don't care. I don't want Walks Quietly to pay for something he didn't do."

"Maybe we can help you," I said.

Her eyes darted to me and she looked skeptical. "How? You're here on vacation. What do you know about finding a murderer?"

"Ahh," I stammered. "In the past, I've had a little experience catching killers."

Tink's head jerked back. "Yeah? Like what?" she said, disbelief in her voice.

"Never mind," I said. "The truth is we're not on vacation, we're here to find out what happened to Brandi Peters."

Tink's face twisted in disgust. "I didn't like her. I was glad when she left."

I leaned forward. "Why didn't you like her?"

"She was always flouncing around, acting like she was better than everyone else. And she never wanted to do her chores," she said, her tone derisive. "Winnie *hated* her. I heard Winnie complaining to Juliet about Brandi."

"What did Winnie say?"

Tink shrugged. "Not much. She was tattling on Brandi for sneaking out." She released Abby's hand and sat back. "How does Brandi leaving have anything to do with Duane Hobbs?"

"I don't know. But I think Duane might have known something about Brandi. Maybe that's why he was killed."

She looked at me carefully. "Does Winnie know why you're here?"

"Probably. We told Juliet yesterday."

Tink nodded. "Then she knows. Juliet tells Winnie everything." She gave a little snort. "Guess they won't be trying to convince you to join the group after all."

"What do you mean?"

"They wanted you to help them with the research Jason's always talking about. I heard them say you were psychics." Tink scooted her chair closer to the table. "Are you?"

"Ahh." I looked at Abby.

She gave me a slight nod.

"Yes."

"Ha, I bet Juliet and Jason are so jealous of you." Her face took on a satisfied smirk.

"Why would they be jealous?"

"They want to be psychic so bad. They practice all the time."

"What about you? Do you want to be psychic?"

Tink picked at her thumbnail again. "No."

Abby looked at Tink sympathetically. "Sometimes we don't get a choice. We are what we are. And we're given the gift for a reason."

Tink stood up. "I don't want to talk about it."

"Why not?"

Her pale face screwed up in a frown. "I don't like all this psychic stuff, that's why. Hearing voices, feeling cold spots, seeing shadows that aren't there. It's crazy."

Tink was a medium. Astonished, I glanced at Abby, but she ignored me.

"Do *you* see shadow people, Tink?" Abby asked, her face serious.

Tink squirmed under Abby's watchful eye and lowered her head. Her hair fell like a curtain around her face, masking her expression. "No," she mumbled.

The hum of a passing boat floated up from the lake. A squirrel rustled the pine boughs next to the deck. No one spoke, and the minutes ticked by.

Tink finally cracked under the weight of Abby's gaze and began pacing back and forth. Abruptly stopping, she cast an angry look at Abby. "What if I do? It doesn't mean they're right, it doesn't mean I'm crazy."

Unruffled by Tink's outburst, Abby motioned for her to resume her place at the table. "You're right, you're not crazy. You've been given a gift few people have. You have the ability to help lost souls."

"You mean like Duane?" Tink made a face. "Gross. I didn't like him."

Abby chuckled. "We'll talk about helping people we don't like later, all right?" Her voice dropped to a gentle, reassuring pitch. "Tink, do you have your necklace?"

"Yeah."

"May I see it?" Abby asked quietly.

"I suppose." Tink leaned back in her chair and reached in her pocket. Drawing out a small pouch, she laid it on the table.

Leaning forward, but not touching the pouch, Abby slipped on her reading glasses and studied it. "Interesting." She pointed to the quill design on the flap. "Did Walks Quietly make this for you?" she asked, taking Tink's hand.

Tink nodded.

"Do you know what the design means?"

"No."

"Would you mind slipping it out of the pouch for me, Tink?"

Tink picked up the pouch and shook the necklace out onto the table. The silver web with its dark red stone sparkled in the sunlight.

Without releasing Tink's hand, Abby closed her eyes and passed her other hand over it several times. "Just as I thought," she said with a shudder. "How do you feel when you wear the necklace, Tink?"

Her mouth tightened in a frown. "Like I'm walking around in some kind of fog. It gives me the creeps."

"Would you like me to change that for you?"

A wary look crossed Tink's face. "How?"

Abby winked. "I have my ways," she said, and squeezed Tink's hand.

Tink rolled her eyes.

"You don't have a lot of trust, do you, kid?" I asked.

"Why should I?" Tink shot back. "I don't know you and your grandmother."

"You're right. You don't. But when you look at Abby, what do you see? What do you feel?"

Tink tilted her head and gazed at Abby with a speculative look, all the time holding tight to Abby's hand. "I see mountains. Women in log houses. People asking the women for help. A garden with lots and lots of plants." She narrowed her eyes. "Peace. And the air around her kind of sparkles."

"Hey, that's pretty good for a kid," I said, nodding my approval.

She gave me a cheeky glance. "Wanna know what I see when I look at you?"

"No thanks."

Last thing I needed was a reading from a budding psychic and medium.

Abby jiggled Tink's hand to catch her attention. "Do you want me to fix the necklace so it isn't creepy?"

"Okay." Her tone sounded unconvinced.

"Ophelia, would you come and stand behind Tink, while I get some supplies out of the cabin," she said rising, but not letting go of Tink's hand.

I gave Abby a perplexed look. "But—"

She nodded toward her hand holding Tink's, and I understood. Abby was using her energy to protect the girl from whatever was imprinted on that necklace. If she let go of her hand, Tink would start feeling "creeped out" again.

I crossed to stand behind Tink and gently laid my

hand on the girl's shoulder. She looked up at me with a question in her eyes, and I gave her a vague smile. At the same time, I tried to keep the wisps of energy I felt from the necklace at bay.

In a moment Abby returned with her salt and a small bundle of herbs wrapped tightly together. She made a thin circle of salt around the necklace. When finished with the salt, she brought a lighter out of her pocket and lit the bundle of herbs. Soon the air was filled with the aroma of burning sage. Abby wafted the smoking bundle over the necklace.

Later I would swear my eyes never left the necklace. Maybe they did, maybe they didn't. I don't know. But I do know while Abby sent the purifying plumes of smoke over the necklace, the sparkling silver became tarnished, almost gray. But the change in the metal wasn't the most bizarre thing that happened. No, what freaked me out the most was the spider that suddenly appeared through the smoke and crawled across the necklace.

# Twenty-seven

Tink shrieked as the spider crept away from the necklace and toward the circle of salt. But when it hit the circle, the spider curled into a tiny ball and died.

Satisfied, Abby extinguished the sage and picked up the necklace. Placing it in her open palm, she rested her other hand on top of it. Closing her eyes, she held the necklace for a moment.

I stepped away from Tink. She was safe now, and Abby, by holding the necklace in her hands, was taking care of whatever leftover negative energy it might hold. And in the process, she was charging the necklace with positive energy, energy that would protect Tink, not control her.

Smiling, Abby opened her eyes, and after polishing the necklace on the tail of her shirt, drew the necklace over Tink's head.

"There," she said as she settled the necklace in place around Tink's slender neck.

Tink winced as the necklace passed over her head, but once Abby straightened it, she grinned. "Hey, the necklace feels different," she said.

"It's supposed to," Abby replied, her smile widening.

Taking the remainder of the sage bundle, she used it like a whisk broom to sweep the salt and dead spider into a plastic bag she'd pulled from her pocket. "I'll get rid of this later." She laid the bag under the table.

Abby crossed to where Tink sat and took her place beside her again. "There's something else I'd like to show you, Tink." She took the girl's hand in both of hers. "You see things and hear things sometimes, don't you? Things that no one else can see?"

"Yes," Tink replied in a shy voice.

"Would you like to be able to control that?" Abby asked gently.

Tink's face glowed. "Yeah."

Abby's eyes twinkled at Tink's enthusiasm. "Okay, close your eyes . . ."

The girl's eyelids dropped down.

"Now," Abby continued, "imagine a white light surrounding you. Inside the light you feel calm and at peace. You see the world around you, but nothing can penetrate the protective barrier of light. Do you see it?"

Tink's body relaxed. "Yes."

"Now imagine that your gift is a flower, held deep inside your soul. The flower is curled tight right now, but any time you want to use your gift, close your eyes and imagine the petals slowly unfolding. Can you do that?"

"Yes, I see it. I see the flower."

"Very good," Abby said, squeezing Tink's hand. "Are the petals open or closed?"

"Open."

"Now allow the petals to close."

Her face screwed with concentration while she did as Abby instructed. "Wow. I can see the flower shut."

Abby smiled with pleasure. "You may open your eyes, Tink. How do you feel?"

Tink's gaze flitted over the deck and back to Abby's face. "I feel really good," she said in amazement.

"Wonderful," Abby said, leaning forward and hugging her. Sitting back, she laid a hand on Tink's cheek. "Whenever you feel threatened or scared—"

"Of shadows?" Tink broke in.

Abby patted her cheek. "Yes, of shadows. Imagine the white light to protect you and keep you safe." She looked at her watch. "You've been gone a long time, Tink; they'll be looking for you." She hugged her again. "You'd better scoot."

Tink popped out of her chair and hurried to the edge of the deck. She paused and looked over her shoulder at us with a worried expression. "You won't forget about Walks Quietly, will you?"

"No, dear, we won't," Abby said.

The worry fell from her face and she grinned. "Thanks . . ." Her hand touched the spider's web necklace. ". . . for everything."

"You're welcome," Abby said to thin air. Tink had already disappeared around the corner of the cabin.

Abby slumped against the back of her chair.

I placed my hand on her shoulder. "Are you okay?"

She reached up and laid hers on top of mine. "I'm fine. Don't worry." Motioning to the chair next to her, she said, "Sit and tell me what your impressions were."

I sat in the chair. "Tink's obviously a medium," I said, "and she needs to learn control. Hopefully, the visualization you taught her will help. Along with the shielding."

"Yes," Abby agreed. "Tink needs to be the one to control her gift, not someone else."

"Do you think that's what the Finches were trying to do?"

"I don't know, but whoever is dabbling in magick, they don't understand what they're doing. The spell on that necklace was poorly done, and for the wrong reasons."

"Witch wannabes?"

"Yes." Abby's eyes closed as she stroked her face.

I lightly touched Abby's knee. "You're tired. Why don't you go inside and lay down?"

She bolted upright in her chair. "No."

Her sudden movement took me off guard. "What's wrong?"

She sighed deeply. "The cabin makes me uncomfortable." A look of confusion marred her face. "And I don't understand why. I smudged the inside and put a protective circle around it." Pursing her lips, she thought for a moment. "And I keep detecting the scent of lavender and roses, but I can't find where it's coming from."

"The smell disturbs you?"

"Yes."

I leaned back in my chair. "Yeah, the smell bothered me, too. That's why, after they gave me the bag, I put it in an empty drawer. It—"

"What bag?" Abby asked, grabbing my hand.

"The bag Tink—"

Abby abruptly stood and hurried into the cabin. A few minutes later she returned, holding the pouch in her fingertips like a dead mouse. "This bag?"

I nodded, frowning. "What's the deal?"

With a look of disgust, she put the bag in the center

of the table and made another circle of salt. Picking up the pouch, she dumped the contents inside the circle.

Sprigs of lavender and dried rose petals fell in a tidy little heap. Leaning forward, I examined the pile without touching it. The petals appeared to have a fine layer of dust coating them.

"What's with the dust?" I asked, looking up at Abby.

Her face wore a tight frown and her arms were crossed at her chest. She didn't answer my question. "Was it Tink's idea to give you this?" she asked.

"Not really. Jason prompted her. He said she made them to sell at craft shows."

"Humph," Abby snorted. "I doubt they'd sell this to anyone. It has some added ingredients." She snapped her fingers. "Just a minute." She hurried over to the edge of the deck and around the corner of the cabin.

I rushed after her, and by the time I reached her, Abby was crouched down scrutinizing the circle of salt around the cabin. She picked up a few grains of salt and rubbed them between her fingers. Holding her hand to her nose, she sniffed.

Her face puckered with distaste as she wiped her hand in the grass. She stood and marched back to the deck.

I scurried to keep up with her. "Hey, what's going on?"

By the time I reached her, she'd already lit the sage and was sending smoke across the pile on dried flowers.

"Abby, you're scaring me," I said, trying to catch my breath.

"You should be scared." Her eyes never left the clump on the table. "It's goofer dust and gunpowder."

*"What?"*

She looked at the sky and shook her head. "Ophelia, you really need to read those journals." Glancing over at me, she said, "Goofer dust is dirt from a graveyard. Someone added it to the bag Tink gave you."

"Yuck." I shivered.

Crushing out the smoldering sage, Abby brushed the pile, salt and all, into the bag already containing what was used to cleanse Tink's necklace. "And either before, or after, you received the bag, they sprinkled gunpowder around the cabin to negate the protective barrier created by the salt."

At a loss, I stared at her. "Why?"

"Goofer dust and gunpowder—two very nasty elements. Especially when used together." She fisted her hands on her hips while her eyes shot green fire. "Someone is trying to put a curse on us."

"Hey guys." Darci bopped through the sliding doors and onto the deck.

In unison, Abby and I whirled toward her.

She took one look at us and the smile she wore disappeared. "Ahh, maybe I'd better go back inside and put the groceries away," she said, pointing over her shoulder.

"No, Darci, it's okay," I said, rubbing my forehead. "Don't worry about it. Abby just informed me that someone is trying to put a curse on us."

"You're kidding?" she said, sinking down on the chaise.

Abby quickly filled her in on what had transpired that morning.

Darci listened quietly, with a thoughtful look on her face. "Walks Quietly is off the suspect list, then?"

"I think so. My feeling is he's trying to help, not harm," I replied while I leaned against the railing. "We're down to the Finches. Maybe Rick was right. Jason is more sinister than I thought he was."

Darci curled her long legs underneath her. "What about Winnie?"

I gave her a disgruntled look. "Winnie? She wouldn't know a spell if it hit her on the head."

"Oh I don't know," she said, twisting her head slowly back and forth. "She doesn't like you. And if the way she acted in the grocery store is any indication, I don't think Winnie would like it if you're invited back for another cozy dinner at the compound."

"You saw Winnie in town?"

"Yup. And it's a wonder I didn't drop dead on the spot when she saw me."

"Really?" I said, my voice incredulous.

She nodded. "She's very jealous of you, said some very nasty things about people who butt in where they're not wanted." She smiled sweetly at me. "I think she was referring to you, Ophelia."

Made sense. Abby said whoever was experimenting with magick wasn't adept at it. That description would fit Winnie. Maybe she was the one who put the spell on Tink's necklace.

I pushed away from the railing. "I guess I need to talk to Winnie. I'll—"

"No," Darci said, stopping me. "You need to call Rick. Tell him to meet us at the library in Brainerd." She uncurled her legs and rushed to her feet. "I have a plan."

I eyed her with suspicion. "What plan?"

I'd had experience with Darci's plans, and they usually involved me getting in some kind of jam.

She hurried over and grabbed my arm. "I know what you're thinking, and no, the plan doesn't involve breaking and entering."

"That's a relief," I said as she tugged me toward the door. "Are you going to be okay alone?" I called to Abby over my shoulder.

"You girls go on," she answered, ignoring the helpless look on my face. "I need to clean up around here."

And I knew she didn't mean sweep and dust.

# Twenty-eight

Darci marched up to the library in Brainerd.

Well, she marched as best one can in platform sandals. But she still made it hard for me to keep up with her, and I was wearing sensible tennis shoes.

"What are we looking for? And why do we need Rick?" I asked, panting and wheezing in the hot, humid air.

"You and I are going to look for information on this Von Schuler Winnie mentioned. And Rick's going to check out the archives to see if there's any mention of Violet Butler's brother," she said.

"Why don't we just ask the Finches about them?"

She looked at me like I'd lost my mind. "I told you, I think you've worn out your welcome. Winnie won't let you near the place."

I gave up arguing and followed her into the library.

Rick stood over by the counter waiting for us. He still hadn't shaved, and the beard he'd let grow for the past four days was losing its scraggly look.

I couldn't help but wonder what his fiancée would think of his new image.

"Hi girls," he said with a crooked grin. "You want to explain to me again what we're doing here?"

I shoved my hands in my pockets and shrugged. "Don't look at me. This is Darci's idea."

"Darci?"

"It's like this," she said, urging us away from the counter. "Abby and Ophelia both believe Walks Quietly's telling the truth, so he's off the hook. That leaves the Finches . . ."

Rick shot me an "I told you so" look.

She continued. "But other than that they were the last ones to see Brandi, we don't have any proof they know more than they're saying—"

"In other words, nothing new has turned up," Rick interrupted.

Darci held up a finger. "That's not true. We know Tink's a psychic and someone at the compound is playing around with magick. And whoever that someone is, they've been worried enough about us being here that they've tried to put a curse on us."

"Have you considered the spells were done out of jealousy?" Rick asked.

"By someone like Winnie?" I interjected.

"Could be." Rick scratched his beard. "This is all pretty strange. I feel like we're fighting phantoms."

Darci gave him a knowing look. "Maybe we are."

"Come on, Darci." Rick frowned. "I can buy into the magick thing, but evil ghosts lurking around, kidnapping a young girl, murdering Duane Hobbs? That's crazy."

"Fine," Darci replied, her chin shooting up a notch. "Don't help us, then. Ophelia and I will find out what we need to know by ourselves." She propelled me forward. "Come on, Ophelia, the card catalogue is over this way."

Rick let out a long sigh. "Okay, okay." His voice

sounded defeated. "We don't have anything to lose. What do you want me to do?"

Darci's face brightened. "The newspaper archives— go through them and see what you can find out about Violet Butler's brother."

"Why him?" Rick's eyebrows drew together.

"Walks Quietly thinks he was the one who lived in the abandoned cabin—"

"The place where Ophelia saw the ghost lights."

"Yeah." She nodded emphatically. "And the place where both Abby and Ophelia think there's some kind of nasty energy. Ophelia, you and I are going to look up twentieth century magicians."

"In particular, a magician named Von Schuler," I said.

"Yup. We're going to see if there's some reason he popped up in your dream."

Rick wandered off with a muttered "What the hell," while Darci and I headed toward the card catalogue.

We found four references to Frederick Von Schuler. After finding the books, we started reading.

Twenty minutes later I turned and looked at Darci, sitting beside me. "These references don't say much. Not even much is written about what kind of magic he performed. Are you finding anything?"

"Hmm." She peered at the pages she'd been reading. " 'Born 1880; performed telepathic routine with help of assistant; retired 1929.' " She flipped the book shut and leaned back. "None of that information's very juicy."

I tucked a strand of hair behind my ear and glanced down at the thick volume. "It seems to me he wasn't very famous, not like Houdini and Blackstone." Looking back up, I tapped my finger to my chin. "I wonder why Jason Finch is so interested in Von Schuler?"

"I don't know," she said, throwing up her hand. "Maybe it's the telepathic thing. Jason wants to know about all things psychic, and maybe this Von Schuler was better than people thought at the time. Maybe he really was a psychic."

I looked down at the pages again. "Do any of your books mention when he died?"

She flipped open the second book. "This one says, 'Believed to have died in 1933.' "

I quickly scanned the text. "Mine says, 'Date of death unknown.' " Raising my head, I arched my eyebrow. "Why wouldn't his date of death be listed?"

"He could have retired and slipped into obscurity. He wasn't all that famous to start with."

Shutting the books, I pushed them to the side and crossed my arms. "Any more ideas?"

"One—"

"Find anything?"

We both jumped. We'd been so intent on Von Schuler, we hadn't noticed Rick slip up behind us.

"No," Darci said, her voice heavy with disappointment. "Did you find anything?"

Rick waved two photocopies in front of our noses. "These."

Darci made a move to grab them, but Rick, with a smug look on his face, held the papers out of her reach.

"I'll read them to you." He crossed to the other side of the table, pulled out a chair, and sat down. "It isn't much, but it raises some questions."

I rolled my eyes. "We're supposed to be finding answers, not more questions, Rick."

"Let me read them, and then you can tell me what you think." He laid out the papers in front of him. "Okay, the first one is only a couple of lines about the death of Vio-

let Butler's brother." He looked down at the paper. "Re-
fers to him only as her brother, his name isn't mentioned.
It also does not mention any other siblings."

"So you're assuming it was just Violet and her
brother?"

"Yes."

"Then the niece the Butlers raised would've been the
brother's child?"

"Right," Rick answered.

He pointed to a line on the paper. "But the last line
struck me as odd. The article ends with, 'May the spirits rest in peace.' "

"Not may *his* spirit rest in peace?" I said.

Rick raised his head. "No."

Darci's eyes darted to mine and she mouthed the
word "ghosts." I shook my head and sighed.

Rick saw the exchange and smiled.

"What year was this article written?" Darci asked,
turning to Rick.

"Nineteen thirty-three—"

Darci's eyes flew wide. "That's the same—"

"Shh." I placed my hand on her arm to silence her.
"Let Rick finish."

"Once I found that article, I decided to dig a little
deeper." He paused for a moment, pride at his discovery flitting across his face. "Care to guess what I un-
covered?" he asked, drawing out the suspense.

I narrowed my eyes and scowled at him. "Would you
cut to the chase?"

"Oh, okay." He picked up the second piece of paper
and held it out with a flourish. "This is a short announce-
ment concerning the marriage of Victor Butler to the
former Violet Von Schuler—"

Before he could finish, I grabbed the page out of his

hands and scanned it quickly. "Violet Butler was Frederick Von Schuler's sister?"

"Yes."

"That means—"

"Juliet Finch is the granddaughter of Frederick Von Schuler," Rick said, finishing the sentence for me.

I chewed the inside of my lip, thinking. The connection explained several things. Why the Finches lived at the lake. Why Jason was fascinated with Von Schuler. And if Von Schuler truly had been a psychic, the relationship could explain Tink's psychic talent. She inherited her gift from her great-grandfather.

I looked over at Darci. "You didn't read anything about Von Schuler being a medium, did you?"

Darci opened the books and reread the passages swiftly. "Nope, nothing in here about that. Why?"

"No reason," I replied distractedly. My mind was locked on Tink's tie to Von Schuler.

I pushed back my chair and stood. "I guess that's it. This information is very interesting, but it doesn't help us find Brandi." Picking up the books, I headed toward the counter.

"Wait." Darci hurried to catch up with me. "I have one more idea."

I slowed my steps. "What now?"

The question was pointless. I had a pretty good hunch what Darci's next idea would involve. Rick wouldn't like it, but for once I agreed with her.

"We need to go to the abandoned cabin," she whispered.

"Okay," I said, and walked away, leaving Darci with a stunned look on her face.

\* \* \*

We hurried out of the library and left Rick with a non-committal "See you later." But before Darci pulled away from the curb, I placed a hand on her arm, stopping her.

"Darci, are you sure you want to do this?"

She looked at me in surprise. "Yeah, I'm sure."

I thought about the last time I'd been at that cabin, and I shivered in spite of the heat. "I don't know if it's a good idea for you to go along."

She whipped her head around and glared at me. "I don't care. I'm going with you." Her eyes became narrow slits. "And if you sneak off without me, I'll follow you."

"I don't know if I can protect you from whatever's in that clearing. What if it attaches itself to you?"

"I've already thought about that." She fluttered a hand in my direction, dismissing my concern. "I'm not a psychic. I won't be as open as you are."

"Darci—"

"Quit worrying about it. If anything happens, you can exorcise me later." She gave me a wink.

"Darci, that's not funny." I picked at the hem on my T-shirt. "I have so many things to learn about magick yet. I don't know if I have enough skill to protect us."

"We could take Abby."

"Oh Lord, no," I exclaimed. "The cabin is deep in the woods. I can't let Abby tramp all that way."

"I guess it's up to you, then." She calmly pulled away from the curb.

I exhaled slowly and thought about what I needed to do. Suddenly an idea hit me, and I pointed to the sign I saw on the left. "Darci, pull over to that gas station."

She whipped into the parking lot, and I hopped out and ran inside. A few moments later I was back in her car with a piece of paper in my hand.

"Here," I said, handing it to her. "We need to find this address."

She read it quickly. "What is it?"

"A New Age shop. We're going to buy a few supplies."

Lucky for us, the store was only a few blocks down the street. By now it was late afternoon and stores were starting to close. Darci slowed to a stop. I jumped out and ran into the store while she found a place to park.

The door chimed as I walked in, and the woman behind the counter gave me a pleasant look. Long crystal earrings dangled from both her ears and ropes of beads hung over her ample chest.

"May I help you?" she asked, strolling out from behind the counter.

"Yes." My eyes scanned the store. "Where are your crystals?"

"Over there." She motioned with a ring-covered hand to a shelf on the other side of the store. "Is there a particular stone you're looking for?"

"Lodestone." I held up my hand, stopping her when she made a move toward the shelf. "That's okay, I can find them."

I rushed past the books and the scented candles, over to the crystal display. While I looked over the bins of crystals, I heard the door chime again. Glancing over my shoulder, I saw Darci come in.

I motioned for her to join me.

"Wow, what a cool store." She took a deep breath. "I love the way it smells in here." Her eyes strayed across the shelves. "Do I have time to look around?"

"Darci," I hissed, "we're not here to shop. Now which stone do you like?" I asked as I held out two black rocks.

"This one," she replied, touching the stone with a long red fingernail.

"Okay." I turned back to the bins and selected one for me and one for Abby. Stepping over, I examined the crystals in the next bin. Picking one up, I turned to Darci.

No Darci.

She'd wandered over to the books and was engrossed in browsing through one. Abruptly, she looked up and waved wildly for me to join her.

Shaking my head to myself, I replaced the crystal and crossed to where she stood.

"Look what I found." Her voice vibrated with excitement. "It's a book on nineteenth century spiritualists. Frederick Von Schuler is in here."

"Great." I handed her the crystals and took the book.

I opened it to the index and found Von Schuler's name. Quickly, I found the pages that referred to him.

The author had written a very complete biography of Von Schuler that covered the time until he disappeared. And, yes, Von Schuler had been a very talented medium. In addition to his magic show, he had conducted many séances for the wealthy throughout the country.

My eyes moved rapidly down the page with a growing sense of dread.

Von Schuler had soon grown tired of only contacting the dearly departed; he figured out a way he could use his gift to increase his own personal power. Or so he thought. Instead, his experiment had led him down a path of scandal and self-destruction.

Von Schuler had gone mad after summoning a demon.

# *Twenty-nine*

I paid for the three lodestones and the book and hustled Darci out of the store.

"What *is* wrong with you?" she asked when we were on our way again. "You look like you've seen a ghost."

"No," I mumbled, staring out the window at the passing stores. "A demon."

"I must not have heard you right." She gave a nervous laugh. "I thought you said a demon."

"I did." I watched Darci's reaction. "Frederick Von Schuler became involved in what most people call the 'black arts.'"

Her mouth dropped open but no words came out.

"My thoughts exactly," I said sarcastically.

"What are you going to do?" she asked when she got her voice back.

"I don't know." I tugged on my lip. "Darci, promise me you won't tell Abby about Von Schuler?"

"I promise. But don't you think we should? She'll figure out we're hiding something."

"I'll take the risk. I don't want her near that cabin until I figure out what's going on."

"Are we still going?"

"I don't know." I hesitated. "Let me rephrase that. I don't know if I'm going. I do know you're not."

Darci's face took on a mulish look. "Last time I checked, I was overage, so I don't think you can tell me what to do, Ophelia."

"I can this time." My voice rose. "And you're not changing my mind."

"I'll follow you."

"No, you won't," I said, my tone final.

She shoved back against the car seat and her fingers drummed an angry beat on the steering wheel. The rest of the ride back to the lake passed in silence.

She parked next to the SUV, shut off the motor, and jumped out, slamming the door. By the time I reached the cabin, Abby stood in the center of the kitchen with a perplexed look on her face.

"Why is Darci so angry?" she asked. "She tore through the house and out to the deck."

I shoved my hands in my pockets. "I suppose I should go talk to her," I said, and took a deep breath.

I took another breath and let the difference I felt inside the cabin sink in.

No headache, no buzzing, no sudden nausea.

"Abby," I said, my worry over Darci's anger momentarily forgotten. "The atmosphere feels great."

A smile teased at the corner of Abby's mouth. "A bunch of amateurs. It took me no time at all to get rid of their spell." Her eyes twinkled. "And this time I added a little extra something to protect us. If they try it again, they're going to get a surprise."

"Do you think it's the Finches?"

She nodded. "Or Winnie." Her eyes lost their sparkle. "I'm concerned about Tink. She's very sensitive, and she's never been taught how to guard herself. It's like she's a sponge, soaking in whatever energy comes her way. I'm afraid all this fooling around with magick could have a damaging effect."

"But you showed her how to shield this morning."

"Yes, but as you know, proficiency takes practice."

One more worry to add to my already full bag. I'd think about Tink later, right now I had Darci to deal with. I started to cross to the sliding glass doors.

Abby's voice stopped me. "I'd leave Darci alone for now, if I were you, dear. Whatever it is that's bothering her, give her time to work through it."

If Abby only knew, but I had no intention of telling her. Abby would be as insistent as Darci about going with me, and a lot harder to dissuade.

My hand found the lodestones in my pocket. I pulled one out and handed it to Abby.

"What's this?" she asked with a pleased smile.

"I didn't know if you had a lodestone or not. And with everything going on . . ." My voice trailed off when Abby gathered me into a hug.

"It's very sweet of you, dear," she said, stepping back.

I withdrew the other stone and handed it to her. "I bought one for Darci, too. Would you give it to her when she comes in? I want to do some reading in my room."

"Of course. I'll charge it with protection, too." Abby looked at me with a hint of suspicion in her eyes, and I saw the questions flitting across her face.

I beat a hasty retreat to my bedroom before the questions were asked.

My decision had been made as I listened to Abby talk about Tink. Abby had called the girl a sponge for energy—like the energy that lurked around the abandoned cabin. She would be an easy target for whatever prowled that clearing.

The lodestone I'd selected for myself was perfect for what I had in mind. A large stone, with one side relatively flat. First, I intended to charge the stone with the purpose of absorbing negative energy. My next step would be to write a bindrune—a group of runes combined together in such a way that they created a design on the lodestone. The runes I selected would be those known for their powers of protection. I had a feeling I would need it.

The procedure would take a couple of hours. All I had to do was figure out a way to avoid Abby and Darci in the three-room cabin for two hours. And not raise their suspicions in the process. Easy, right?

I groaned and paced the small bedroom.

Drug them? Naw, that would be a bit severe, and I'd never drugged anyone before. It seemed kind of cold for my first attempt to be on my grandmother and my best friend. Send them on a wild goose chase? Where? Brainerd? Maybe I could enlist Rick's help?

The cordless phone was on the end table next to the couch. All I had to do was steal down the hall, reach around the corner, grab the phone, and make it back to my room. Undetected.

I peeked out the door of my bedroom and listened. I didn't hear any activity in the kitchen. Slipping out the door, I skulked down the short hallway toward the main room. The cabin was silent.

I felt like a teenager sneaking out of the house, while I tiptoed across the tile floor. Two more steps and I'd be within snatching distance of the phone.

The shrill ringing had me skittering and sliding all the way back to my room. From my position, with my back plastered against the door, I heard Abby answer on the fifth ring.

"Ophelia, it's Rick," she called.

Fate was smiling on me.

Composing my face, I opened the door a crack and took the phone from Abby. "Thanks."

"Ophelia—"

"Got to talk to Rick," I said with a bogus grin while pointing to the phone in my hand. "Hi, Rick."

"I know the last few days have been hard," he said, "and I think it would be good for the three of you to get away from the lake for the evening. How about joining me in Brainerd for a pizza?"

I mouthed a silent thank-you.

"Gee, Rick, I'm tired, but let me find Abby and Darci. I'm sure they'll be happy to meet you. Hang on."

Flying down the hall, I found them in the kitchen. "Rick wants to take everyone out for pizza. How about it?"

Darci gave me a stony look and turned her eyes to Abby, who nodded in agreement.

"Yeah Rick, they'd love to come," I told him, and wrote down the directions to the pizza parlor.

After a quick good-bye, I handed the slip of paper to Abby. "Here are the directions. Rick will meet you in a half an hour, so you'd better get going."

Abby's eyebrows knitted together in a frown. "Aren't you coming?"

"No, I'm tired. The last few days have gotten the best of me," I said with wide-eyed innocence. "The cabin feels so much better, I think I can get a good night's sleep tonight."

Abby walked over to me and laid a hand on my forehead. "You're not running a fever, are you?"

I stepped back from her touch, afraid of what my clever grandmother might pick up. "No, I'm fine. You and Darci go and have a good time." I gestured toward my bedroom. "If you don't mind, I think I'll take a look at those journals."

"Good for you. It's time you started studying them," she said with a pat on my arm. A look of pride crossed her face. "Those journals contain the history of our family, Ophelia. Every spell, every cure, what worked, what didn't. I recommend you start with my mother's. It's on my nightstand."

Abby's pleasure that I'd finally read those old books was apparent. And here I was lying about it. How rotten did I feel?

I stole a glance at Darci. She leaned against the counter and watched me with a steely look in her eye.

She wasn't buying it, but I knew I could trust her to keep her promise. She cared about Abby as much as I did, and she wouldn't risk Abby's safety by spilling what we knew about Von Schuler.

After they left, I checked the time. Twenty minutes to reach the restaurant, a good hour for dinner, and twenty minutes to get back to the lake. An hour and forty minutes. I had just enough time if I hurried.

I heard each second tick by as I rushed to make my preparations. After a purifying bath in sea salt, I grabbed my great-grandmother's journal and flipped through the worn pages, looking for the correct runes to carve on the lodestone to create the bindrune. They had to be exactly right or the spell wouldn't work. Finally, I found three that, when placed in a design, would not only be pleasing to the eye, but would give me the most protection.

One problem—how to carve them on the stone?

*Hadn't thought that far ahead, had you, Jensen?*

I ran to the kitchen, pulled out drawers, and dug through them until I found something sharp enough to mark the stone. My fingers hit on a piece of metal.

A nail. The pointy tip would be sharp enough to scratch the runes into the stone.

I snatched the nail and began to swiftly carve the symbols on the lodestone.

*Careful, Jensen, careful. The symbols must be made correctly.*

Taking a deep breath, I concentrated on making calm, deliberate strokes, and while I did, visualized a shield of energy reaching out from the lodestone to surround me. To protect me.

Twenty minutes later and I was finished. My eyes flew to the clock. How much time did I have before Abby and Darci returned?

Quickly, I added up the elapsed time in my head. *Yes.* I pumped my fist. *Thirty minutes to spare.* More than enough time to change and get down to the lake.

Finally, dressed in jeans and T-shirt, I was on the dock, hooking up the motor to the boat. My windbreaker lay in the bottom of the boat, and my lodestone, with the bindrune written on it, rested safely in the left pocket of my jeans. Even now, I could feel its energy circling around me. A flashlight and backpack were also in the boat.

The moon had been waxing for the last four days, and it gave enough light for me to see the opposite shore. I glanced over my shoulder as I prepared to cast off, and then I saw the light.

The hair on my arm stood up while I watched it bob and weave as it had four nights ago.

The ghost lights were back.

I fought down the fear creeping up from deep inside me. I thought about Tink, about Abby, about Darci. All could be at risk. Something, or someone, unknown prowled around the woods across the lake, and I couldn't fight it if I didn't know what it was.

I had to go.

Turning back to my task, I cast off the rope and stepped to the back of the boat. I took one last look at our cabin and almost fell overboard when two shapes stepped out of the shadows.

"You weren't planning on leaving without us, were you, Ophelia?" my stubborn grandmother asked.

# Thirty

I grabbed one of the pilings and scowled at Darci in the darkness. "Darci, you promised—"

"Darci didn't talk, Ophelia," Abby cut in as she and Darci made their way down to the fishing boat. "Do you think I didn't know you were up to something? The lodestone, the hustling back to your room? But I didn't think you'd be foolish enough to attempt going to the cabin by yourself."

In the dim light of the moon, I felt the weight of Abby's stare.

"When Rick mentioned at the restaurant that you'd learned of the magician's relationship to Juliet," she continued, "all the pieces fell together. I insisted Darci and I leave immediately. And then when you weren't in the cabin . . ." Her voiced trailed off. "By the way, you left the journal lying on the counter."

I exhaled a long breath. "I don't suppose you'd believe me if I told you I'm going night fishing?"

"No," Abby replied tersely.

I quickly filled her in on what had happened that afternoon in Brainerd.

"Ophelia Jensen," she said while she paced the

length of the dock, "of all the foolish tricks—attempting to take on whatever is in those woods by yourself."

"Abby, I'm prepared." I explained to her about the lodestone and the bindrune.

Mollified, she stopped her pacing and stood on the dock near the boat. "It's still not wise to go alone. I'm going with you."

Darci, who'd remained silent while Abby scolded me, stepped forward. "I'm going, too."

Abby and I exchanged looks in the moonlight. Abby gave a small nod.

This secret mission of mine was turning into quite a party.

I looked both of them over. Darci wore the shorts she'd worn earlier in the day, and Abby had on one of her long skirts. "I give up—you both can go with me, but you can't go dressed like that."

Abby threw an arm around Darci's shoulders and led her back to the steps leading to the cabin. "Let's go change. I expect you to still be here when we get back," she called over her shoulder.

"I will. Oh, and Darci, don't try and make a fashion statement. Jeans and tennis shoes will work," I said as they climbed the steps.

Ten minutes later they had returned and we were on our way across the lake. Both had changed into jeans and sensible shoes. Darci had shoved her blond hair under a baseball cap, and she carried a light jacket like mine. Abby held a sweater, my backpack, and a flashlight in her arms. The scent of lemon and something else hung around them.

Keeping my hand on the tiller, I leaned forward and sniffed. "Jeez, did you guys have garlic pizza, or what?" I wrinkled my nose.

"No." Darci reached in her pocket and drew out a small clove of garlic. Its scent filled the small boat.

"I don't believe this," I said in exasperation. "We're not hunting vampires, Darci."

Abby touched my knee lightly. "I gave the garlic to Darci. I have one for you, too." She handed me a clove. "There's a reason that the old tales mention garlic. It absorbs negative energy."

Without arguing, I stuck the clove in my pocket, next to the lodestone.

The closer we got to shore, the more I felt the apprehension building inside me. At home, Abby hiked through the woods all the time, but these woods were unfamiliar to her. When I'd stumbled onto the clearing, it had been full daylight and the cabin still hung in shadows. What would it be like in the middle of the night? What if Abby tripped and broke a bone? Was it too late to turn around?

Yes. My jaw clenched. Abby and Darci were determined to find out about the cabin, and there was nothing I could do to talk them out of it.

I eased the boat toward shore. Darci and I hopped out barefoot and pulled the bow far enough in that Abby could step out onto dry land. Slipping on my shoes and jacket, I swung the backpack to my shoulder and we were off, flashlights in hand. Our beams bounced through the trees as we climbed the hill.

At the top, I stopped to get my bearings. Once sure I knew my directions, I pointed to my right and we began our hike. Darci walked on one side of Abby, and I on the other, ready to reach out if she so much as faltered.

In the half-light of the moon, I saw Abby's smile. "Girls, I'm not decrepit, you know."

I touched the sleeve of her sweater. "Humor me, okay."

Walking in silence, I concentrated on leading us through the trees. I was relieved when our flashlight beams caught something shiny in the distance. The wire fence was directly ahead, its hole visible.

Reaching the hole, I held the wire back while Darci scrambled through and then helped Abby from the other side. I tossed my backpack through the hole and joined them.

"The cabin's this way," I said, pointing my flashlight through the trees.

While we walked, the darkness became more complete as the tall pines thickened, hiding the moon. The air around us was totally still, and a sense of something waiting just beyond our wavering lights came over me. My eyes traveled to Abby, walking beside me.

"Yes," she said, her voice hushed. "I feel it, too."

"Wait." Darci halted suddenly. "Is that the cabin?" she asked, moving her flashlight in a wide arc ahead of us.

The light reflected back at us from one of the broken panes of glass.

She took a step forward, but Abby stopped her.

"Slowly, Darci." She turned toward me. "Ophelia, how close were you to the cabin when you found the circle of cedar?"

"About fifty feet."

"Hmm, it's so dark, it's hard to judge the distance," Abby said.

Remembering the zap I received when I tried to cross the circle of cedar, I glanced at Abby. "You'll feel it when you touch it."

Abby stiffened her spine. "Let's go."

Side by side, the three of us approached the cabin, one small step at a time. I noticed the beam of Darci's flashlight trembling on the ground in front of us, shaking like the hand that held it.

I didn't blame her. My fear churned inside me, too. The only one who radiated calm was Abby. I felt her energy expand until it seemed to wrap both Darci and me in a protective circle.

Without warning, Abby's hands shot out and pulled the both of us back.

She released us and extended her hand. "Right here."

I closed my eyes and tried to feel what lay in wait on the other side of Walks Quietly's circle. Again I detected the smell of rotting things, but this time the scent of garlic seemed to overpower the odor.

Grasping our hands, Abby looked first at Darci, then at me, before returning her gaze to the center of the clearing. "We're going to step over the circle, but we don't have a lot of time to reach the cabin. We'll need to move fast. Ophelia, when we're inside, lay out everything I've brought in your backpack. Darci, you hold the flashlights."

"O-Okay," Darci stuttered.

Abby cocked her head at a defiant angle, and giving our hands a quick squeeze, urged us forward.

Together we rushed across the clearing. Through the fabric of my jeans, I felt the lodestone grow warmer and warmer with each step I took. Abby's energy surrounded us like a bubble, but from beyond the protective layer, the darkness swirled in an evil cloud.

We hurried up the broken steps and through the crooked door. Stopping just inside, Darci and I quickly scanned the room with our flashlights. The wooden floor was missing several boards, exposing the ground beneath the cabin.

I released Abby's hand and gave my flashlight to Darci. Stepping over the holes in the floor, I crossed to the center of the room and emptied the backpack on an old table sitting there.

Darci and Abby followed. And so did the cloud.

Abby snatched a pouch from the table and scattered the contents around the room as if she were sowing seeds. She crossed to the door and laid a thick layer down at the threshold.

Without being told, I lit the two black candles Abby had brought. The wicks sputtered and popped before the flame finally flared to life. Picking them up, I placed them at both ends of the table.

As I did, the darkness that I'd felt chase us across the clearing grew smaller and smaller in the light of the candles. It sank like a heavy mist and receded out the door.

I exhaled the breath that I didn't know I'd been holding.

Looking over at Darci, I gave her a weak smile. "You did good, Darce."

In slow motion her knees gave out and she sank to the floor.

Abby was at her side in an instant, and crouching down next to her, she took both of Darci's hands in hers. "Are you all right?"

"I—I think so." She rested her forehead on Abby's shoulder. "I don't think I've ever been so scared in all my life."

Abby stroked her back. "We're safe for the time being, but we can't linger. Whatever that thing is, I haven't banished it. It's still sneaking around somewhere—"

Releasing Abby, Darci jumped to her feet. "What do you want us to do?"

"Look around. See what we can find," I answered. Making a slow circle, I scanned the room.

Two doorways were to my right. Both had curtains hung across them. I walked over to the first and pulled the curtain back to look inside. "Darci, bring me a flashlight, will you?" I called over my shoulder.

After she handed it to me, I shone the light around the room. It was empty.

I wandered into the next room. The beam of the flashlight revealed a rusted metal-frame bed sitting in the middle of the small room. Covering the mattress was a tattered blanket. The floor was littered with what appeared to be food scraps. A bundle lay in one corner.

I disappeared inside the room and returned holding the bundle—a fatigue jacket. "Hey, will you look at this," I said, shaking the jacket out.

Darci and Abby were crouched over one of holes in the floor. They both looked up when I called out.

Darci squinted in the dim light to see what I held in my hands. "Duane Hobbs wore a jacket like that."

"I know." I stuck my hand in the pocket, hoping to find some ID, but all I came up with was a can of tobacco and a half-chewed toothpick.

"What if it is Duane's? Is there any blood on it?" she asked.

"Yuck." I held the jacket as far away from me as possible and peered at it in the candlelight. "Nope, I don't see any."

"Maybe it's not Duane's," she said with a shrug. "But look at this. Someone has ripped up these boards on purpose." She held up a crowbar. "Abby found this laying by the stove."

"Someone is looking for something?" I asked.

Abby pursed her lips and nodded. "I think so."

"Duane?"

"Hard to say, but I'm more interested in *what* they're looking for. Something Frederick Von Schuler left behind?" Abby held her wrist in front of her face and examined her watch. "It's late. Whatever dwells in this clearing will gather strength after midnight. We need to leave. Now."

# Thirty-one

Abby didn't have to say it twice. Darci and I flew around the room, extinguishing candles and loading everything into the backpack. I shoved the fatigue jacket in the bottom.

The three of us paused at the door, and I felt again Abby's energy circle us. We took a step onto the rickety porch.

The presence of whatever had chased us across the clearing was no longer there, but we didn't waste time wondering why. We dashed over the ground and across the circle of cedar.

Abby took the backpack from my shoulder and quickly removed her sea salt. Starting at the northernmost point of the clearing, she walked in a clockwise direction and poured a thin layer of salt next to the cedar. Finished, she returned the salt to the bag.

"One last thing—there should be a plastic bag in the front pocket of the backpack. Will you please hand it to me?"

When I did, she opened the bag and held it out. "Drop your cloves of garlic and the lodestones in here."

"What? Toxic waste?" I plunked my stone in the bag.

"Yes. The lodestones and garlic are full of negative energy now." Abby passed a hand in front of her eyes, and in the glow of the flashlight, I saw her sag.

I grasped her arm and steadied her. "We need to get you back to the cabin."

Darci clasped Abby's other arm, and we returned to the boat. Within twenty minutes we were safely back in the cabin.

I insisted Abby go straight to bed, and for a change I took care of her. Armed with a tray of hot lemon tea and lavender oil, I knocked on her door.

She sat propped up on her pillows, a journal lying across her lap, when I walked into the room. The soft light of the bedside lamp illuminated the weariness on her face. Scooting over, she patted a spot next to her.

"What have you got there?"

I placed the tray on the nightstand and handed her the mug. "Lemon tea and lavender oil. I thought the oil might help recharge you."

Abby handed the mug back to me and shook out a couple of drops of oil in her palm. Immediately, the room filled with the sweet scent of lavender. After spreading the oil on her fingers, she massaged her temples. The fatigue in her face faded, and with a sigh, she eased back on her pillows.

"That's lovely, dear. Thank you."

I tucked the blankets around her. "You're welcome." My face tightened with concern. "Are you going to be okay?"

"Yes. I'll be fine. An experience like tonight is very draining." Her eyelids drifted shut.

I leaned forward and kissed her forehead. "I'm leaving now. Get some rest."

Her eyes shot open. "Wait. What are we going to do about Tink?"

"Abby, I don't think we can do anything about her," I said with a frown. "The Finches are her legal guardians."

She stroked the end of the braid hanging over her shoulder. "Living at the compound is not good for her."

Sitting back, I studied her. "You think the Finches are behind this?"

"Or Winnie."

"You agree with Darci?" I gave her a skeptical look. "I don't think Winnie's clever enough."

She tilted her head and watched me with amusement. "It doesn't take cleverness to make up a spell." The humor fell away. "But it does take wisdom to use the spell correctly."

"And the person behind this isn't wise?"

"No." Abby's whole body stiffened with irritation. "To use magick without proper understanding is anything but wise. It's foolhardy and dangerous."

"Yeah." I picked up the journal from her lap and ran my hand over its worn cover. "Just ask Frederick Von Schuler. He didn't understand, and messed with forces he couldn't control. He lost his mind as a result."

As I stroked the journal, Abby laid her hand on mine. "That's why each woman in our family kept her own journal—to record her journey down the right path."

A chill seemed to creep into the room. But what if someone chose the wrong path? Would that journey be recorded, too?

\* \* \*

I watched the sun rise over the lake from my bedroom window. My bed had not been slept in. I'd spent the entire night adding up what I knew, but coming up with the wrong answer. I knew Jason admired Frederick Von Schuler. I knew Von Schuler had chosen to engage in the black arts and went mad. His tortured soul had spent his last days in that wretched cabin. I also knew, after listening to Abby speak with pride about our family's journals, that Frederick Von Schuler had a journal, too. He would have wanted to chart his course on his path to unlimited power.

I slapped my forehead in frustration. For a psychic, I couldn't be much denser. All along, the clues were there. My dreams had repeatedly shown me a book, but I had ignored them. The runes had foretold finding magic, and I had—black magic.

Abby and I had come to search for a lost girl who'd never belonged, and we'd found one, but it was the wrong girl. What were we going to do to help Tink? Abby was worried. So was I. But the Finches were her family, and we had no proof they were involved in anything illegal. There was no reason for us to become involved in Tink's life.

I'd always heard curiosity killed the cat, but I needed to look around the area near the cabin. I wouldn't be stupid enough to visit the clearing again until I was better prepared, but maybe something in the woods would give me an idea of what I was dealing with.

After throwing on jeans and a T-shirt, I slipped past Queenie and Lady and out of the cabin without alerting anyone. In no time at all I was in the fishing boat and on my way across the lake.

In the early morning light, a mist hung like a shroud along the shoreline, and the only sound was the low hum of the fishing boat's electric motor. The air around me seemed thick and heavy and carried the promise of a day hotter than the one before.

Banking the boat as I had last time, I got out and looked around. The last time I headed east, I had walked to the clearing with the abandoned cabin, so this time I'd head west, staying close to the shoreline. I hadn't walked far when I noticed a heap of brush at the water's edge. The branches seemed to be piled in a systematic order. I moved closer to investigate. Setting the top branch aside, I found the curved bow of a canoe.

Someone had a boat stashed at the water's edge.

Removing the rest of the branches, I flipped the boat over, and the owner of the canoe became obvious. Tink. A small life jacket lay under it.

I fisted my hands on my hips and looked around. I was standing at a point where the shore jutted out. Directly across from where I stood, the land projected out on that side, too, causing the lake to form a wide channel. Wouldn't take long at all to paddle across the lake at that spot. I scanned the opposite shore until I found what I was looking for. A familiar plume of smoke floating above the pine trees. Smoke from Walks Quietly's cabin.

Now I knew one of the ways Tink managed to escape from underneath the watchful eye of her aunt and uncle.

I flipped the canoe back over and covered it up. Tink would never know that I'd found one of her secrets.

I'd finished covering the boat when the breeze moving through the pines carried the sound of a human voice.

Tink singing one of her songs?

But the voice wasn't Tink's. I followed the sound up the hill, away from the lake and through the pines.

In a small clearing, with her back toward me, Winnie crouched in front of a fire ringed with stones. From where I stood hidden in the trees, I couldn't make out her words, but she repeated them over and over in a singsong voice. And as she did, she threw something into the fire.

What do you know? Winnie was doing a little dabbling on her own. Should I confront her, or move away undetected?

The decision was made for me when I took a step away from the tree and stepped on a stick. The sound of it breaking echoed in the quiet. In an instant Winnie was on her feet and staring right at me.

"What are you doing spying on me?" she demanded without a preamble.

Spying? Gee, I seemed to be getting accused of that a lot lately.

"Hi, Winnie." I plastered a pleasant expression on my face. "I didn't mean to disturb you."

Winnie crouched down in front of the fire and began shoving things into a canvas sack. "Why don't you go away and leave us alone? You've brought nothing but trouble."

I walked closer to the fire and peered over her shoulder, trying to make out what she was putting in her bag.

Her head whipped toward me and she hunched forward, blocking my view. She scooped up what was left and dumped it all in the bag.

"How have Abby and I caused you problems, Winnie?"

She stood abruptly and, with her eyes full of anger, watched me. "You just have, that's all. Ever since you showed up, Juliet and Jason have been upset. You've disturbed our peace." She took a step toward me. "Jason is an extraordinary man, and you're interfering with his work." As she talked, her face became mottled with angry red spots. "You have no right. No right."

Backing up a few paces, I tried to sound reasonable. "How have we interfered, Winnie?"

Behind her glasses her small eyes narrowed into slits. She opened her mouth to speak, but then snapped her jaw shut. Without another word she spun on her heel, grabbed her sack, and marched away.

Brilliant, Jensen, I thought. My interrogation skills left a lot to be desired and I'd blown my chance to corner Winnie. *What do I do now?*

I lifted my head and looked around the clearing. Glancing down, I saw that Winnie's fire still smoldered. Faint curls of smoke slithered from whatever Winnie had thrown on the burning sticks. Stepping closer, I took a deep breath. Basil, an herb used to either banish what you don't want or draw what you do want. Now why would she be using basil? And in this spot?

My eyes scanned the clearing for a clue. A low row of juniper grew at the top of a slight rise beyond Winnie's campfire. Blue, almost purple berries hung in clusters from the branches. On all except one. It was in the center of the row, and the needles were brown and brittle, a sharp contrast from the rich green foliage of the rest of the bushes.

I waded through the hedge till I reached the dead bush. Bending down, I saw exposed roots where the dirt had sunk in a deep indentation around the trunk of the bush. I picked up a stick and started to probe the hole.

"Sneaking off again?" said a voice from behind me. Jumping to my feet, I whirled around.

Darci—with her arms crossed and looking none too pleased with me.

## Thirty-two

"How did you find me?" I said, standing.

"Walks Quietly's boat," she said, and started off down the hill. "Abby sent me. We need you back at the cabin. Tink's missing."

I rushed after her. "What do you mean, Tink's missing?"

"Walks Quietly found a message under a rock by his front door this morning," she said over her shoulder. "Evidently, Tink had been there, and when she couldn't find him, she used some paper from his cabin to leave a note. She wanted him to meet her down by the lake. But when he reached the lake, she wasn't there. He found her bicycle in the woods across from our cabin—"

"She'd stopped by our place?"

At the bottom of the hill, Darci looked over at me from where she'd moored the boat right next to mine. "We don't know. Neither Abby or I heard her." She untied the boat. "What about you?"

"No," I said, untying mine. "I was up at first light and came over here."

Darci pushed the boat away from shore and stepped

into it. "Well, Abby and Walks Quietly can fill you in when we get to his cabin. Abby's there."

I followed Darci across the lake to Walks Quietly's dock. Once there, we docked both boats and headed up the hill to his cabin.

Walks Quietly's little cabin consisted of one main room with two bedrooms in the back. Rough-hewn stairs to the left led to a loft above the main room. A cook stove, much like Abby's, stood along one wall, near a planked table. The remains of his breakfast still sat there.

"What's going on?" I said as Darci and I entered the room.

Abby stood quietly in the room, and Walks Quietly stopped his pacing and began to remove the dishes from the table. "I had troubled dreams last night, so I went to the sweat lodge at daybreak to find guidance." His face tightened in a frown. "But I learned nothing. Tink must have come while I was in the sweat lodge." He picked up a piece of paper lying on the table and handed it to me. "I found this on the porch, under a rock."

I read the note quickly. It was as Darci had told me. Tink had wanted him to meet her down by the lake. No reason given, just that she had something important to tell him.

I noticed the jagged edge on the pad of paper. "She came in the cabin to write this?"

"Yes." Walks Quietly moved to the old sink and began rinsing the plate and silverware. "Tink never comes in the cabin. We always have our talks by the lake, even in the winter."

I turned to Abby. "What do you think?"

She shrugged.

"Darci said you found her bike in the woods," I said to Walks Quietly. "Has anyone talked to the Finches?"

"Of course. I went to the compound after I found her bicycle, but no one was there." He turned away from the counter. "The place is deserted, empty."

"It can't be," I said, confused. "I saw Winnie in a clearing directly across from here on the other side of the lake."

"I tell you, the place was deserted."

"Should we call the sheriff?" Darci piped in.

"And tell them what, dear?" Abby asked.

Darci pulled out a chair and plopped down. "I don't know."

"Has anyone called Rick?" I asked.

"I did," Abby replied. "But he wasn't in his room. I left a message for him to come to the lake as soon as he gets back."

I turned toward the door. "I'm going to the Finches. Someone has to be there."

Darci sprang from her chair. "I'm going, too."

"Darci—" I stopped. One look at her face told me I'd be wasting my time arguing. "Okay, let's go." I glanced over my shoulder at Abby. "You stay here and wait for Rick."

Fifteen minutes later Darci and I stood on the Finches' porch, knocking at the door.

"Walks Quietly was right. No one's here," Darci whispered.

I arched an eyebrow. "Why are you whispering?"

She rubbed her arms. "It's so quiet here that it's spooky. Don't you feel it?"

She was right. The air was totally still, and a feeling of abandonment hung over the place.

Turning the knob, I found the door unlocked.

Opening it and sticking my head in, I called out, "Hello. Anyone home?"

Silence was the answer.

"Let's go in," Darci said, pushing passed me.

"Wait a second." I made a move to grab her arm but missed. "We can't go barging into someone else's house."

"Yes we can." She was already down the hall.

Following her in, we did a quick search of the rooms downstairs. Nothing. It did look like the Finches had left. Even Juliet's loom was gone from its spot by the windows.

"Do you suppose that's what Tink wanted to tell Walks Quietly? That they were leaving?" Darci asked from the middle of the room.

"Maybe." My eyes traveled the empty room. "Let's go outside and look around."

We went back out the way we came, carefully shutting the door behind us. We had rounded the corner of the house when I saw Winnie, with her head down, scurrying up the hill from the boathouse. In her arms she carried a bundle of what looked like clothes.

I grabbed Darci's arm and pulled her behind a tree. Putting a finger to my lips, we hid while Winnie hurried by. Once she reached the top of the hill, I motioned toward the boathouse. Like a couple of characters out of a spy novel, Darci and I moved from tree to tree until we'd reached the building. We dashed around the corner and were finally out of sight of the main house.

Leaning against the boathouse, I took a deep breath and exhaled slowly. "Made it," I said in whisper.

"Winnie sure seemed anxious to get away from here, didn't she?" Darci asked.

"Yeah." My eyes slid toward Darci. "Let's see why."

We climbed the rickety steps leading to the upper story. I tested the wooden door. Unlocked. Swinging it open, we stepped inside the room.

Cardboard boxes were stacked everywhere, and an old cot was shoved against one wall. Next to the cot was a large, black-lacquered box, taller than I was and wide enough for two people, wrapped in chains.

"Darci," I said, crossing over to it. "This must be one of Jason's props. And look, the padlock isn't shut."

Darci joined me while I removed the lock and let the chains drop to the floor. Turning the small knob, I let the door swing open.

"Whoa, what *is* that smell?" I pinched my nose to block the pungent aroma that filled the room.

"This," Darci said, reaching inside the box and pulling out a ratty blanket. "Gosh, it smells like somebody died in there . . ." Her eyes widened as she stared at me. "You don't suppose—"

"Brandi?"

"I told you to go away, but you wouldn't listen," said a voice from across the room. "Now I have to punish you."

Darci and I whirled to see Winnie standing in the center of the room.

Strands of hair straggled around her face, and her eyes darted back and forth between Darci and me. In her shaking hand she held a gun, its barrel waving wildly.

Panic fought with fear inside me. I could see Winnie's finger tremble on the trigger. Any second the gun could go off. Maybe we could make a run for it. But Winnie blocked our way to the open door.

I hooked Darci's arm and edged sideways, pulling her with me. "Winnie, put that gun down. You might shoot someone," I said with false bravado.

Her mouth twisted in a snide grin while she kept the barrel trained on us. "That's the point, isn't it?"

The blanket slipped from Darci's limp hands, and she clutched my arm. "Ophelia." Her voice was tight with fear.

I ignored her and took another step to the side.

Winnie grabbed the gun with both hands and motioned with the barrel toward the box. "Get back over there."

I released Darci's arm and held up my hands in surrender. We moved until we were in front of the box again.

"Get inside."

I glanced over my shoulder at the dark interior and shuddered.

"Go on," Winnie said, drawing my attention back to her.

"You don't want to do this," I pleaded. "I know Jason is looking for Von Schuler's book. The book is evil, Winnie. You have to get away from him. We can help you."

Winnie seemed to sag, and the barrel of the gun dropped.

I took a step forward, but she stiffened and brought the gun up sharply.

"You don't understand. I can't leave. I have to do what they want." Her chin jutted out. "And you're too late. We found the book. You led us right to it. It was buried under the bush you were digging at this morning." The gun quivered. "Now get in the box."

Betting my will was stronger than hers, I crossed my arms and glared at her. "No."

Wrong bet.

The gun stopped shaking, and Winnie's pudgy face

filled with determination. "Either get in the box or I'll shoot you both."

What a choice—in the box or die. I picked in the box.

Grasping Darci's arm, I pulled her in with me.

In an instant Winnie crossed the room and shut the door, extinguishing all light. From inside I heard the clank of chains as she wrapped them around the outside. The last sound was the tiny click of the padlock closing.

Seconds ticked by in silence while I pondered what to do next. Not like I had a lot of choices. We were shut inside a box, in total darkness. Nothing to do but wait.

"I don't feel so good," Darci moaned in the darkness.

I waved my hand until it came in contact with something solid. Darci.

"You can't get sick," I said, shaking her arm. "It smells bad enough in here."

My hand lost contact as I felt Darci slide to the bottom of the trunk. I inched my way down until I was kneeling next to her. "Take deep breaths and put your head between your knees."

The sound of Darci's deep breathing filled the darkness. Suddenly, the sound stopped.

"What if we run out of oxygen?" Darci asked in a voice full of panic.

"We won't. This isn't airtight." I found Darci's shoulder and patted it. "We'll be rescued. Abby will turn this place upside down to find us."

"Can you reach her, umm, you know, 'mentally'?"

"I can try."

I sat back and leaned against the side of the box. Closing my eyes, I tried to picture Abby's face. Silver hair, green eyes full of worry at our disappearance—once I had the image fixed in my mind, I concentrated on where we were. Dark, alone. My eyes shot open.

That's what Abby had said when she looked at Brandi's pictures. While I was having dinner with the Finches, Brandi had been just a short distance away—shut inside this box.

The thought sickened me.

"Anything?" Darci asked.

"No." I patted her knee. "Don't worry. They'll find us."

Darci's breathing became rapid. "We're going to die in this stupid box."

Dang, she was hyperventilating.

An idea popped in my head. "Darci, you believe I'm psychic, don't you?"

"Well, yeah," she gasped. "Sometimes I wonder how good you are, though."

*You and me both.*

"Okay, since I'm psychic, I should be able to tell your future, right?" I said, trying to sound confident.

Her breathing slowed. "Right."

I found Darci's hand in the darkness and placed my other hand on top. Nervous sweat dampened my palms. What if I didn't see anything? Would that mean we were both going to die?

I shook my head. Darci was going to get a positive reading even if I had to make something up.

Slowly, images began to appear in rapid succession behind my closed eyes. I saw Darci standing before a crowd of people. Everyone was smiling and nodding their heads in approval as they watched a man in a suit hand Darci a plaque. Darci, with a radiant look on her face, shook the man's hand. When she did, the crowd clapped with enthusiasm.

Darci's hand clenched mine. "What do you see?"

"You're going to win some kind of award," I said, opening my eyes. "And the whole town will be there, cheering you on."

She snorted. "Yeah, sure. Everyone in Summerset thinks I'm an airhead."

"But I know you're not." I squeezed her fingers. "Really, Darci, something's going to happen, and you're going to receive the recognition you deserve."

"That would be nice," she said in a small voice. "I get tired of people thinking I'm stupid."

I released her hand. "Do you feel better now?"

"Yeah, except—" She cleared her throat, and I felt her squirm. "I drank too much tea this morning."

"Oh God, Darci," I groaned. "Not now."

# Thirty-three

"I can't help it. I—"

A sound in the room outside caught my attention. "Shh." I cocked my head and listened. I heard it again. "Do you hear that?"

"Hear what—"

We both jumped when we heard the clatter of chains hitting the floor outside the box.

I sprang to my feet and shoved the door. It swung open easily, and the darkness was filled with blessed light. Shielding my eyes from the sudden brightness, I pulled Darci to her feet and turned to the door in time to see Walks Quietly move toward the boathouse door, a large gray dog at his side.

Scrambling from the box, I tripped and fell face first on the dusty floor. "Wait," I called after him, but he didn't turn around. In a moment he was gone.

"Did you see that?" I asked Darci as I scrambled to my feet.

"What?"

"There!" I pointed at the door. "Walks Quietly."

"Who cares who opened the door?" She tugged on my arm. "Let's get out of here."

We rushed out of the boathouse and had made it to the bottom of the steps when I heard my name called. My eyes flew to the top of the hill, where Abby stood with Rick next to her. Relief flooded through me.

Darci and I ran up the hill to the main house, and I threw my arms around Abby.

"Brandi was here the whole time, in a box, in the boathouse." The words poured out of me. "We have to stop Jason. He's going to use Von Schuler's spells. They've found the book—"

"Slow down," Rick said gently. "Do you know where Brandi is now?"

I turned away from Abby. "No, I don't know what Jason did to her, but I bet we can find him at the abandoned cabin. I don't know about Juliet or Tink. Maybe he did something to them, too." I clutched Abby's sleeve. "Where's Walks Quietly?"

A perplexed look crossed her face. "Walks Quietly?"

"Yeah." I pointed down the hill. "He was—"

"Hey," Rick said, looking around. "Where did Darci go?"

"I'm right here," she said, walking toward us from the house. Her cheeks were tinged a faint pink.

Abby stepped away from me and looked up at the sky. "If we're going to the cabin, we'd better get going."

My eyes followed hers to the clouds above. Great dark thunderclouds tumbled against one another, and in the distance I saw a flash of lightning. If we didn't hurry, we'd be caught in a downpour.

"Which way is the cabin?" Rick called over his shoulder as his long strides put distance between us.

"To the east," I yelled after him. "But shouldn't we call the sheriff?"

"The phones in the house don't work," Abby replied as she trailed after Rick. "We've already tried."

I caught up with her. "What about cell phones?"

Rick pivoted. "No service, and we don't have time to drive back to your cabin."

"You said Jason has the spell book," Abby said without breaking stride. "If we don't stop him—" She shook her head. "What's been held at bay all these years in that clearing is nothing compared to what he could unleash if he uses the book. He doesn't have the skill to control it."

I shivered. "Do we?"

Abby's eyes hardened with determination. "We'll find out." She drew two pouches from her pocket, and as we walked, handed one to me and then the other to Darci. "Put these on. Walks Quietly gave them to me."

The pouches were made of supple leather and hung from a thin strip of rawhide. I slipped the talisman over my head and tucked it beneath my T-shirt. As I did, I felt the energy radiate from within the leather sack. Whatever the sack contained, I sensed its power. It expanded until the force seemed to settle around me like a cloak.

Between Walks Quietly's medicine and Abby's magick, the four of us should be safe. I hoped.

Our pace quickened as we neared the clearing. The storm was drawing closer, and a sense of urgency hung in the air. Tiny beads of sweat, either from nerves or from the heat, gathered on my lip. I wiped them away.

"You okay?" Darci asked.

I gave her a shaky smile and patted the hidden pouch. "We'll be fine."

Abby put a finger to her mouth to silence us. We had reached the circle of cedar ringing the cabin.

From our vantage point at the edge of the clearing, we could see the flickering light of candles shining through the broken panes. A figure moved in and out of the light, but we were too far away to see who it was.

Rick motioned for Darci and me to move to the opposite side of the clearing and pointed to the porch.

*Got it.* Darci and I would approach from one side of the porch, while he and Abby came in from the other side.

I nodded and took the position Rick had indicated.

He gave us a signal, and with a deep breath, I stepped across the cedar.

Nothing. Nothing swirled around us with dark intensity like the last time. Were we too late? Had the evil already taken up residence in the cabin?

Slowly, the four of us stole across the clearing and up onto the porch. I crouched and peeked into a window.

Black candles with strange signs carved on them lit the room. And in their flickering light I saw someone hunkered down in the corner. The glow of the candles made the dirty orange hair shine dully. Brandi—we'd finally found her.

Another figure, in a black robe, stood before the table. A figure whose face was hidden by the deep folds of the hood covering their head, just like in my dream. Only this time I knew it was Jason's face beneath the hood. And in his hands he held Von Schuler's book.

The other figure from my dream was there, too. Tink, dressed in white, lay stretched out on the table. Bowls of smoking incense burned at her head and feet, filling the air with billows of smoke.

Winnie was nowhere to be seen.

Rick caught my eye from his side of the porch and held up one finger. With a shrug, I nodded. He moved slowly to the door. Darci and I gathered behind him. With a kick, he forced the door open, and we surged through.

Jason dropped the book and whipped his head toward the opposite corner of the room, where Winnie sat huddled with the gun lying at her side.

*Whoops—I forgot to tell Rick about the gun.*

But before Winnie could grab it, Rick launched himself toward her, rolled, and came to his feet, gun in hand.

Jason's whole body shook with rage, and with a jerk he turned toward the three of us still standing in the doorway. And as he did, his hood fell back, revealing an angular face with hazel eyes. It wasn't Jason after all. It was Juliet.

With a howl, she bent and scrambled on the dirty floor until she found what she was looking for. She righted herself and stood, holding the book, now open, tightly in her hands. In a voice tinged with madness, strange words came rushing from her lips.

Lightning flashed outside the windows, and for an instant the cabin was as bright as midday as the walls shook with the explosion of thunder. Winnie let out a shriek, while the rest of us stood transfixed, unable to move. The smell of ozone thickened the air.

Tink seemed to be the only one capable of movement, and she rolled her head toward the three of us planted in the middle of the room. Tears ran down her cheeks, but her body seemed to glow in the shadowy light.

*Yes. She's shielding, as Abby taught her.*

The lightning blazed again, and in the instant of light, I saw a murky mist gather in the corner behind Juliet. Long tendrils snaked out and wove their way toward where Tink lay vulnerable on the table. Fingers of black curled around the table legs, inching closer and closer to Tink. One thin wisp drifted toward the light she emanated, poking and prodding as if testing the strength of Tink's shield.

Tink felt the evil, and her face screwed in concentration while she fought to keep the black cloud at bay.

*Do something! Do something!* A voice inside my head screeched, but I couldn't move. Helplessly, my eyes sought Abby.

Standing next to Darci, her head was bowed as she tried to send some of her strength to Tink. I felt it pulsing in the air around us, but it couldn't make it past the barrier of darkness that threatened to surround Tink.

The thunder roared again, and a voice called out, "Juliet, stop!"

Jason stood in the open doorway, his face a map of sorrow.

Juliet raised her eyes from the book, and the cloud ebbed. For a second her eyes lost their madness and her face softened. But the cloud surged and the madness flared in her eyes again.

"Jason, I have to do this. It's my destiny," Juliet said in a wheedling voice.

Jason took measured steps toward the table. "No," he replied calmly.

Her eyes widened and her voice dropped almost to a whisper. "Think of it, my love, unlimited power." Her gaze fell on Tink. "We can use her. We can channel the power through her."

Jason inched closer to Juliet. "Frederick went mad."

A sly smile brightened her face. "I won't go mad. Frederick didn't understand the power and how to control it, but I do." Her smile fell away. "I tried to explain this to Miranda, too. She laughed at me. Told me I was insane. Wouldn't use her gift to help me." A faraway expression filled her eyes, and she pulled the book close to her heart. "It's not my fault she fell down the stairs."

*Oh my God, she killed Tink's mother, and then blamed it on Tink.*

Lightning flared again, and the sky opened, sending torrents of water, each drop sounding like pebbles hitting the roof. Jason used the sudden distraction to make a grab for Juliet.

Startled, she raised her hands to push him away, and the book fell with a thud to the floor. She struggled against him while he fought to control her. And all the while, fed by the conflict and Juliet's fury, the dark mist swirled at their feet.

As if released from bonds, I took a step toward Tink, but Abby motioned for me to help Brandi. Darci and I rushed to the corner and hauled the half out of it girl to her feet, while Abby helped Tink.

At the same time, Rick jerked Winnie up and urged her out the door.

After both Brandi and Winnie were safe, away from the cabin, I rushed back to help Abby. As I ran toward the cabin, I thought I saw a shadow move swiftly through the trees on the other side. Not pausing to look, I flung myself through the door.

The black cloud had almost completely engulfed the struggling couple, but Abby had freed Tink and was helping her off the table when it happened:

Their struggles had tipped one of the candles over, and a thin line of fire twisted its way across the old wooden table. Busy helping Tink, Abby didn't see the flame rushing toward her. I watched in horror as the fire caught the tail of the shirt Abby wore over her jeans, igniting it.

"Abby!" I hurled myself at them.

Before I could help her, Tink began beating the flames out with her bare hands.

I ripped the shirt off Abby and flung it, still smoldering, to the floor, and with an arm around both Tink and Abby, I guided them to the door and out into the rain.

Rick and Darci had moved Brandi and Winnie over to the shelter of trees, but when he saw me emerge from the cabin, he ran to me and scooped Tink up in his arms.

As he set Tink on the ground, I eased Abby down next to Darci and Brandi. Crouching, I studied her face. "Are you all right?"

"I'm fine—a little singed. The shirt was heavy, and Tink got the flames out before they burned through." She scooted away from me and over to Tink. Gathering the girl in her arms, she rocked her slowly back and forth, crooning.

Tink's ragged coughs echoed with the thunder.

A sudden crash drew our attention.

The old cabin was going up like a torch, and part of the roof had already fallen in. Through the flames, we watched Jason stagger out of the cabin with Juliet over his shoulder.

Rick ran to them and helped the couple to a spot under the trees.

Then a howl rent the air, and the old cabin collapsed, sending sparks into the sky.

Again I saw the shadow by the trees. I nudged Darci and pointed to them.

In the illumination of the burning cabin, Walks Quietly stood just outside the circle of cedar. Motionless at his side was a wolf, its eyes glowing in the half-light. A badger growled at Walks Quietly's feet. And on his arm perched a snow owl.

"Humph," I grunted. "Now he shows up to help."

A confused expression crossed Darci's face. "Who?"

"Walks Quietly," I said, pointing back to the spot by the trees.

Darci's eyes traveled to where I pointed. "I think you better have a doctor check you out once we get out of here." She shook her head. "You must have inhaled too much smoke."

"Look," I said, and waved my arm toward Walks Quietly. "He's standing right there. He's got a wolf, a badger, and a snow owl with him."

Darci took my hand and squeezed it. "You'll be okay. You've been under a lot of stress lately." She stood and looked down at me. "Ophelia, I hate to tell you, but there's no one there."

I watched in disbelief as Walks Quietly smiled and raised a hand in farewell. Then he disappeared like a puff of smoke.

# *Thirty-four*

"Okay, let me get this straight." I glanced over at Rick. "Juliet was behind all of this the whole time?"

Darci, Abby, Rick, and I had stepped out of Tink's room while the doctor checked her over. We sat in the waiting room, drinking what seemed our tenth cup of coffee. The sheriff had already taken our statements, and Brandi's grateful parents had arrived. After spending the night at the hospital with Tink, I felt punchy and unable to comprehend the simplest of ideas. And God only knew, there had been nothing simple about the past few days.

"That's right. She held Brandi down in the boathouse, with the help of Winnie. Where, by the way, the sheriff found an axe with blood on it and some hair. They won't know for sure until the forensics comes back, but they're reasonably certain the axe was used to kill Duane Hobbs."

"Juliet?"

He nodded. "Walks Quietly identified the axe as his. My guess is Juliet stole it and intended to frame him for it, but things happened too fast. She didn't have time."

"Will they get fingerprints?" I asked.

"Sure."

"And she killed her sister?"

"Yeah. Tink still doesn't remember that day clearly, but Jason has already talked to the sheriff about it. They're going to reopen the investigation into the fire that killed Violet, and Mona, too."

My mouth dropped open. "You're kidding me."

"Nope." Rick scratched his beard. "The arson investigator always thought there was something not quite right about the fire, but couldn't prove anything."

"But now they can?" I asked.

"Maybe. It's been a long time. We'll see." Rick let his head fall back against the couch. "Even if they don't, Juliet's going to be locked away for a long time. Either in a mental institution or prison," he said, and closed his eyes.

I zeroed in on Abby. "What do you think her plans for Brandi were?"

"Human sacrifice—"

Darci made a gargled sound.

"Afraid so," she said, tucking a strand of hair behind her ear. "Evil demands evil."

"But it's gone now, right?" I tried to keep the desperate note out of my voice.

She smiled reassuringly and patted my knee. "This evil is, but there's always more out there."

I didn't like the sound of that.

"Oh, don't worry about it." She wiggled back in her chair. "Whatever happens, we'll deal with it."

Darci nudged Rick. "Is the sheriff going to charge Jason?"

"Don't know," Rick replied in a weary voice. "He's in custody now. He swears he didn't know what Juliet was doing, and he has proof he was in Brainerd yesterday afternoon. He did admit he knew Juliet wasn't well, that she'd been acting strange. That's why he disbanded the group a couple of nights ago and told them all to leave. The sheriff is rounding them up for questioning, too." He exhaled slowly. "Too bad Winnie slipped away during all the commotion. She knows the answers to a lot of these questions."

I shuddered, remembering Winnie and her beady little eyes staring at me down the barrel of her gun. "I don't care if they do find her. I certainly hope I never see her again."

A smile flickered across Abby's face, and she patted my knee again.

"What?" I narrowed my eyes at her. "Do you know something I don't?"

Abby radiated calm. "I said we'll deal with it."

"Oh peachy," I muttered to myself. "More circles to be closed."

Abby sat forward. "There's one question you haven't asked, Ophelia."

"What's that?" I asked, puzzled.

"What's going to happen to Tink?"

"Oh man," I groaned. "Her guardians are both locked up. Will they put her in foster care?"

"They'll have to," Rick said, his head still tipped back.

Sadness squeezed my heart. "With people who don't have a clue how to help her with her talents."

"We could help her," Abby said in a soft voice.

I jerked forward. "Us? Foster parents?"

Abby chuckled. "Not me, dear, I'm too old. But you could do it. Take Tink back to Iowa; give her a real home, a real family."

Momentarily robbed of speech, I searched my mind

for something, anything, to say. I thought about Brandi. From what Rick had told me at the beginning, Brandi never belonged, never fit in. And look where those feeling had led her. As Tink grew older, she'd feel the same way. Without those around her who understood her special gifts, she'd always be an outsider. I'd been lucky—I'd had Abby to help me. Could I help Tink?

I sighed. "Even if I thought I could do it, Social Services wouldn't let us take her out of state."

Rick sat up. "I could put in a good word for you, and I can see if my editor might pull a few strings. Get you some recommendations they can't ignore. He has friends in high places," he said with a wink. "Stranger things have happened."

I snorted. He had that right.

Moving my eyes from face to face, I looked at these wonderful people. Each one had a place in my heart, but for different reasons. Darci and Rick for their friendship in spite of my prickly ways. And my beloved grandmother, whose unconditional love I'd relied on all of my life. I knew I could count on them, anytime, anywhere. And deep inside, it felt right to want to give back some of that caring and love to a young girl as alone as Tink.

I lifted my chin and looked Abby square in the eye. "Let's go for it."

"I'm proud of you, Ophelia Jensen," a voice behind me said.

I whipped around to see Walks Quietly standing in the corridor. "What do you mean?"

"I talked to your grandmother, and she said you want to take the little one home with you."

A hot blush crept up my neck. "Yeah, I think Abby and I can help her."

"I think she can help *you,* Ophelia. It is not right for people to be alone."

"Oh yeah," I said, cocking my head at him. "What about you? You've been alone."

"You're right." He nodded, his brown eyes twinkling. "I might have to reconsider some things."

I laid a hand on his arm. "Does that mean you might visit us in Iowa? You're always welcome."

He placed his hand on his heart and gave his head a slight bow. "Thank you. That will be one of the things I consider."

He turned to walk away, but I stopped him.

"I do have one question for you. I saw you in the clearing yesterday, and you had a wolf, a badger, and a snow owl with you. I didn't know you had any wild animals as pets."

"I don't. A wolf, a badger, and a snow owl are my spirit guides."

"I saw you, and them," I said, pointing a finger at him. "But Darci didn't. How did that happen?"

He twitched his shoulder. "I wasn't there."

My eyes narrowed. "Yes, you were."

A smile played at the corner of his mouth. "When you return home, Ophelia, read about spirit walks." He turned on his heel and walked a few paces down the hallway. Turning around, he faced me again. "One last thing—when you are troubled, look to the sky and a hawk will guide you."

I sat on the edge of Tink's bed and watched her. She plucked at the blanket with her bandaged hands.

"Am I going to like Iowa?" she asked in a shy voice.

"I hope so. You'll have Lady and Queenie around all the time—"

"And you," she said with a shy glance at me.

I chuckled. "Yeah, and me. But there might be some people who would argue that's not such a great deal." I paused. "Listen, kid, I've never raised a child, so I don't know much about being a parent. But I think we can both figure things out as we go along. Are you okay with that?"

"Sure." She smiled. "This is going to be kind of cool. Since my mom died, I've never really had a family." Her smile vanished. "With Juliet and Jason, I always felt like I was in their way. Hey," she said, her face lightening, "can I have friends?"

"Sure," I said with a grin. "Friends are a great thing to have. Just no wild parties, okay?"

She rolled her eyes. "Okay."

"And," I said, smoothing her hair, "I've already invited Walks Quietly to come to Iowa."

She threw her arms around my neck. "You're the best, Ophelia."

"Yeah, well, we'll see how long you think that," I said with a smile, and hugged her back. Just like Abby had hugged me so many times when I was growing up.

This felt right. Everything was going to work out.

Setting Tink back against the pillows, I tucked her blankets around her. "When we get back, Darci's going to take you shopping for clothes. No more white stuff. And—"

The door swung open and Abby stuck her head in the room. "Excuse me, but Mrs. Sanford from Social Services wants to talk with us, Ophelia. She's waiting down the hall with Rick."

A look of fear crossed Tink's face.

"Don't worry," I said, standing. "Abby and I can be pretty persuasive. And with Rick there, too . . ." I threw my hand in the air. "He can charm the socks off somebody without even taking off their shoes." I gave her a wink. "Mrs. Sanford doesn't stand a chance."

I moved to the door, but paused. Turning around, I looked at Tink. "One thing I should probably know, before I talk to her—just in case she asks. What kind of name is 'Tink'?"

"It stands for Tinkes Belle," she said with a grin.

Oh my God, her mother had named her Tinkes Belle. What kind of a name is that to stick on a poor kid?

She saw the shocked look on my face, and her grin turned to a smile. "It's not my real name. It's a nickname."

"So what is your real name?"

Tink inched her way up in the bed. "I've always been small for my age, so my mom told me that she decided she'd have to call me something else till I grew into my wings."

She folded her hands in her lap and lifted her head. A look of pride filled her incredible violet eyes, and I saw a glimpse of the woman she would one day be.

"My name is Titania."

Of course. Her mother had named her well. I could think of no other for this child who, from the first moment I saw her, reminded me of a wood sprite.

Titania—Queen of the Fairies.